# Contraindications

*by Pen Darke*

*Illustrations by Ash Finley*

# Contraindications

Production copyright FurPlanet Productions © 2018

Text Copyright © Pen Darke 2018

Illustrations and Cover Artwork by Ash Finley 2018

**Published by FurPlanet Productions**
Dallas, Texas
www.FurPlanet.com

ISBN 978-1-61450-457-3

Printed in the United States of America
First Edition Trade Paperback 2018

# Table of Contents

# Contra-Dedications

This book is not dedicated to: asshole weightlifters, homophobes, transphobes, pushy horse cops, kidnappers, and other jerks like that. Tell them to find a different book.

# Chapter 1

Matt sat cross-legged in the doctor's office, waiting for her to return. He felt more nervous than he expected to, his palms and finger webs sweating. Reviewing a few simple blood tests shouldn't take that long. Finally, the door opened and Dr. Jann, his primary care physician, strolled in, her striped, feline tail swaying under the bottom of her lab coat. She ruffled through a few printed papers, all stapled together.

"Hi, Mr. Stafford. Sorry to keep you waiting. But I have good news."

Matt brightened. "Oh yeah?"

"Yep," she said. "Completely normal. You're a perfectly healthy, young, male otter."

His face fell, his small, round ears drooping. "But—but that's not possible. I mean, my sex drive! And my workouts! I *have to* be low in testosterone. What other explanation is there?"

Dr. Jann looked at him contemplatively for a moment, then sat down in the chair across from him, leaning forward, her white-clad elbows resting on her knees. "You know, Mr. Stafford, sometimes things like this have a medical cause, but sometimes not. Sometimes it's just the way we're made. As far as I can tell, you're perfectly healthy. Now. You say you're weightlifting, and you're not making any gains. There are things you can do about that. You might try different programs, for example. You can try increasing your caloric and protein intake, and these things will help some. But you're an ectomorph—you've got the high metabolism most people dream of, but it's going to make it very hard for you to put on the kind of muscle mass that you seem to really want.

"I don't want to step on your dreams here, but I think that going for a fit and toned body is going to be a more realistic goal for you, and it's just healthier anyway. This is the body you were given. Learn to work with its strengths and compensate for its weaknesses, but if you try to change it, you're going to be disappointed. If you like, I can refer you to some physical trainers who can help you with a weight program more tailored to your needs."

As she spoke, Matt could feel himself slowly sag in his chair, his narrow shoulders slouching forward. He lowered his eyes to stare down at his webbed paws, folded in his lap. He had been so sure this was the answer, that this was why his year-long efforts in the gym had been useless. And that was one more hope dashed.

"As for your problems with your sex drive, we'll try a low dosage of Wholebutrin. It's an antidepressant, but it's been shown to increase sex drive and sensitivity in most people. If you start getting feelings of anxiety or aggression, I want you to stop taking it immediately, all right?"

He nodded.

"And don't take it with any other medications without checking with me first."

"Yeah, okay."

\* \* \*

Matt drove home, trying to fight the feelings of frustration and disappointment away. He'd always wanted to be big—really big, even huge—ever since he was a pup. He wasn't really sure why; otters weren't supposed to get all massive and bulky, but as a fantasy it persisted. and only intensified with age. For a long time, he'd been sure he didn't have the dedication to really get big at the gym, but finally he'd decided to give it a go. He'd shelled out more than he could afford for a good trainer, and more beyond that for a gym membership at the local Demigods', where some of the guys were as wide as he was tall. After a few weeks, he started making big gains in strength, but two months after that, they tapered off, and he'd seen little, if any, difference in size. A year later, and he was still stuck at that same plateau. He'd tried different workouts, he'd tried cramming proteins (mainly tuna) down his throat until he was sick of it, he'd tried creatine and taurine and arginine and a whole lot of other shit that ended with –ine. Nothing had helped.

His boyfriend Stetson was supportive as hell; he dug big guys too; he just didn't want to be one. At nights, he'd whisper in Matt's ear about how hot it would be to get fucked by the big, bulging otter he knew Matt would become. But as the workouts continued to fail, Stetson didn't seem to know how to handle Matt's frustration and disappointment. He'd tried to soothe and comfort him and keep him encouraged, but Matt sensed he was getting tired of the effort. He could also tell that he was getting increasingly unhappy with Matt's low sex drive.

They'd both been hopeful that the doctor would get Matt on a prescription to amp up his hormones. Matt wasn't looking forward to sharing the bad news: that it wasn't a problem with his health or his hormones. It was just him.

Turning right to head out of the commercial district, he noticed the local WNC on the right, and thought, what the hell. Might as well come home with *something* that might help. Maybe there was something new that actually wasn't snake oil. He pulled into the strip mall, parked, and trudged into the store.

A lone raccoon, who would have been pretty cute if not for the look of extreme boredom on his face, sat at the counter, flipping through a magazine that had more beef on the cover than the supermarket had in its entire deli. "Hey," he said, not looking up. He was kind of small for a WNC employee, but still filled out his shirtsleeves decently. Matt felt a pang of envy.

"Hey," he said. He looked up and down the aisles. He'd been here before for creatine and such, but never any of the more exotic supplements, which he'd been reliably informed time and time again were nothing more than scams to bilk gullible meatheads out of their cash.

The more expensive supplements were all locked away in a plastic case to keep shoplifters from running off with them. They all had pictures of huge guys on their labels: tigers and bears and bulls with more muscle than any two people combined had a right to. Muscle which they certainly hadn't grown using the supplements. The labels were plastered with various ridiculous claims, asterisked to remind the gullible that these claims had not been validated by the FDA.

Matt looked up at the selection wistfully, the locked case placed securely at six feet, just over his head. He glanced at the clerk. "Any of this stuff for real at all?" he asked, jerking his thumb in the direction of the case.

The raccoon snorted. "Sure, if you like caffeine and placebos. That's pretty much all any of that stuff is. Or amino acids you don't need. You wouldn't believe what people do to market this stuff. Like myostatin—that stuff that tells your muscles when to stop growing? They found there's a chemical compound that can block it, and there's something kind of vaguely similar to it in seaweed. So these companies start selling seaweed pills as myostatin blockers, with the price jacked up fifty times what it actually costs to process it. Take it from a friend, man. There's no replacement for hard work."

Matt nodded. "I figured as much. It's just that hard work hasn't been doin' anything for me either. I'm getting desperate."

The raccoon's mouth quirked wryly to one side. "Truthfully, dude, the only stuff that really works is 'roids, and you don't strike me as the type."

Matt heard himself saying, much to his own surprise, "At this point, I'd try anything."

There was an awkward silence. "Yeah, I'm not a hookup, man. Guys are always coming in here droppin' the hints, and I'm like, okay, dudes. No freakin' way."

The otter felt his face flush and burn hot. He tried to cover for himself. "No, no, I didn't mean that at all; I seriously wasn't asking you about that. Oh god."

"It's all right, man."

The raccoon leaned back on his counter; not focusing on his face, the otter found himself staring at the label-stamped nametag: Terry. The otter's eyes wandered back up to the rounded, grey-furred biceps filling the red shirt, and he sighed again wistfully. "Okay, well, I didn't see anything I needed. I'll be back early next month, I guess."

"Take it easy, dude." The raccoon went back to his magazine as Matt headed out, then said, "Oh, look out for the—"

Matt felt something wet and slippery under his toes and before he realized what was happening, he slid forward, his webbed feet slipping out from beneath him, past the yellow CAUTION—

WET FLOOR sign. Flailing, his paws grabbed at the closest object, which, unfortunately was a mop handle and which did nothing to catch his weight. He slipped to one side instead, his shoulders slamming against the shelves and knocking bottles to the floor as he crashed against it. He clutched at the shelf for support, short claws scrabbling, and the whole thing slid with him as he fell, pulling right off the rack. He dropped heavily, banging his head against the floor, and for a moment or two, everything went dark and distant.

"Oh shit, oh shit," he heard someone saying. "Dude, are you okay? Dude?"

He opened his eyes and saw a masked face staring down at him. His back was wet. His shirt was clinging to his narrow chest. His muzzle was wet too, and his tongue felt heavy and coated. His head was throbbing too much for him to remember exactly what had happened.

"Oh man, my boss is totally gonna kill me," the raccoon groaned. "Just tell me you're okay."

"I think so," was what Matt tried to say, but it came out as "Aggh," as clumped powder in his muzzle slipped to the back of his throat. It felt caked and thick. He tried to swallow, but it stuck, and then he couldn't breathe. He gagged.

"Shit," said the raccoon and dashed away. Matt clawed at his tongue—it tasted bitter, and whatever was on his fingers stung a little. He still couldn't breathe, and was starting to panic. Then the raccoon was back and opening a bottle. "Here, dude, drink this." He put something in Matt's paw, and Matt chugged it back, forgetting that he was lying down. Cold liquid splashed over his face, but a good bit got in his muzzle and he felt the caked powder dissolving. He tipped the bottle more gently, trying to fight back the panic, and washed the powders down his throat, feeling a thick wad of gelcaps bulge in his esophagus as they got washed down too. He gave a quick gasp for breath, swallowed again and again, quickly draining the bottle, and started coughing. Terry helped him to sit up as he coughed; he noticed the bottle was a grape-flavored post-workout protein drink that he'd had before and avoided since because it tasted so awful.

"Oh crap," he finally managed. "What happened? I think I fell."

"You did," Terry said. He still looked wide-eyed and panicked. "When you grabbed the shelf, the whole thing collapsed. Please, man, tell me you're not gonna sue us. For god's sake, please. I'm in enough trouble already with the loss of product."

Matt shook his head. "No, I'm not gonna sue, don't worry. People fall. Shit happens. Plus, you had that wet floor sign up so I'm pretty sure you're not... liable." It occurred to him he probably shouldn't be letting the company off the hook that easily. He looked down at the mess he was sitting in: a mixture of clear and orangish yellow liquids, and caking powders sprinkled with a variety of different gel caps. "What product?"

Terry gave a faint groan. "It's all the good stuff, man. Top of the line shit. I mean, still fake, but *top of the line* fake."

Matt frowned, still feeling confused; he hoped he didn't have a concussion. "I thought you kept that stuff locked up in the case. And uh, in closed bottles and stuff?"

The raccoon made a rueful face. "Only the stuff for display, you know, so people don't steal it. We put the spares on the upper shelves behind everything." He stood up, reaching out to help Matt up, and very deliberately leading him away from the spill. "That's gotta be like six hundred dollars of spilled product." Then he turned a concerned face toward the otter. "The shelves crushed everything open when they fell. A lot of it went in your mouth. I don't *think* there was anything dangerous in there, but legally, I should probably advise you to contact poison control or somethin', dude."

Matt shook his head. "I don't think I swallowed that much. Really, I'll be fine, okay?"

Terry shrugged as if to say he tried. "Your choice, dude."

\* \* \*

When Matt finally got in the door, he was really ready for a shower. The spilled powders and liquids were solidifying like cement into his fur. He groaned as he walked in, grateful for the cool air of the air conditioning.

A white-furred rabbit looked up from the couch. "Hey th—holy shit, what happened to you?"

12

Matt rubbed his head. "Short answer is: I fell."

"Are you okay?" Stetson asked. He hopped up from the couch, wearing only a pair of boxer-briefs, his lean, slightly rounded abs flexing under his fur in that way that always gave Matt a pang of jealousy. Stetson was slightly built without even trying. Probably something in his rabbit genes. He had the typical club body: solid arms and shoulders, a decent chest, and thick lapine legs, slightly buff without being beefy. And he didn't work out for it at all. He slid around the furniture and gave Matt a careful kiss on the muzzle.

"Yeah, I'm fine, I just gotta clean up. Doctor said I'm fine, btw. All the hormones are normal."

"Oh." Stetson paused. "Well that's good, right? Good to know you're healthy and everything's working right." That was Stetson, always trying to put the bright side on everything. Most of the time it was nice, but sometimes it was irritating. Sometimes Matt just wanted a little sympathy.

"Yeah," he said. "Yeah, I guess. Doctor gave me a prescription anyway, said it might help my sex drive."

Predictably, the rabbit's expression brightened. He'd always been somewhat insatiable, and Matt felt guilty that he had never been all that interested in sex. Maybe this would help things a little after all. "I can't wait to find out," Stetson breathed excitedly. "You're gonna take it tonight, right?"

"Yep, just as soon as I get cleaned up." He gave the rabbit a powdery kiss back and headed to the bedroom. He set his prescription on the counter, and showered off, taking a long and steamy one, letting the hot water dissolve all the supplements, some of which he guessed had been cut with corn starch and sugar, out of his tan fur. It clumped in the drain, and he stepped on it with his webbed toes to push it down. God, what an awful day.

Being an otter, drying off didn't take long, and soon he was standing in front of the mirror, staring at himself. He was so damned lean, barely a bulge anywhere, his flat chest scarcely rounded at all, thin arms like sticks, ribs showing at his sides. He sighed, feeling that familiar sense of self-loathing. Nothing to be proud of there. Even his sheath and balls were undersized—not childish or practical joke small, but definitely below average. An erection barely filled his

webbed paw. He grimaced and looked at the rather large bottle of Wholebutrin. Dosage, 1 per day.

He took out one of the pale blue pills. The small round thing sat in his palm like a pastel punctuation mark. His sex drive was pretty low. He was pretty sure Stetson would be happy to go two to three times a day if possible. Matt's low sex drive had been a real sticking point with them early on, and their solution had been to opt for an open relationship. Technically, he was allowed to fuck other people on a regular basis, if he wanted. True, he never did, but he was pretty sure Stetson was blowing off steam multiple times a week. It was okay. It had never been any kind of problem with them, and if the ability to get his rocks off meant the rabbit stayed happy and satisfied, Matt sure as hell didn't begrudge him that liberty.

He paused a moment, then took a second pale blue pill from the bottle, cupped it in his palm, and gulped them both down, washing them down his throat with a glass of water from the sink.

\* \* \*

In the middle of the night, Matt's eyes snapped open. The room was dark, but he could see okay. He felt slightly euphoric, a faint but persistent buzz making him feel like he was floating under the covers. The light contact of the sheets against his short fur felt good, and gradually, to his surprise, he felt himself going hard. This wasn't entirely unusual; he periodically woke up during the night with wood, but this time he felt really aroused, the low throb of desire in his loins rising rapidly to a sense of urgent, pressing need. He looked to his right; Stetson was asleep with the sheets wrapped tightly around him, a faint but cute snore coming from his mouth.

Matt didn't want to wake him. He slipped out of the covers, suddenly feeling very awake, his cock almost painfully hard against his boxers. It must be the Wholebutrin, he thought. Holy shit, that stuff really works. Quietly he made his way back to the bathroom and stood in it with the lights off. He unhooked his boxers from around his erection, and curled his webbed fingers around the shaft, feeling its familiar length fill his paw, and gave it a few squeezes.

Electric pleasure shot up its length, rooting itself in his balls. He gasped in shock, toppling forward, barely managing to catch his weight on the bathroom counter. He squeezed at his cock again; it was unusually hot, harder than he'd ever felt it, and another wave of intense pleasure shot through him, and then all of a sudden, before he was even ready, before he'd even had a chance to stroke it, he was cumming, the spurts of his seed spattering against the doors of the sink cabinet in a few quick bursts. His knees almost buckled beneath him, and he cried out once, then gasped for breath, feeling his balls draw up.

A strange feeling rushed through him. As his cock pulsed in his paw, he felt every muscle in his body tensing hard, flexing, making his back arch, and each time it flexed a little harder than before. It felt like it should have been painful, but coupled with his orgasm, it felt oddly pleasurable. One paw gripped the counter firmly as he gasped, trying to stifle himself so he didn't wake Stetson, but then it was over. Panting more from surprise than anything else, he grabbed the still-damp washcloth from the shower and cleaned off the cabinet and the floor where his cum had dripped down. It looked like he had blown a full tablespoon of seed, and he had trouble collecting it all in the washcloth, but he got the area clean, rinsed out the cloth, hung it in the shower, and then tugged up his boxers over his still slightly hard shaft and headed back to bed.

\* \* \*

He woke dimly, faintly, not completely aware, as he nestled up against his soft, warm rabbit, slipping one arm over him. He felt really good. His cock was hard again, and had worked its way through the hole in his boxers. He wriggled closer to Stetson, feeling the achingly hard tip nestle up between the bunny's rounded, soft-furred rump. A low growl came from his throat, surprising him. He knew it wasn't too early, dimly aware of the morning light on his eyelids. Stetson stirred in his arms. His hand slid down toward the rabbit's hips, pulling back against him, and the skin of his tip pulsed as it pressed up against the under the spade tail.

16

"Matt?" the rabbit murmured blearily, but the otter just gave him another soft growl in return. He flexed his cock, and felt sudden warm wetness against the flesh at his tip. So this was what it felt like to make pre. He wriggled his hips, feeling a surprising amount of slipperiness. Maybe that would be enough. He gave a little push, and the rabbit gasped, now aware of what was going on, aware enough to be into it, not to stop it.

Matt reached forward from the hips a little and felt Stetson's prodigious length, already erect. He wrapped his fingers around it, sliding it up the good ten inches his boyfriend had been endowed with. Stetson gave a low moan and then pushed back suddenly; there was an explosion of heat around Matt's tip as he felt himself sink into his boyfriend, and he surprised himself by crying out at the incredible pleasure. He didn't get long to enjoy it. Of its own accord, his cock flexed once, twice, then exploded cum into the bunny's ass, making Matt moan again, clutching at Stetson's side with one paw, his slender body arching with the pleasure. He came again, and again, and then that feeling from last night came over him again, every muscle in his body tensing hard, then harder, then harder, his arm squeezing involuntarily at Stetson as he groaned with the pleasure. His cock was only half-buried inside his mate, but suddenly there was the strange feeling of it sinking in a little deeper, maybe a half-inch or so, burrowing its way into that tight ecstasy.

Finally, Matt relaxed, panting, leaning back as his still-hard shaft slipped slowly from Stetson's tight passage. He let his hands rest on his belly as he waited for himself to go soft, waited for the buzz to fade from his mind.

Next to him, Stetson leaned up on one elbow. "Well," he said. "That was a surprise. Guess that prescription you got works after all, huh?"

"Uh huh." Matt stared upward, and nodded wordlessly, still amazed.

The rabbit chuckled, stroking a fuzzy paw down Matt's chest and side. "Well, that was unexpected and wonderful, love, but maybe next time a little lube, hmm?"

Matt nodded again. "Sure thing."

The rabbit patted his side and rolled out of bed. He stretched, looking down at Matt. "Hey, you know, I know you're disappointed about what that doctor said, but I think you're underestimating yourself. The gym is definitely working for you."

"What?" Matt leaned up on one elbow.

"I'm just saying, I can see a difference. That's all." Stetson winked at him and headed into the bathroom.

A difference? Really? Matt got up out of bed and looked in the closet mirror. He felt his jaw go slack. He was bigger.

# Chapter 2

Matt turned from side to side, staring at himself in the closet mirror. Okay, yes, he was still embarrassingly scrawny, but his chest now had a slight roundness to it, the lines of his pecs defining them up to visible caps of muscle across his shoulders. He curled his arm into a tentative biceps—making sure Stetson had left the room, as flexing always embarrassed him—and was gratified to see wiry cords thicken and rise on his arm. He looked lean still, but in a hardened way, like an endurance runner.

He held his breath in his chest, not sure he believed what he was seeing. It had to be what happened in the WNC yesterday. But that was crazy. Granted, he'd swallowed a lot of different stuff, but it was all junk. It was just wishful thinking. Maybe, in fact, he just had been making progress all along, and had been just too down on himself to see it. He thought for a moment. Wholebutrin was an antidepressant. Maybe he was like anorexics, who no matter how thin they get, always look fat to themselves in the mirror... but instead of looking fat to himself, he just looked small and scrawny, and maybe the antidepressant was helping him to see past all that. Yeah, that had to be it. There are no magic potions, no quick fixes. To get big, it takes hard work, and that's what he'd been doing at the gym for a year now. Hard work, and it was paying off.

Matt's tongue lolled from his muzzle. Seeing the change in himself was starting to get him excited. He felt his cock sliding up from his sheath again, slowly becoming erect. He looked down at it in the mirror; even it looked bigger than before. Like maybe as much as half an inch bigger. That had to be his imagination. No exercise in the world could make your dick grow. But, he thought, the medicine was making his erections harder, so it stood to reason they'd be bigger, too.

He licked his lips, trying to keep from getting more aroused. A drop of wetness appeared at his tip, pointing right up at his nose. He

19

could smell a faint odor, bestial and kind of salty somehow. Trying to push the thoughts out of his mind was strangely difficult, but he was sure his balls would ache if he tried to cum a third time in less than twelve hours. That was just nuts. He forced himself to think about unstimulating things, like what he was going to have to do at work in two days. His schedule there was both full and expressly boring, the work tedious and frustrating. He hated working with the people and came home tired and—yeah, that did it. Good and soft. He tucked the hole in the front of his boxer-briefs closed again and got dressed.

Stetson was making an omelet when Matt came out to the kitchen in a sleeveless tee and gym shorts. He cocked an ear and looked over. "Hey, hon. Off to the gym today?"

Matt felt his stomach growl. "Yeah, gonna do chest and biceps today." He came up behind the rabbit and put his hands on the other's waist. "You gonna make one of those for me?"

"That's what this is. Just the way you like it."

Matt sniffed. "God, I'm hungry. Could you make it twice as big?"

"You? Hungry?" Stetson chuckled. "Must be a blue moon. Still, I guess you did work up an appetite this morning, huh?"

The otter felt himself flush under his fur. "Not like it took very long."

"It was a pleasant surprise all the same." Stetson flicked his tail, and Matt gasped a little, feeling it brush against his belly. His sheath was growing thick again in his shorts. What the hell was wrong with him? This stuff just worked too well. The silky fabric of the workout shorts felt good against his tip as it poked up from his sheath.

"Ungh," he said out loud, and stepped away, grabbing the elastic ties for his shorts and pulling them tight. The swelling feeling receded.

"Hmm?" Stetson asked, turning partway around.

"I said, um," Matt said. "I woke up in the middle of the night last night too, and had to... relieve myself."

The corner of the rabbit's muzzle quirked in a half-grin. "Really? I thought that was what you were doing in there, but I was mostly asleep. Wow, I'm really glad to know this prescription is working for you. Might want to take it a bit easy, though. Maybe cut your dosage in half, eh? Don't wanna overdo it so soon."

Matt looked the rabbit up and down again, thinking of the nicely-muscled, furry frame under those clothes. He cinched his waistband tighter. "Even if I could take you three or four times a day?" he asked.

"Th…" Stetson turned around, holding the frying pan in one paw. "Three or four times a day? Seriously?"

Matt leaned up on the table, bracing both paws. "I feel like I could go again. How about you?"

The rabbit paused, slowly setting down the frying pan on the stove. "You really mean it?"

The otter opened the knot on his waistband and groaned in relief as his shaft slid into freedom. "What do you think?" He dropped the shorts to the floor. His shirt hung baggily on him, but the bottom hem hooked above his jutting erection, pink against the white of his t-shirt.

Stetson gaped for about two seconds in surprise, then pulled his own shirt up over his head, exposing a thick, white-furred chest and a visible six-pack. His thick finger fumbled at his jeans, undoing the clasp. "I don't know where you found this new Matt," he breathed huskily, "but I like him." He lifted his broad, leporine paws out of the fallen jeans, his own erection rising with his heartbeat.

Matt turned around and grabbed the plates off the table, setting them on the chair. "I'll do you over this," he said. His sudden directness surprised him.

"Lube." Stetson nodded eagerly. "We need lube."

Matt scanned the cooking supplies on the counter. "Grab the butter."

Stetson's eyes widened, but then he turned around and grabbed the half-stick of butter in one paw. He was at Matt's side in about two seconds, and took the otter's cock into the other paw. Matt cried out at the sudden stimulation, his shaft jerking, feeling as if he was about to release immediately, but instead, a few drops of pre slid down onto the rabbit's paw.

The rabbit leaned in close, letting his breath tickle Matt's whiskers, his chest rising and falling heavily. "You keep that up, hon, soon we won't be needing lube," he whispered, and then he pressed the cool stick of butter to Matt's hot flesh. Matt shuddered and leaned forward, his paws on Stetson's shoulders. The butter melted faster than he expected as his mate rubbed it around and around his shaft, quickly slickening it. He patted the otter's chest with his clean hand. "Okay, that should do it."

Matt stepped back, feeling almost possessed by lust as he watched his boyfriend lean across the kitchen table, muscled legs spread, rump bared, tail lifted. He'd never felt this aggressive, this sexual, this masculine before. Melted butter and pre dripped from his tip onto the floor, slippery under his webbed toes when he stepped forward. *Don't fall this time*, he thought to himself, almost hysterically. Putting a paw on each of Stetson's hips, he placed his tip firmly against the puckered flesh. The rabbit went tense under his paws.

The urgency of mating was consuming him, he could barely hold back enough to be gentle, his cock pushing steadily into his mate's ass. Stetson moaned low, and Matt matched him with a soft growl. The intensity was incredible. Squeezed tightly all around, his cock sent steady waves of pleasure rolling up his body. He gave one last little push and then shuddered, chest resting against Stetson's muscled back, his hips pressed firmly to the rabbit's rounded cheeks.

"Oh god…" he groaned. He breathed in deep, smelling the mix of omelet and butter and the musky scent from before. Looking down, he watched the pink flesh slide halfway from that rump, and then he drove forward again, burying into his mate once more. His cock flexed involuntarily. There was a knocking sound, and Stetson cried out. Matt pulled back, gave another thrust, and again came that sound from the table and the rabbit gave another little "Ah."

Concerned, but too driven to stop, Matt rocked into his rabbit, and the knocking sound continued. "You okay?" he grunted, still thrusting.

"Ah… hah…" Stetson groaned. His fingers clung hard to the far side of the table. "Cock… hitting… underside… of table…"

Shit that's hot, was all Matt had time to think, and then he came, his sac rising up as he slumped across Stetson, buried as deep as he could get. His teeth clenched. He felt himself unload again and again. Climaxes never lasted this long when jerking off. Maybe there was something to this sex thing after all! Once again he got that strong surge of pleasure through his whole body. Every muscle tensed hard,

his legs pushing. Stetson cried out as the table skidded across the floor, making a grinding noise. For what felt like a full minute, Matt came, his fingers gripping tightly at the rabbit's sides, and then he felt the rabbit somehow seem to squeeze around him, getting a little tighter, his cock sinking just a little farther into him than before.

He panted heavily into the white fur, making it damp, as he slowly pulled back. "Oh, bunny," he managed. "How did you do that?"

Stetson arched his back as the otter pulled out of him. In his eyes there was an expression of admiration. "How did *you?*" he asked.

\* \* \*

Matt felt grateful the urges had waned after that screw on the table. Not a great idea going to a gym filled with hugely built guys if he was going to be that easily aroused the entire time. After cleaning butter off a very sensitive bit of flesh in the shower, he'd had not two but three omelets before he felt full. It was true: sex did give you an appetite.

Now he felt comfortably full, and surprisingly, his balls weren't sore at all after the three climaxes in one day. Though they did seem a bit swollen, his underwear hugging more tightly around them than he was used to. It was a Saturday, so the gym was mostly empty, and he'd have the run of the place to himself. He signed in and headed for the dumbbells, figuring he'd start with biceps and then move to chest exercises. There were maybe three other guys in that area, all bigger than him, and two of them downright huge. He wasn't feeling particularly aroused, but he looked away just in case. If he set himself going there, there was no way to know what he'd do. Or how others would react. He focused on the crappy music they were blasting; club mixes and variations on the Top 40. That'd take your boner away.

He grabbed his normal pair of twenty pound weights and started curling them, watching his shoulders lift under the t-shirt. The dumbbells were oddly light, feeling more like tens. He frowned and set them back in the rack, moving up to twenty-fives. That felt more like what he was used to lifting, but he'd been stuck using the twenties for six months now. Finally some improvement? Again the thought of what he'd swallowed at the WNC occurred to him, and he dismissed it. Nonsense. It was just hard work.

He finished two sets, feeling a pleasant, hard pump in his biceps, and looked at the thirties. Why not give them a try? The thirties were properly heavy; he could feel the weight tugging at his traps as he hefted them. No way could he curl these, but it was worth putting the effort into it anyway. He clenched his teeth, straining, feeling the muscle knot up in his arms, and then he managed a full rep. Releasing slowly, he went for another, and then another. Four times he managed to curl a pair of thirty-pound dumbbells before his arms gave out, and just a week ago, twenties had felt like nearly too much.

He was stronger. He moved on to his other arm lifts, and found the same results. In each, he was able to lift around ten to twenty pounds more than last week. He felt himself start to get aroused at the thought. Bigger, stronger, more sexual.

He shook his head, trying to keep his mind from going there, but it was so difficult. Best to distract it with more exercise. Chest work was next, and that always started out with the bench press. Normally he just pressed the bar, a cool forty-five pounds, on good days with a five plate thrown on each side. But he was feeling pretty good about it today. He put twenty-five pounds on each side.

Stretched out on the bench, he stared up at the bar. Ninety pounds, twice what he was lifting before. This was stupid. It was a huge jump in weight, and he had no spotter. He could hurt himself. He curled his fingers around the bar. He felt confident, strong. He could do this. He pushed hard, and the bar budged, and then lifted up out of its stirrups. He gaped in surprise, and then felt his right triceps shudder, then his left, and he barely managed to push the bar forward enough as it fell to keep it from landing across his neck. It impacted across his chest painfully, sliding slightly to one side.

Okay. Too much weight. Now what to do? How to get off the bench? He didn't want to do the roll of shame, the embarrassing push of the barbell down his chest and belly until he could sit up. Even if no one was watching.

He pressed his thick tail against the bench for balance, gripped the bar, and pushed as hard as he could. At first it didn't budge, then slowly it rose, his arms shaking as he lifted it higher, and then all the way up above him. He slammed it back into the stirrups and then let his arms fall, gasping with relief.

It didn't last long. He felt something pushing against his waistband and groaned. The confirmation of his strength as he'd pressed those ninety pounds up had also made his cock slide out from his sheath again, and this time it had pushed up beyond the top of his shorts to nestle against his belly, beneath his t-shirt. Suddenly realizing he'd have a very odd tent going on if he lay there, he sat up quickly. Fuck. To the bathroom. He rolled to his paws, hunching over a bit so his erection wouldn't show, and headed for the bathroom.

"Hey buddy," a voice said.

He looked around, keeping turned away. A large, incredibly well-built husky was standing behind him, wearing a stringer tee that seemed like it was about to be burst apart by bulging traps and a huge chest. Obviously a pro bodybuilder. Matt felt the heat rise to his ears. "Yeah?"

"You comin' back, or you want to rerack those weights?"

Matt's cock strained, and he realized with sudden horror that he could actually *smell* it even through his t-shirt. "Sorry!" he said. "I gotta go right now! Emergency!"

Staying hunched, he headed for the locker rooms and didn't look back.

Thankfully, the locker rooms were empty, and so were the showers. The room smelled sharp and pungent and sweaty. *Sex*, thought Matt's brain. *No!* he told it. A cold shower would help.

Matt never showered at the gym. He couldn't stand the idea of being naked around others, and was generally shy to begin with. It wasn't that he was worried about popping a boner—up until today, the interest just hadn't been there, but he didn't feel comfortable undressing and showering with others. Today, though, he didn't hesitate. Although, granted, the showers were empty. As quickly as he could he pulled off his shirt and shorts.

His cock was hard and throbbing, and it looked even bigger than he remembered it. He put his thumb on the tip and felt it go warm and slick. *Mate*, his brain suggested.

"No," he said out loud, and turned on the cold water. That scent was getting stronger in the room, and the water in the air seemed to make it spread. Shuddering at the cold, he stepped into the spray, letting the droplets soak his fur, run in rivulets down his chest and legs, and spatter against the hard flesh of his erection. It wasn't going down. He put his paws against the shower wall, facing into the shower, trying to force the lust out of his mind. "No," he said again, louder. The cold water was starting to feel good.

"No?" said a voice. "You all right?"

Matt turned around. The husky stood there, completely naked, and without his clothes even bigger and better-shaped than Matt had thought before. Matt looked down at his erection, ashamed, but then his eyes crept back up to the well-formed lines of the husky. He stood, staring, in the cold water, pink cock framed against the white fur of his groin. "It won't go away," he said apologetically.

The husky snorted, looking down. "Sometimes happens when you're lifting, kid. Don't worry about it. Happens to the best of us." He sniffed the air. "What is that?"

He looked back at Matt, sniffing again.

Matt looked down slightly. The husky's sheath was filling, a bright red tip appearing at the end and slowly sliding upward. The otter caught his breath, stepping forward, toward the dog, out of the cold water. He looked down at his erection, then looked over at the husky's.

"Uh…" the dog said. His tail was still, ears alert. He sniffed the air again, then came toward Matt, still sniffing. He went down to his knees and inhaled deeply, looking up at Matt. His erection was a red pole against his white-furred, fluffy abdominals. "Oh my god. What… what the hell? I just… I just need to…"

Pre bubbled up from Matt's tip.

The husky leaned closer. His breath huffed against Matt's aching flesh.

"You don't understand," the husky murmured. "I'm not gay."

"That's okay," Matt said. "I am."

# Chapter 3

The large husky bunched his shoulders, pulling back slightly and looking up at Matt. There was confusion and fear in his eyes, but behind that, lust. He shook his head. "I don't want to do this," he groaned.

"Then don't," Matt heard himself saying. The husky nodded, as if relieved, and slowly, almost regretfully, up. He towered head and shoulders over the otter, and the cold spray of the shower matting his fur only made his thick musculature more obvious. Matt found himself almost nose to tip with the dog's erection. He snorted at it, letting his breath puff across the hot flesh, just as the husky had done to him. "But it looks to me," he continued, "like you want to do it very, very much."

A low whine came from the husky's muzzle. He paused for a minute, and then quickly dropped to all fours, his padded palms soaked in the cold water splashing across the shower floor. He opened his mouth and the thin curl of his tongue flicked out and slid briefly up the length of Matt's erection. The otter shuddered, electric pleasure flashing through him and running up his spine. He felt his cock spasm of its own accord, and a thick drool of his pre arced out and spattered on the husky's wet, black nose, the clear fluid running down in a line to his chin. The dog snuffled in surprise, and then did it again, more slowly, nostrils flaring. His tongue slipped from his muzzle again and licked over his nose, cleaning the pre away. He looked up at Matt, jaws gaping slightly. Matt couldn't read his expression.

Then the husky suddenly grabbed his ankles, pulling them forward toward him across the slippery shower floor. "Hey, what are you—" the otter managed, and then he fell backward, catching himself on his palms and landing on his ass. The husky didn't let him finish, pushing him down to lie flat on the shower floor, the cold water raining down and spattering his face and chest. The husky moved forward over Matt; from this position, he looked positively gigantic; he could do anything he wanted, and there was no way Matt could stop him. One paw was still on the otter's chest, holding him flat against the shower floor and making it difficult to breathe, but the husky paid no attention to his struggles, instead immediately bending that thick neck down to coat Matt's cock with smooth strokes of his tongue.

"Oh god," the otter gasped, managing to arch his back despite the weight on his chest, pleasure rocketing through him. The husky was greedily licking up his shaft as if it were candy, in long, regular strokes, his breath huffing through his nostrils, tickling Matt's skin. Matt felt his rump tighten as he pushed up with instinctive mating movements that he couldn't quite control. The licking stopped briefly, and he caught his breath in near-relief, only to find himself holding it as he found his sac suddenly cradled in warm jaws, his balls rolling against the husky's undulating tongue, grazing lightly against those predatory teeth. He hoped faintly that the dog wouldn't come to his senses just now, but then the husky closed his jaws slightly, suckling his balls deeper into his muzzle, that long, dexterous tongue slipping out below them to lick up between his thighs. The otter gripped at the arm holding him down, pushing at it, but could feel nothing but cold, matted fur and steely, unyielding muscle bulging beneath it. Warmth spread across his belly; he was faintly aware that this was more pre spilling out of him, the cold water washing it from his belly quickly. It was odd. He had never been messy like this before in his life, ever, but he couldn't focus on that right now. There was a snuffling sound as the husky caught the scent of his precum again, and slid up, dragging his tongue up the length of Matt's cock toward the tip, and then he pushed his muzzle down around it, engulfing it.

Sudden heat surrounded the otter's shaft, and he heard himself cry out, his hips pushing up as his paws darted out to grip the husky's cheek ruffs, fingers digging into the fur. He was able lean up a little despite the pressure on his chest; apparently his movement caught the dog by surprise. His hips pushed up again and again, the dog's nose mashing against his belly. He gave five, maybe six pumps against the husky's muzzle and then convulsed, his cock feeling painfully hard as he came.

Again and again he felt his cock pulse with cum, and each time the pleasure increased, his whole body going tense and hard, biceps flexing at his side, flaring back lifting off the floor, his chest squeezing together and pulling his shoulders forward, feet kicking against the slippery shower tiles. The husky made odd gulping sounds, half chokes, his head pulled forward, paw shoving back against Matt, the movements of his tongue making it seem to Matt that he was pushing even deeper, the tip of his cock pressing against the husky's muzzle somewhere deep.

Finally Matt began to relax. He slid back, panting for breath and sitting up in the shower spray. The husky let him go. Matt couldn't believe it. What the hell had just happened? He never did this kind of thing, never *could*. And now he'd got a giant straight dog to blow him in the gym showers. This was nuts. He looked up at the husky, who stared back at him with wide, almost panicked eyes, clearly just as shocked by this as Matt had been. The floor between his knees was spattered with white that was slowly sliding toward the drain; sometime during the blowjob, the husky had climaxed. Matt felt with some relief his cock sliding all the way back into his sheath, all thoughts of lust and desire fleeing him. He stood up, letting the water run through his fur, cleaning it out.

The husky got to his feet too, still looking slightly stunned. "My... my name's Devon?" he said as if uncertain. Matt couldn't avoid noticing the dog was still hard.

He nodded. "Thanks for a good time, Devon."

The dog just stared at him. "How... how did you just do that? That's amazing!"

A deep voice from across the room said, "Well, what the fuck is goin' on in here?"

Matt turned to look and felt his gut seize in fear: two huge, nude wolves, obviously pro bodybuilders and bigger than the husky by far, were standing in the entrance. How much had they seen? They lumbered in, thick thighs rolling around each other in a weightlifter's gait, but they were moving toward the husky who, Matt noticed, had rather quickly lost his erection.

One of the wolves put a finger on the husky's chest, and the dog's ears went back, his tail curling between his thighs. "You botherin' this little guy, queerboy?" one said.

The otter knew he had to speak up. "Er... no, guys. He wasn't botherin' me. Just, you know how it is. Sometimes happens when you're lifting. Happens to the best of us, right?" He moved to the side, hoping they'd let him leave.

The other wolf growled low. "Maybe." Suddenly he sniffed the air. "What's that smell? Is that...?" His thick sheath started swelling of its own accord.

"You see?" Matt offered, as a pair of red lupine shafts began rising before him. "To the best of us." And then he slipped to one side and bolted for the locker room.

To his immense relief, no one followed, and he was able to dress quickly and head out, but as he passed by the entrance to the showers on his way out, he heard low moans resonating in the room. He did not dare to look.

\* \* \*

He drove straight home, but his mind was racing. How could this kind of thing happen to him? He wasn't a stud—no model, no rock star, no celebrated athlete. But he'd just got a blow job in a gym shower from another guy whose name he hadn't even known. The constant arousal, harder erections, even the increased amount of cum and pre he seemed to be producing could be explained by the Wholebutrin, but to be literally pounced by a complete stranger who claimed to be straight? There was no explanation for that!

He tugged at his shirt, which was pulling at his arms and chest uncomfortably. You're just reading into it, he told himself. Clearly that was one repressed puppy; a lot of bodybuilders couldn't deal with their latent homosexuality. They all claimed to be straight, but it stood to reason that anyone spending that much time looking at and trying to achieve male beauty had to develop some kind of appreciation for it.

So yeah, maybe he'd just been at the right place at the right time for all that husky's gay repression to give way. Placebo effect, that's what this was. He was trying to attribute anything and everything different than normal to the drug he'd taken.

The otter grunted, pulling down at the legs of his gym shorts, which were riding up uncomfortably, chafing a bit at his inner thighs. He felt his paw brush against his crotch, and then it swelled. "Oh no," he told it.

That was definitely enough for today. He made himself think about work again, and how stressful it had been, and all the shit he was going to have to put up with when he went in on Monday. He thought about that asshole anteater from Accounting who gave him orders as if Matt were his own personal assistant. What a dickweed. Yeah, this was working. Matt felt the pressure in his shorts subside. He sighed in relief, though his balls ached a little. Probably were overtaxed, the poor little things.

He couldn't get wait to get home and relax. And get a protein shake. Always gotta drink one of those within an hour after lifting, no matter how awful they taste.

His stomach rumbled. Good grief, he was hungrier than he thought. He must have burned off a lot of calories lifting at the gym—it *had* been a lot more weight than he was used to—and then the sex in the shower afterward. Maybe he shouldn't wait until he got home for the nasty butterscotch-flavored thing, just stop and grab some lunch on the way back. His stomach growled again, and he burped. He suddenly felt starving; cravings for fat and protein and starches clawed at his insides. His belly felt hollow and raw. Yeah. Definitely stop and get some food now; suddenly it was almost all he could think about. There was a burger joint a few blocks down the road. He headed that way and pulled into the drive thru.

"Clath mah hufpsel yum?" squawked the drivethru speaker.

Matt scanned the order menu. Everything looked delicious: cold chocolate shakes, crisp, salty steak fries, and fat burgers bulging with glistening meat. Drool ran down the corner of his muzzle. "Uh, yeah," he said. "I'll have a half-pounder with bacon and swiss, in a combo." His stomach growled louder. "Uh, better make it two… no, three of those." Maybe Stetson would want one, he told himself. Never mind Stetson hated burgers. Come to think of it, so did he. But right now, they sounded like steaming heaven on a toasted sesame seed bun.

"Dumsy wuff stoo sigh?"

"Supersize?" Matt paused. "Yeah… why not?"

* * *

Stetson busied himself over the kitchen sink while waiting for his boyfriend to get back from the gym. What had gotten into that otter this morning? Could it really be the medication he'd got from the doctor? If so, Stetson intended to send that woman a fruit basket. Still, he'd never heard of any medication having that much of an effect on libido. Matt was like a teenager, maybe even worse.

Huh, maybe that was it. Most guys learn how to deal with their raging hormones when they're teenagers, learn how to control them and not be controlled *by* them. But if Matt had always had low libido, he would never have learned how to deal with them. So now he had a normal, healthy male's reproductive urges, but no coping mechanisms for suppressing them. Stetson nodded to himself. That had to be it.

He scrubbed out the greasy frying pan he'd used to make the omelets. It was nice to see Matt with a healthy appetite for once, as well. The otter was always complaining that he didn't grow in the gym, but he never ate well enough to support his growth. Poor guy. He wanted to be big so badly. The rabbit wasn't entirely sure why, but it was a driving force for Matt. He had to give him props, though.

Stetson's own build came from a combination of lucky genetics and his job, which involved a moderate amount of exercise. He was pretty used to guys noticing he was in shape and then they'd start talking about how they really needed to start going to the gym, needed to get in shape, start lifting, yadda yadda yadda. But none of them would ever do it. Matt hit the gym four times a week like clockwork, and even though he never seemed to get anywhere, he never quit going. That, at least, was worthy of respect.

Stetson rinsed out the frying pan and put it in the draining rack, and then his ears caught the sound of the side door opening. He almost turned, assuming it must be Matt, but then he caught the reflection of the intruder in the glass of a photograph above the sink, and it was definitely not his boyfriend—the reflection showed a thickly built character, someone broad and tough looking. He froze, his rabbit heart racing with the prey panic innate to his species. *Run*, his mind told him. Instead he reached slowly over to the draining rack and took out the knife he'd used earlier to chop onions. He watched the glass as the figure came into the kitchen.

"Hey, hon," a voice said. It sounded like Matt, but the voice was a little deeper. The rabbit turned around, fingers gripping the handle of the knife tightly.

If it wasn't Matt, the resemblance was uncanny. The otter standing there wore Matt's face and clothes, but the clothes didn't fit him very well. His t-shirt was stretched tightly across a broad chest, the bumps of his nipples clear through the taut fabric. The sleeves bunched up around healthy, round biceps, wrinkled at broad shoulders. His shorts were riding up on thick thighs, each of the muscles bulging prominently through the otter's short fur, above rounded calves. Hell, even his *tail* looked thicker and bulgier. He held out what appeared to be an empty bag that said Barnyard Burgers on the front.

"I got you a burger," he said, with an apologetic look on his muzzle, "but I ate it. Sorry. I was just crazy hungry."

Stetson felt himself nod. "S'okay."

The large otter pulled out a kitchen chair and sat down in it. He tried to cross his legs, one over the other. Matt always sat that way, hooking his paws around one knee as if holding on. But this otter couldn't cross his legs like that; the bulges of his thighs pressed against each other. He tried a couple times, frowning a little, then set his foot back down, settling for sitting with his knees close together. "Guess I'm still a little stiff from the gym today," he said. Then he frowned. "Though I didn't do any leg exercises. Huh."

"M… Matt?" Stetson asked. He realized there was a real danger of him dropping the knife, possibly on his foot, so he put it back in the draining rack.

"Yeah?" The otter leaned one elbow on the table, and then tugged at his shirt sleeves as if they were bothering him, which, considering the fit, they probably were.

So it really was Matt. Of course it was. It had to be. But… what had happened?

"How... how did it go?" Stetson tried to sound casual, as if nothing was wrong. No reason to alarm the otter.

Matt's face lit up. "Oh my god," he said. "You'll never believe what happened."

"I—I think I might," Stetson heard himself croak. He needed a chair. "Try me." He crossed to the other side of the table and sat down.

The otter nodded, turning to face him, his paws splayed as he always did when he was telling a story he'd rehearsed beforehand. "Okay, so, the pills have made me really horny, right? I mean, I came last night, then again this morning, and then with you on the table."

"Yes," Stetson said. *Oh god, yes.*

"Okay, so I was thinking that had to be it, that there's no way I'd be ready to go again, so I'm at the gym lifting, and I guess it was because I was doing so well, because I started getting off on how much better I was doing. So I'm thinking, oh shit, I can't have a boner in front of all these guys, so I go off to the showers to cool off, yeah? And this friggin' giant husky comes in all naked, and I'm standing there with a boner, freaking out, thinking he's gonna, I dunno, beat me up or something. But he's cool, and then he starts sniffing the air. And then guess what two things he does?"

Stetson just shook his head. "No idea."

"He tells me he's straight, and then he freakin' blows me right there in the shower." The otter paused, grinning at him broadly, waiting for the look of disbelief, which fortunately Stetson was still wearing from before.

"You—you got a blow job from a straight guy in the gym showers," Stetson repeated. Despite his confusion, he felt himself getting a little excited, a stiffness in his sheath.

The otter nodded emphatically. "I know, it's crazy, huh?"

"You're damn right, it's crazy," Stetson said. "What if you'd gotten caught? You could have lost your membership, or even been arrested! What were you thinking?"

The otter looked down. "Well, I mean, I knew it was a bad idea, but I just couldn't help it. I was so freakin' horny. And it kinda didn't matter anyway. There was nothing I could do. That husky was twice my size and he basically held me down." He frowned, staring at his forearm, tilting his head a little.

"So he assaulted you? Is that what you're saying?" Stetson could barely believe what he was hearing; he probably wouldn't have if he weren't already having to believe what he was *seeing*.

The otter shook his head. "No. I mean, I invited him to do it." His ears twitched. "I wanted it sooooo bad. Nothing like that's ever happened to me before!" He twisted his forearm from side to side, making a fist, making the thick muscles bunch up hard, stretching his skin tight. Then he looked up with a puzzled expression. "Do I look bigger to you?"

Stetson's jaw dropped a little. "Do you..." he trailed off. "Get up. Come with me."

The table creaked as the otter leaned on it slightly, getting up from his chair. Stetson led him back to the bedroom and showed him his reflection in the closet mirror.

Matt—he finally had to accept it really was Matt—frowned, as if he didn't know what he was seeing, then gaped. "I... I grew again? I mean, I mean..." he staggered over to the bed and sat down heavily on it. Stetson quickly sat next to him and put his arm around his boyfriend's back, feeling strange new bulges there under the tightly-stretched t-shirt. He squeezed a little, feeling the resistance. Matt shook his head. "Okay, this morning I noticed I looked bigger, and you did too, and I thought, you know, maybe I'd really been making progress all along and was just in denial, but now... well, I guess there's only one thing that could have caused it."

Then he told Stetson a story about going to a sports nutrition store, and having an accident, and swallowing a bunch of random stuff that wasn't supposed to work. Stetson listened quietly. If he weren't sitting next to a boyfriend who was now much larger than he was twenty-four ago, he'd never have believed it, but physical proof was hard to argue with.

"So why didn't you go to poison control?" Stetson asked when he had finished.

Matt shrugged, the push of those broad shoulders bumping against the rabbit. "All the stuff in those ingredients is junk, you know, snake oil."

"Clearly not."

The otter nodded, getting up. He turned to the mirror again, staring up and down at himself, then curled a bicep up into a flex. The shirt sleeve stretched tight around a bicep that balled up slightly smaller than a tennis ball. He clearly lost some kind of battle to keep a broad grin from spreading across his face. "This is awesome!"

Concerned as he was, Stetson had to agree; this newly built otter was pretty damned hot. And it was great seeing Matt get what he'd always wanted so badly. Still, maybe he should encourage Matt to check out a doctor, just to be sure. This kind of thing could have disastrous side effects, maybe even cancer. He'd have to talk the otter into making an appointment as soon as possible, even if it---

He lost his train of thought as Matt gripped the bottom of his shirt and lifted—no, more like *peeled* the tee from his body and tossed it onto the bed, revealing a thick, heavy chest and below it a magnificent set of taut, rounded, lightly-furred abs. "Holy shit," the otter murmured. Stetson was inclined to agree. Matt flexed his chest, and the pair of pecs lifted and bulged huge. "I didn't even know how to do that before!" the otter exclaimed. "I mean, move my chest by itself. Now I can feel it, make it move!"

Stetson nodded, and got up, walking over and putting his paws on the round chest, brushing his fingers through the short fur. "It's very, very nice, but don't you think that—" he broke off. Something odd was sticking up from the waistband of Matt's shorts. "What's this?" He reached down and brushed it with a thumb, and Matt gasped.

"Come on, you've seen that before, it's my..."

Stetson pulled Matt's shorts down to his knees, then stared. "Sheath?!" It was. Matt's sheath had grown significantly, climbing up toward his new abs until the lip of it just barely protruded above his waistband, though granted, the loose shorts the otter usually wore tended to ride rather low on his hips.

The otter's fingers slid down to brush against the furry sleeve. He gasped, and the thick muscles across his back bulged in response. "It's bigger," he said slowly. About an inch and a half bigger, by Stetson's estimation, and as his fingers brushed against it, the pink tip of his cock poked up from the end. The otter groaned, then, and

pulled his shorts back up, cinching the waistband tight above the top of his sheath.

"What's wrong?"

Matt shook his head. "Trying to keep from getting... aroused. I mean, I came three times today before I even left, and then I could barely work out, I was so horny... then I got blown in the shower, and then on the way home I had to run for a public restroom and cum again." He sighed heavily through his nose.

Stetson felt his own sheath thickening at the thought. He pawed at it reflexively and felt it pulse satisfyingly in his fingers. "Well, none of that sounds so bad. Sounds pretty nice, actually."

His otter grinned weakly. "Yeah, it was all very, very nice. Seemed to get better each time. But I don't know. I don't really want to lose control, you know? I'm feeling better now. I'm supposed to take that Wholebutrin twice a day, and I didn't take it this morning, so I guess it's wearing off. Otherwise, just from... just from looking at myself in the mirror, or having you pull down my shorts, or maybe from nothing at all, I'd probably be doing you hard against the bed right now, whether you wanted it or not."

Oh gods, yes. Stetson felt his erection pushing up uncomfortably into his shorts, the fabric dragging along his tip. "Well, you don't need to worry about that, Matt. I always want it."

"Even if it's five times a day?" Matt asked. "Or more, if I had taken my second dose this morning?"

Stetson licked his lips. "Yeah, I think so. Even then."

Matt grinned at him. "Randy little fucker. But all the same, I think I should take it easy, yeah? Re-evaluate. There's apparently a lot happening to me now that we don't understand and can't explain. I can maybe ask the doctor for a lower dosage or something."

Stetson nodded slowly, feeling a slight disappointment. "Yeah, that's probably for the best, I suppose." He paused. "So... you're really not feeling horny at all right now?"

"A little," the otter said. "But just until I get a grip on things, can we wait until tomorrow?"

"Sure," Stetson said.

"Thanks." Matt stood up, rather obviously ogling his new beefy bod in the mirror. "I'm gonna go make a protein shake; I forgot to have it after the gym."

"Okay." Stetson watched that wider back sway as the otter left without a shirt, which was a victory in and of itself. Matt had always been far too self-conscious to go without a shirt; he didn't even like being looked at shirtless by Stetson. Well, he didn't have anything to be self-conscious about now. He was positively beefy. Okay, not bodybuilder level, but he had the whole club body thing going on, nearly as built as Stetson himself. Stetson resolved to talk to him tonight about making an appointment to see the doctor, and maybe also heading back to the sports nutrition store to find out what exactly had been in all those supplements he'd taken.

He did feel really disappointed that Matt didn't want to take the Wholebutrin anymore, though. Their relationship hadn't been suffering, exactly, but the lack of physical intimacy wasn't making it any better. And Matt was never going to learn how to deal with his new urges if he just tried to squash them down whenever they arose. He thought for a moment or two. What he was considering was probably a really bad idea, and if Matt found out about it, it might even hurt his trust in him, but damn it, sometimes in a relationship you just have to make an executive decision.

Stetson got to his feet and went into the bathroom. The little orange bottle sat on the counter. He opened the cap and shook a pale blue, round pill into his palm. This was for Matt's own good, he told himself. And for them, for the relationship. He'd slip it into something at dinner, something Matt would be likely to swallow whole and not chew. A sardine, yeah. And tomorrow, well, they'd just have to see what happened.

\* \* \*

"Coming to bed, hon?" Stetson called.

"Yeah, just a minute." Matt was still staring at himself in the mirror. He was gorgeous, if he said so himself. Or, well, thought so himself. He had an underwear model build, almost, and his sheath was nice and plump. Even his balls were bigger: round, and large around as a couple of small chicken eggs, pulling the skin of his furred sac tight around them. He brushed his fingers over his abs, feeling their hard curves, then shuddered as his sheath visibly plumped. No.

Not tonight. He had to stop doing this until tomorrow at least, try to get control of himself. Maybe he'd limit himself to… five times a day. Yeah, that should be enough.

If you can do it that many times, his brain told him. Remember, without the Wholebutrin, you're not really interested are you?

Yeah, but there's no point in being sex-crazed.

Why not compromise? Take half a pill instead of a whole. Stetson will be pleased, and you'll be frisky, but able to control it. Yeah.

He opened the pill bottle, shook out a pill, and then bit it in half. It was bitter—absolutely foul on his tongue. He filled a glass of water and chugged it down as quickly as he could.

"Okay, coming!" he said. He looked up and down his new body in the mirror one last time, then headed, completely naked, for bed, thick tail swaying contentedly behind him.

# Chapter 4

Stetson awoke to a low groan. It took him a moment to realize who it was. Matt's voice was a little deeper than it had been before. Not much, but a little. That was another thing he should remind his boyfriend to ask the doctor about. He opened his eyes slowly, blinking at the clock. About 3 a.m. Matt groaned again, and the rabbit rolled over to look at him.

The otter was lying on his back. He took up a little more of the bed than he used to, and the moonlight spilled across his chiseled chest and abs, delineating them in a canvas of glow and shadow. The sheets were curled around his thighs, but above them, his erection jutted, large and heavy. Stetson marveled at it. It must have grown three inches larger than it had been two days ago, and it was much thicker. Over eight inches long now, it was suspended over the otter's abs and pulsing with his heartbeat. Still not as large as what the rabbit had been blessed with, but if today was anything like yesterday, he'd surpass him soon. Stetson had to admit, this was making him feel nervous, not because he was envious or felt threatened—in fact, he liked his men bigger than he was—but there was no indication as to what was causing this and when it would end. It must have been something the otter had swallowed at the WNC. Hopefully they'd be able to figure it out later today.

He leaned up, looking down at his boyfriend. Matt turned his head in his sleep, and a low sigh came from his muzzle again as his cock flexed hard. Poor little guy. Well, not so little anymore. But he must be positively sore by now, what with all the activity he'd been having. His muscled chest rose and fell with his breath. Stetson looked at that jutting shaft, then leaned down close, letting his whiskers tickle against it.

Matt moaned in response, his cock flexing hard, and then a spill of clear fluid arced from his tip and pooled on his belly. Stetson caught his breath. Was that all pre? He couldn't believe it. His boyfriend had just, in his sleep, dumped a bigger load of pre on his belly than he used to cum. It collected in the ridges between his new abs, and pooled in his navel, a little trickle running down from his stomach toward his side. Had the pill Stetson slipped him caused this?

Quickly, but as quietly as he could, the rabbit slipped out of the bed and crept into the bathroom. He opened the cupboard under the sink and took out two large, fluffy towels. Then he tiptoed back to the bed and nestled those towels on each side of Matt's belly. No sense in having to change the sheets if they could help it.

He climbed back into the bed next to the otter and leaned down again, letting his whiskers tickle along the length of his boyfriend's cock. It had to be more than an inch and a half thick. Matt tensed, and another copious spill of pre spattered down onto his abs, soaking into the fur, sliding down his side to the towel. Stetson breathed in, impressed, and caught the strong, pungent scent of male otter. Sudden images flickered through his head, images of being pinned down and rutted hard, of meticulously and slowly adoring every inch of this lutrine god with his tongue, of sliding that pulsing cock deep down his throat and swallowing until he choked.

He caught himself, shaking his head. What was wrong with him? He loved Matt, to be sure, he loved sex with him, but he'd *never* pictured the otter in those kinds of fantasies. But he was so gorgeous... Stetson reached down and pulled the sheets back, exposing the otter's stretched sheath, revealing the sac, stuffed with two separate and large bulges, cradled between muscled thighs. He breathed in deeply again, smelling that imperative, masculine scent, and sudden need hit his mind. He felt his back arch, his tufted tail lift, rump pushing into the air. The tip of his cock suddenly hit the soft linen of the bed and he barely bit back his surprise. He hadn't even felt himself go erect. Why was he behaving this way?

Suddenly he remembered what Matt had told him yesterday, about the husky in the shower who had claimed to be straight, and then blown him. What was it he had been doing right before putting his tongue on the otter's cock? Sniffing. Suddenly, Stetson thought he understood. It was some kind of pheromonal response. How it was possible, why it worked on males, he wasn't sure, but it was definitely having an effect. He felt a warm dampness on the sheets—shit, he was leaking pre himself. He turned on his knees so that his tip was against the towel, and that put him almost nose to shaft with the otter, his whiskers brushing smoothly down the length of his boyfriend, who gave a low growl, and then spattered his own chest with clear pre.

Stetson gasped in surprise, a sharp inhalation. He smelled masculinity, then opened his eyes to find that his tongue was licking eagerly up Matt's underchannel, and while he tried to process how this had happened, he felt the tip of the otter's cock push between his teeth. Was he doing this? He must be, he thought. Matt was still sleeping.

Stetson gave a soft, desperate keening noise as his rump pushed higher into the air, his ten-inch cock furrowing the sheets where he ground it in. He licked down the otter's length once more, and then Matt's whole perfectly chiseled body went tense, the otter's back arching as he gave another growl. Stetson backed away instinctively, the growl flickering prey instincts through his pheromone-addled mind.

There was a sudden, wet *thwap*. Stetson looked toward the head of the bed where the sound had come from, and saw a large gob of cum, a whole teaspoon's worth at least, sliding slowly down the headboard. Matt grunted, his body bucking, and then there was another *splat*, and a second dollop joined the first, adding its weight to the fluid, which slid down toward the pillow. Good god, Stetson thought, scooting farther back, the adrenaline pulling him out of his daze. He watched the otter convulse in his sleep as load after load jetted from his cock, none going so far as the first two, but hitting him in the face, chin, above one shoulder, and then a whole mess of it collecting on his chest and belly.

Stetson started to creep forward, sure it was over, but then something really strange happened. Matt's cock started to stretch slightly larger. It was so subtle an effect, it might almost have been his imagination, but no, it grew steadily larger. His sheath grew too, the whole thing pulsing as it swelled perceptibly bigger, its opening creeping a little further up toward the otter's well-formed abs. Stetson's drew back to watch, trying to catch all the effects. He saw

Matt's sac stretch tighter as its contents inflated to large, round eggs, and then it loosened as the skin grew to make more room.

Then the rabbit noticed that wasn't all that was growing. As Matt's body tensed with his climax, each muscle flexed, and after it flexed, it didn't *unflex*, but then seemed to be relaxed before it flexed again even larger. Pecs thickened and broadened on his chest, his shoulders pushed farther apart, the traps leading up to his neck bulging from straight lines into defined arcs. The otter's abs pushed up more clearly from the cum covering them, and his arms bulged rounder, looking far stronger than they had a moment ago. Beneath his larger sac, his thighs swelled larger, pushing each other apart. The otter's calves swelled up to the size of small grapefruits clinging to the backs of his legs, even the muscles layering over his shins thickening noticeably.

Stetson couldn't believe what he was seeing. This was impossible. He bit his lip, then shook his boyfriend. "Matt! Matt, wake up?"

Matt grunted. "What… what?" His eyes opened. "What's wrong?" He looked down at the mess spread across his chest and belly, at the tip still drooling a thin stream of cum onto him. "Oh, god. Did I have a wet dream?"

"Yes," Stetson said at first, then realized sooner or later he was going to have to be honest. "I mean, no, not exactly, but listen. I found out what's making you grow. I mean, what causes it to happen."

Matt blinked, clearly much more awake now. He pushed backward with thicker arms, sat up in bed, the mess on his chest slowly sliding down, his still-erect cock dripping onto his thighs. Stetson reminded himself to take shallow breaths, to breathe through the mouth, not the nose. "What do you mean?" the otter asked.

"Okay, just now, when you came, as soon as you started climaxing, you grew," the rabbit said.

Matt rubbed his eyes. "What do you mean, I grew?"

"I mean I saw you get larger. You came, and then your cock grew, your balls, your muscles. You grew all over." Stetson bit his lip. "I think that when you cum, you grow."

Matt stared at him. Then stared at him some more. "That's crazy," he finally said.

"Is it?" the rabbit asked. "I mean, you're bigger, right? You know you're bigger. It happens when you climax. I felt it yesterday morning when you were in me. As you came, you seemed to push in just a little more. I thought you just… I don't know what I thought. But I felt it."

Matt nodded. "Now that you mention it, I was wondering what was happening whenever I came." He reached forward to put his paw on top of his tip, then groaned, but it didn't sound like the groan of someone too sensitive after climax. It was an interested groan. He squeezed around that length, and Stetson fought back the urge to help him. The pheromones must be getting to him, even breathing through the mouth. "It's definitely bigger than when I jerked it yesterday," he said.

Then his face fell. "Oh, shit, Stets. Shit."

"What?" The rabbit felt his heart jump in worry. "What's wrong?"

"You know how I said I wasn't going to take the Wholebutrin again? Well, I did. Not a full one, but a half of one. That must be why I came in my sleep. If this keeps happening, and I'm as horny today as I was yesterday… who knows what could happen?" He looked down at the huge shaft attached to him, stretching eagerly upward.

Stetson's stomach was heavy in him; he wanted to throw up. But he had to tell Matt. "Matt," he began, then backed away, clutching his hands at his belly. "Matt, I have to tell you something."

The otter looked back at him, wide-eyed and trusting. Stetson wished he could kick himself in the teeth. "I—I was disappointed when you said you weren't going to take the pill anymore. I thought it would be best if you learned how to control your sex urges instead of just not having them." He looked down at the floor, noticing that his own erection was, at least for the moment, thankfully, gone. "And," he admitted, "I really wanted you to want to have sex with me as much as you did yesterday. So I slipped a pill into your food last night."

He didn't hear a response right away, so after a moment, he looked up. Matt was gazing down at the end of the thick organ he gripped in both paws. "Well," the otter said, "I guess you figured out pretty quick that giving me a drug that I didn't want to take in the first place is pretty goddamn unethical and untrustworthy."

Stetson winced, feeling like he'd been kicked.

"And that," Matt continued, "it demonstrates a real lack of respect for me."

"I don't disrespect you," Stetson said. "I guess I just wasn't thinking clearly." He managed a faint smile. "It's hard to do that around you lately, you know?"

Matt nodded and gave him a quirky smile back. "Unfortunately, yeah. I've had trouble thinking around me lately too. Which is, I suppose, why I'm not as mad as I should be."

The rabbit nodded. "But you're right. It was incredibly wrong to do. And I'm sorry." He couldn't keep from glancing out of the corner of his eyes at that still-erect shaft pushing out Matt's paws. "So what do we do about that?"

The otter looked down. His paws squeezed at his girth, and another stream of pre drooled down the underside. "Oh gods," he groaned. "I just… I really need sex." He licked his lips, looking back up at Stetson. His eyes were clouded with lust. "Wanna fuck like wildcats?"

Stetson gasped, and suddenly felt so empty, so void. He *needed* to feel that cock buried deep into him, the raw, urgent pulsing as his otter held down his prey and mated and mated and…

…the pheromones were getting to him again. He got up from the bed, stepping back, and his paw tripped on the bedspread. He fell backward on his rump, catching himself on the heels of his hands, and as he fell, felt his tail lift again, his jaws gape open to be crammed with Matt's cock. *What the hell?* He thought. *This is too strong.*

The otter looked unconcerned, getting up from the bed, his broad shoulders swaying, triceps bulging as he lifted his new bulk off the mattress, a long string of pre attaching his red tip to the sheets. "Sure, I can take ya' there on the floor," he growled low.

"No, Matt, wait," Stetson cried. "We can't do this! You'll grow again! We have to keep you someplace safe until the pills wear off!" *Oh gods, I want to so bad.*

"Yeah," Matt said, his voice sounding hungry. "I'll grow again."

"Matt, NO!" he heard himself cry. He scrambled up to his feet, moving backward, then darted through the bedroom door and slammed it shut. He heard a couple of heavy thumps, and then a splintering sound came from the door. At first he thought it had broken, but when he looked up, it was still intact. A low moan came from the bedroom.

"Matt?" he said. He went back to the door. The jamb on his side had pulled free of the door partway. "Matt?" No answer. He opened the door. The muscled otter that his boyfriend now was lay curled up on the floor. His cock had gone soft, retreating into the impressive sheath jutting up from between his legs.

"I hit it on the door," Matt groaned. "Really hard!"

*Oh, thank gods,* Stetson thought. *That at least bought us some time.* He carefully reached down to pet at Matt's side with one hand. "Hang on there, big guy. I've got an idea."

He went to the phone in the kitchen and dialed. The other end rang for six or seven times. He looked over at the clock. About 3:30 a.m.

"Sup?" a sleepy voice on the other end of the line said.

"Saul," he said. "It's me, Stetson."

"Yeah." Saul sounded out of it.

"Look, I'm sorry for calling you this early in the morning, but we've got an emergency."

He heard the rustle of sheets as Saul sat up. "Yeah man, what do you need?"

"It's going to be really hard to explain, and time's a factor. Can you get over here in your truck?"

"Uh… my truck, my truck." He still sounded disoriented. "Yeah, okay. I can be there in fifteen."

"And look, we're gonna need your handcuffs."

\* \* \*

"Holy shit, you can't be telling me that's Matt," an older man's voice said.

"That's what I'm telling you," came Stetson's reply.

Matt blinked his eyes open. He must have been really tired; he'd fallen asleep on the bedroom floor. His stomach felt like its inner walls were touching, he was so hungry. The aching emptiness clawed at his belly.

Above him stood his boyfriend and one of the rabbit's old acquaintances, Saul, a tabby Matt had met only a few times. Saul was lean and a bit rangy, in his late fifties as evidenced by his thinning and greying fur. He'd been part of the gay scene back when that would get you beat to death by the side of the road. He still looked damned good, though, for an older guy, Matt thought.

"He has really been hitting the gym lately. Damn," the cat said.

"Yeah, he has, but this is new," Stetson said. "But look, better get him in those things now. Trust me. I don't think he can control himself. And be careful not to smell him."

"Not to smell him?" The tabby laughed roughly. "Honey, I think I can take a little musk."

"Not like this, you can't," Stetson said firmly. "Please, just trust me."

"Sure, sure." Saul shrugged his wiry shoulders. "If it's major enough to bring me down here in the middle of the night, I figure you know what you're doing." The cat strode over and knelt down into Matt's vision. "Hey there, big guy. You wanna hold out your wrists for me?"

"No, behind his back," Stetson said. "We can't let him touch himself."

"Oooh, is this what I think it is?" Saul's ears pricked. "I mean, not that that'd be worth getting me out of bed *this* late, but still, I had *no* idea!"

"I really, really doubt it's what you think it is." Stetson said.

"Okay, put those big arms behind your back, otter."

Matt nodded, still unsure what was going on, and tried to put his arms behind his back. He felt unfamiliar resistance, the backs of his arms pressing against his lats. How big was he now? He bent his elbows, leaning forward so that he could bring his wrists together. Something cold and hard encircled one wrist and clicked into place, and then the other. It was tight and uncomfortable. "You're handcuffing me?"

"That's what your boyfriend said," Saul sung into his ear. "What did you *do*, otter? And can I do it, too?"

Stetson knelt down next to him. "Come on, hon, get up." He put an arm around one of Matt's and grunted as he helped him to stand. Matt felt his thighs press against each other as he got up. The unfamiliar bulges of his body made his sheath start to thicken again. He looked at Stetson, then Matt. He could take them both, one after the other. It would be fantastic. Erotic sensations pulsed through his shaft as it rose, sending shivers of pleasure through him.

"Oh my god," Saul said. "What in the hell is he on? I thought steroids made your balls *shrink*."

"We don't know," Stetson answered. "But every time he cums, he gets bigger. All over. You understand what I'm saying? That's why we can't let him touch himself."

Saul laughed disbelievingly. "You're shitting me."

"Not in the slightest. He got some weird combination of workout supplements. And we accidentally gave him Wholebutrin, and now he's extra horny. He tried to take me in the bedroom earlier, and couldn't seem to control himself."

"I'm not seeing any problem here." Saul grinned. Matt found himself grinning in agreement.

The rabbit frowned, and Matt's grin faded. The worry in his boyfriend's eyes was unavoidable. "The problem," he said, "is that we have no idea what side effects there might be or when it's going to stop. If he grew that much yesterday, how big will he be at the end of today?"

Matt shuddered in pleasure thinking about it. His body felt strong and tense, ready to flex, ready for the slightest excuse to pump larger. His cock was now painfully hard, and he felt a hot trickle spill from the end.

"Oh my *god*!" Saul gasped. "Is that *pre*?"

Matt looked down. A three-inch wide puddle had already formed on the floor.

"Try not to inhale the scent." Stetson put his fingers over his nose and mouth. "Can we take him to your place?"

"Yeah, sure, bring him out to the truck."

The otter found himself being led outside, his broad shoulders bumping into the doorframe as they exited via the front. Saul's old white pickup was parked in the drive.

"He'll have to lie down in the back," the cat said. "There's no room for him in the cab."

"You gonna be okay lying back there?" Stetson murmured into Matt's ear.

Matt nodded, still feeling confused and now a little frightened. His cock was still just as hard, and still dripping pre—it soaked into the fur on his paws and down his leg. "Yeah, but can you please get me some food? I'm starving so bad. I feel like I'm about to die from hunger. Maybe fried chicken? Like, two or three buckets? Please?"

Stetson looked doubtful for a moment, then stared him up and down and nodded. "Yeah, okay. We'll get you all you can eat, guy. Just try to think about something other than sex, okay? Don't rub it against the truck bed or anything."

"Okay."

Matt lay down in the bed of the pickup, trying to brace himself, to keep from rolling back and forth as they drove down the roads. The rumble of the truck sent pleasant vibrations through him and through his cock, which steadily dripped pre onto his chest throughout the drive. The smell of it a foot away from his nose made him think of rutting, of hunting down prey and pinning it to the ground, pushing his girth in just a little too deeply, flooding its body with his virility. After a while he felt the car turn into a drive, his heavy balls rolling back and forth where they were cradled against his thighs, and then there was the squawk of a drive-thru intercom. A moment or two later, and Stetson put a couple buckets of delicious, greasy-smelling chicken in the back of the truck next to Matt. "I can't uncuff you, hon, but don't worry. We'll feed you when we get there."

The truck started up again, but the hunger clawed at Matt's belly. He couldn't wait for the food. He rolled to lean up on one shoulder, which lifted his head higher than it should have, and dipped his muzzle into one of the cardboard buckets, greedily chewing up the pieces of chicken there, trying to avoid the bones even as they cracked between his teeth. He found himself so incredibly hungry he didn't even care when he accidentally poked the tip of his cock over the top of the bucket, spattering his food with his own pre—he ate that too, just as readily, and was of the opinion that it tasted possibly even better that way.

He hadn't finished the second bucket yet, and wasn't close to full, when he noticed the truck finally come to the stop.

"Cripes," Stetson said, "He's been eating it bones and all." Matt looked up, licking his lips, and Stetson swatted him on the shoulder. "Don't you know how dangerous that is? The bones could splinter."

"I couldn't wait," Matt groaned. "I was just too hungry."

Saul's voice came from behind him; he was peering into the back of the truck. "Gods... is all that pre? There's so much of it. It reeks like a—like a—" he looked up to stare at Matt.

"Step away," Stetson shouted. "Don't let the smell get to your head!"

"Well why not?" Saul began to purr. He reached out and let his thin, delicately clawed fingers brush down Matt's shoulder; the muscle jumped instinctively, flexing in response. "Not like I'd regret anything I did with *this* big otter."

"Please," Stetson said. "Just help me get him to the basement."

"All right, all right."

Behind Matt, the tailgate to the truck opened. He made an effort to sit up, which was difficult with his hands behind his back, and scooted out onto his paws.

"Come on inside, big guy," the tabby said, still purring. "We've got a special place for you."

Matt was still hungry, but digesting the chicken was starting to make him sleepy. Blearily, he followed the cat through a door into an old, but tastefully decorated living room with sparse furnishings and abstract art on the walls. It smelled like stale cigarettes.

"Back here," said Saul, and led him to a door in the far corner. He opened it and flicked on a light. Matt followed him down a set of wooden plank stairs that creaked worryingly under his paws. Stetson followed close behind him. As they neared the bottom of the stairs, the otter saw they were in a basement, but not a comfortable one. The walls were stone. There was an odd, flat table in one corner. On one wall hung a variety of whips, ropes, and strange wooden and metal instruments in a rack that seemed custom-built for them. And on the opposite wall hung a pair of black iron manacles with two matching leg-cuffs below.

"Matt," said Stetson, "This is how we're gonna keep you from going nuts during the next twenty-four hours. We keep you down here that long, at least, and maybe by then the Wholebutrin will have worn off and you can get control of yourself." He put a paw on the otter's arm. It felt strangely small and delicate. "Are you okay with this? I really think this is the best thing."

Matt looked at the manacles, and then down at his still-dripping cock. He wanted so badly to use it, to push it deep into his boyfriend, let his hips rock in, flood him with his cum, and then maybe encourage that tabby to suck it dry, and then— Gods, what was wrong with him? "Yeah," he said. "I agree. Chain me up."

He stood against the wall and held up his arms. They felt oddly light as Saul and Stetson clamped the cold iron of the manacles around his wrists in place of the handcuffs. The metal was hard and uncomfortable. Matt found himself wondering what had been done to other people who had been in these chains. His ankles were secured a minute later.

"How does that feel?" Stetson asked him, standing back with Saul.

Matt gave the chains a tug with each arm. He watched his round biceps mound up like an amateur bodybuilder's. God, he looked hot. He leaned his head down, stuck out his tongue, and licked smoothly up the right bicep. It was hard and warm against his tongue. He tugged with both arms as hard as he could, leaning forward, bracing with his thighs, and he felt his chest mound up. I'm dangerous, he thought. So gorgeous, so irresistible, they have to chain me up. At that thought, his cock flexed, and a huge burst of pre spilled from his tip and arced to the floor, forming a spreading puddle. He shuddered, feeling his whole body flex with lust, and another stream spilled out, making the puddle grow.

Stetson sniffed the air and looked over at the tabby. "Saul," he said. "Is this room ventilated?"

The tabby stared at Matt, transfixed. "What?" he said. His eyes were locked on Matt's cock. Matt felt himself grin, and flexed the cock for him, feeling the strange pull of its weight bobbing before him. "What do you mean, ventilated?"

# Chapter 5

Stetson tugged at Saul's wrist. The slim, older cat was still staring at Matt. He reached one arm forward as if to touch Matt's chest, and Matt moved toward him, feeling the bite and chafe of the manacles on his ankles. The tabby licked his teeth, and shivered.

"Don't you understand?" Matt's boyfriend was saying. His voice sounded a little slow and slurred, as if he were having trouble forming the words. "His scent, it's pheromonal. It's making you want sex with him."

Saul looked around to the rabbit, his brow furrowing in apparent confusion. "Honey, it's not the smell that's making me want him. I mean, just look at him! When would I ever have a chance with a guy like that?"

Stetson inhaled deeply. "Yeah," he said slowly, stepping forward, and then shook his head. "No, no, think about it! If he grows every time we do anything with him, he won't be a guy like that for long." He tugged at Saul's wrist again. "Come on, let's get out of here!"

Matt listened to this conversation distantly. It was hard for him to focus. Urgent, desperate need throbbed between his legs. His cock ached with steely heat. Small details transfixed his attention: the curl of Saul's pink, lithe tongue at the corner of his mouth; his slender waist hidden inside his button-down shirt, but revealed in the way he turned; the worshipful, hungry look in his eyes. He shifted his gaze to Stetson when the rabbit spoke, and his lust seemed to magnify. He was so incredibly lucky to have Stetson as a boyfriend. The rabbit was gorgeous, absolutely gorgeous, with a heavy, perfectly lined build, a round, muscular rump, a huge sheath that housed a cock even weightier and larger than Matt's own, and white fur that was whisper-soft, that would feel so wonderful gliding lightly against his aching cock as he slid it slowly down his bunny's back, holding him down, before driving it hard into that tight, hot hole… He shuddered, realizing suddenly that he hadn't been paying attention, that he had no idea what they were saying now. His drowsiness from before was now beginning to overwhelm his lust. His stomach still felt full from the chicken, but not bloated like before, and digesting it was making him increasingly sleepy.

The cat said something about muscles, looked back at him and shuddered. He gazed back at the tabby, wondering what he'd feel like inside, wondering if his new arms would be able to lift that cat up and hold him while he sank his cock deep, standing upright. But no, he definitely wasn't that strong. Still, the thought made his cock flex again, really hard this time. A silvery arc of pre sailed out from it toward Saul and struck him square in the whiskered muzzle.

Matt let out a groan, his unfamiliar voice resonating deep in the basement, a hungry growl. Saul just gaped, his nostrils flaring as he tried repeatedly to catch his breath, and then he dropped to his knees. He reached forward as if to crawl toward Matt, but Stetson crouched down and clasped his arms around Saul's waist, tugging him back.

"No," the cat pleaded, reaching out toward Matt. "No, I need him! And he needs me! He needs this! Just look at him! He needs relief."

Stetson began dragging Saul backward. The cat struggled, kicking his legs, squirming, trying to get free. "I know," the rabbit said. "I want to, too. So badly. But we can't risk it." He reached the stairs, and tried to drag Saul upward.

Matt could tell it wasn't easy for him, but he was managing. He watched his boyfriend fighting his own desires and dragging the cat slowly up the stairs, just to protect him, and through the lust and drowsiness, he felt love swell inside his chest. He knew then that Stetson would do anything for him. And that made him want the rabbit all the more. How strange it was that he had ever been uninterested in sex with Stetson. It occurred to him that it wasn't only now that Stetson loved him enough *not* to have sex with him. It had always been that way.

Halfway up the stairs, Saul stopped struggling. "All right," he said. "I'm all right. Jesus, I don't know what came over me, Stets. I just—it compelled me, you understand?"

Stetson still held on. "Are you sure you can control yourself?"

Saul nodded, standing still. "It's okay, you can let go. I promise. I see what you mean now. That boy of yours is dangerous!"

The rabbit looked down to Matt. "I'm sorry about this, hon. But I guess you can see now why we have to do it. I'll check on you later, okay?"

Matt nodded. "Okay."

"I love you," Stetson said, and then he pushed Saul through the door and exited, closing it behind him.

Matt stood there, letting his arms hang slack in the manacles, feeling the cuffs bite into his wrists. The air smelled of him, rich and masculine, and his erection was not flagging, but he did feel incredibly sleepy. His eyelids were so heavy. How could he ever sleep in these chains? Stetson had said they'd keep him there for twenty-four hours. Maybe when they came back he could ask them to give him a little slack, enough so that he could lie on the floor with maybe a pillow. He leaned back against the wall, shifting his paws forward to find a more comfortable angle, and let his chin rest against his chest, his eyes closing. In that darkness, with nothing else to focus on, the presence of sex in the room became stronger. He smelled the intense, pungent scent of his musk in the room. He could feel his erection so strongly he could almost see it through his closed lids, glowing red and hot in the darkness, occasionally dripping, beads sliding with aching promise of contact down his underchannel, soaking into the fur of his sac. He could feel it throbbing with his pulse, and even, it seemed, feel the heat radiating from it. But drowsiness continued to cloud his mind, and while he never lost awareness of his perpetual need, it entered the realm of semiconscious with him as he sunk into a half-sleep.

* * *

Matt awoke to a strange sound—a kind of wet rasping. He lifted his head up, stretching out his stiff neck, and his eyes blinked open, the light of the room briefly painful. He didn't immediately see anyone, and then a flicker of movement caught his peripheral vision, and he looked down. Saul was crouched there on the stone floor, palms flat, his tail swaying back and forth like a feral cat's. His tongue slid out of his muzzle and licked into the small puddle of pre on the floor.

He looked up, alerted by the jingle of the chains from the otter's slight movements. His long, pink tongue curled out again to lick at the side of his muzzle. Dewdrops of pre clung to his whiskers. "Well, look who's up," he said. "My boy, you are positively *delicious*. I've never tasted anyone better. And if this is just the appetizer..." He leaned his head down and licked into that puddle again. "Imagine what the main course must taste like."

Matt stood up straight. It was time for sex again. The little cat desperately wanted it. He felt himself shivering with urgent need. But no, Stetson had loved him enough not to do this. He could do the same. Fighting his instincts anew in each second, he backed up against the wall. "You said—you said you were all right," he mumbled.

Saul stood up. "I lied," he said, stepping forward, his long, sinuous tail switching behind him. "You can't hold it against me, you know. You're too perfect, too—too *everything*." He grinned, showing pointed, predatory teeth. "I'm helpless against you."

Matt shook his head. "I don't want this," he lied.

The tabby ignored him. "Sure, at first, I thought maybe at first I might be okay." He stepped forward again, deftly avoiding the jutting erection pointing out at him from below Matt's hard-lined belly. Moving to Matt's side, he put one finger to the otter's chest. His touch was light, and began to move in little circles, tracing the lines of the muscle. "But, my hot young friend, you spat that butter of yours right in my face."

Matt was briefly distracted, suddenly remembering the previous morning (was it only a day ago?) when he'd lubed up with butter and slid into Stetson's ass. He groaned, his cock flexing. A few drops of pre spilled from his tip, feeling like a small climax, and Saul's paw shot down suddenly and caught every drop.

"All night," the tabby said, "I could smell you, your cock right in front of my nose, begging me to lick it. For hours, knowing all I had to do was stick out my tongue just a few inches..." He demonstrated, curling that pink muscle briefly into an O as it slid from between his furry lips, and then slowly and delicately lapping the droplets from his fingers. "...and taste you." Then he shuddered, his green eyes fixed on Matt's face.

Matt shook his head. "Saul, think of what Stetson said. You don't want to do this."

The cat actually laughed at that: a light, carefree, disbelieving laugh. "Don't want to do this? My hot young friend, not only do I want to do this, there is nothing in my life that I have ever wanted to do *more than this*." He growled the last three words, putting his hand across Matt's chest again, and nestling close, his shirt buttons pressing against the otter's lats.

Matt felt himself flex his back and chest automatically, hard, felt the new muscle strain against tight skin. He didn't even intend to do it. It just happened. He could feel the cat's lithe, wiry body through the shirt, pressing up against him. It would feel so good to sink into him, just to get a little relief. But Stetson. "No," he said. "I'll stop you."

Saul arched a long-furred eyebrow. "Stop me?" he said. "I'm disappointed in you, Matt. I'm not a rapist. How could you think that?" He trailed his fingers down the fur in Matt's chest, down the new, round bulges of the otter's abs, his touch light, almost grazing. Matt's cock flexed again, as if trying to lift up toward the cat's paw. He was so close, so close. "I won't do anything you don't decide you want," Saul said. His fingers slid outward to Matt's hip. "Just remember, all you have to do to get relief, to get the incredible pleasure an *experienced* gay cat knows how to give, is say one simple word." He slid his fingers down Matt's thigh, dancing around the inside, so delicately near those egg-sized balls. "Yes." At that last word, he pressed his chest firmly up against Matt's side and began to purr loudly, the sound vibrating against the otter.

Matt tried to pull back, his arms tugging at the chains, but there was nowhere to go. Another low rumble rolled from his throat. His balls felt so full, and the cat's fingers were right there next to them. They just needed to be squeezed a little; he just needed to feel that paw slide up his throbbing shaft.

"Mmhm," said Saul. He moved in front of Matt, and put both paws around Matt's lean waist, just above where his new thigh muscles curved inward toward it. He crouched down in front of the otter's bobbing cock, watching it, eyes following it intently. He moved his muzzle closer, so close that Matt thought for sure the soft fur there would brush against his tip, but it didn't. The cat's whiskers twitched, waving near Matt's hips, and then he opened his mouth wide.

Matt felt himself tremble. The cat was obviously about to slide those parted jaws down around his cock, bury his tip deep in that throat. But that didn't happen. Instead, Saul breathed out heavily, letting his hot, damp breath puff across the otter's tip. Matt groaned again, his cock flexing of its own volition as it spat another silvery stream of pre into the air—but it didn't go far, Saul catching it expertly in his muzzle and swallowing it down, his tongue curling out just millimeters from Matt's dick. All he had to do was lean forward...

"Please," he heard himself beg.

Saul smirked coyly up at him. "Please? Please what? Please *suck* me? Please sit on my cock? Oh no, big boy, not until you say yes." He winked one green eye. "Explicitly." The cat stood up again, stepping back. "You want me to undress for you."

Matt shook his head no.

"You do? Hmm, you *are* flirting with disaster, aren't you? All right then." The cat twitched his hip to one side and stepped backward, moving sin a kind of slow, sinuous dance, his tail swaying. He unbuttoned the top buttons of his shirt, exposing part of a white ruff of fur. He tugged upward, pulling his shirt-tails out of his dark slacks, giving Matt a glimpse of a lean belly. "You sure you want to see more of me?" he purred.

Matt huffed his breath out heavily, unable to turn the cat down at this point.

"Well, that certainly wasn't a no!" Saul deftly unbuttoned his shirt, parting it to reveal a toned, lean torso that could have belonged to a man half his age. He tossed the shirt aside, arching his back, his slender shoulders rolling as his tail switched behind them.

I could take him so easily, Matt thought. His fingers flexed toward the cat. If he came in reach, I could pin him up against this wall and.... He shuddered again, drooling pre onto the floor again. Saul immediately dropped into a crouch before him, arching his slacks-clad rump high, his belly to the floor, tail swaying above him as he lifted his head and opened his jaws to catch the pre on his tongue, swallowing it down. The sight of that made Matt pre again, the sensation better than climax had felt as his old self, but only building toward his arousal, not alleviating it. He groaned.

Saul grinned wickedly up at him. "Mmm, it's so much better warm from the tap." He rubbed his fingers in the spilled puddle, stood up, and dragged them down Matt's chest. Matt flexed his chest again hard, involuntarily, watching the two thick slabs of muscle bunch up into striated mountains as the tabby left four dark, matted trails down the middle. The scent of his own musk was suddenly much more intense, drifting directly up to his nostrils. The cat stood up again, backing away, and unbuttoned the front of his slacks. He was wearing striped boxers, bulging up in front with the obvious tent of his erection, pushing out through the parted zipper. "Should I take these off?" he purred.

Matt felt himself nod.

The cat grinned broadly, looking nothing so much like he was about to eat the canary, and then swayed his hips as he shifted his slacks down his slender thighs, over his calves, and then kicking them off his feet. Matt realized he could smell not only his own arousal but, much fainter but still distinct and noticeable, Saul's. The cat's boxers had damp spots on the front, and for the first time, Matt wondered who was really captive here? Himself, or Saul? Maybe they both were, helplessly driven forward by a tidal wave of hormonal instinct. Saul gripped his erection through the fabric of his boxers, making the head outline distinctly against the material. "Should I get rid of these too, muscle otter?" he smiled, looking up.

Matt's arms strain against the manacles as he tried to move forward, tugging against the chains.

"I'll take that as a yes," the cat sighed happily, and pulled the lip of his boxers out to unhook it from his erection. The boxers dropped down around his paws. Saul's cock stood out stiff, six inches of pink flesh that pulsed with his need. His body was slender but well-lined, framing it, and he smiled up at Matt, stepping forward with a confidence divorced of the vulnerability that comes with nudity. Matt stared hungrily, longing to rub his tip up against that sleek belly fur, wanting to see the cat arch his back again, licking up his pre while Matt moved behind him to squeeze into that slight, rounded ass.

Saul pushed his shoulders back a little, swishing slightly as he strode back to Matt, putting his hands on the otter's shoulders and nestling up close against him, careful not to let his side brush against Matt's erection. Matt panted, his breaths ragged and erratic, hips twitching with urgent need as the nude cat nestled up against him. The cat leaned up higher, bringing his muzzle to the otter's neck, stuck out his tongue, and licked slowly from collarbone to just under the side of his jaw. The cuffs bit into Matt's wrists as he tried to reach down and seize the cat. Pleasure radiated from his cock; his pre spattering onto the floor made a regular *pattapat* sound.

Saul sunk down against him, paws sliding down his sides, finger trailing over the bulges of new muscle, moving toward his hips. Crouching, the cat pressed his muzzle against the fur of Matt's thigh and began to lick slowly, steadily, his tongue rasping against the fur as he began to groom the muscled leg in front of him, sliding his tongue slowly up and down Matt's inner thigh before moving to the other leg, his tongue dancing almost painfully close to the heavy sac cradled between them before moving on, licking up the other thigh. He dragged it slowly up Matt's abs, which flexed into hard ridges of their own accord, making his cock bob. Saul deftly avoided it.

Matt's body was aching with need. Why wouldn't the cat just lick his cock, just move his head slightly to the side and touch it, slide those swaying whiskers up the hard and burning length? Why was he going to make him ask for it? At this point, the question of refusing seemed moot. A starving person would, if his hunger were deep enough, do anything, anything for a bite of food. A person who had not slept in days could not be kept awake no matter how urgent the need. And Matt needed sex. He was controlled by it. He could no longer resist.

Saul moved back to hover in front of Matt's cock, and Matt lunged forward, stretching out his arms, reaching the very end of his chains. The cat quickly fell backward, dodging the movement, rolling to his feet again. As Matt struggled at the ends of his restraint, pulling forward with all his might, Saul crouched again, opening his mouth into a perfect O, the tongue curled just slightly between his teeth, his breath panting against Matt's skin. He peered up inquisitively at the otter.

"…Yes," Matt heard himself say. He could not feel regret. He had reached the end of his stamina.

Saul needed not a half-second further encouragement than that. Before Matt could do or say anything else, he dove forward, pushing the otter's dripping tip between parted teeth, his warm tongue curling around it, his muzzle tight, lips sealing around the otter's girth. Matt shuddered at the sudden relief of contact: it was like oxygen, like a drink of water when he was dying of thirst. His whole being shuddered with pleasure as he sunk into the tabby's mouth, filling it with pre as he did so, enough to make the cat's eyes widen in surprise. Saul didn't slow down, though. He swallowed, tongue massaging Matt's cock with the motion, and pushed forward, jaws gaping wider as he squeezed the otter's malehood into the back of his throat and down. Matt cried out in pleasure, his deep voice echoing in the room. Steadily, inexorably, his throat squeezing as it tried to swallow, Saul pushed down around him, until Matt's eight inches were deep in his throat, his nose bumping against the otter's abs.

Matt groaned again, and at that moment, the basement door opened. Stetson stood at the top of the stairs, looking down. There was no surprise or shock in his expression, at least as far as Matt could see. He surveyed the scene below. Saul didn't even pause— merely drew back slightly and then pushed forward around Matt's cock again, his breath huffing against belly fur.

Stetson stared down for a moment, then slowly and quite deliberately sniffed the air a few times. The front of his jeans bulged steadily outward.

"Wait a minute," the rabbit said. "Let me help you." And with that, he descended the staircase, pulling off his shirt as he came.

# Chapter 6

Stetson shrugged his shirt over his head, broad shoulders, a thick, white-furred chest, and taut abdominals. Matt found himself staring, distracted from the cat slurping at his shaft below. He'd always appreciated Stetson's build before, but now it seemed like he was seeing his boyfriend for the first time, lust intensifying his appreciation of the solid lines and bulging strength. And for possibly the first time, his perspective was unclouded by envy of Stetson's Adonis-like musculature.

Through his lust, he did notice that Saul flinched when he heard Stetson's voice, but not for an instant did the cat stop swallowing his cock. It flexed on its own, pulsing as what felt like half a cup of pre shot from the end into Saul's throat, the pleasure rivalling Matt's one-time climaxes in intensity.

Distantly, he felt his hips rocking forward against the tabby, seeming to move by themselves, independent of his wishes. He gave Stetson a worried, apologetic smile, unable to stop thrusting against the cat's face even as a sense of betrayal rolled through him. Stetson had tried so hard to keep this from happening. He'd wanted to fuck Matt so badly—Matt *knew* he had—but instead had summoned all his strength of will and left the room. All for Matt's benefit. All to save him from the outcome. And Matt had let him down. He'd tried so hard to hold out, but had failed.

And yet no reproach hooded Stetson's eyes: the rabbit smiled back broadly, warmly, unzipping his jeans to expose a thick, swollen sheath that made even Matt's look small by comparison. Above it wagged about four inches of rabbit cock, steadily rising before Matt's eyes. He licked his nose hungrily and gave a forceful buck with his hips, ignoring Saul's choked splutter of protest.

Stetson slid his jeans off of his long, white legs and kicked them to the side. His cock jutted pink, his white-furred balls drawn up tight between his thighs. He sauntered—almost *prowled*—over to his boyfriend, shaft bobbing heavily with each step, and pressed himself up against Matt's side, leaning forward to administer a slow, reassuring kiss, his tongue soft and warm, lapping between Matt's pointed canines. Matt moaned, partly from the kiss and partly because Saul had begun rocking back and forth on his cock, his nose thumping against the alien solidity of Matt's taut abs. Matt strained, feeling another thick load of pre slide up his length and well briefly around the cockhead being squeezed by Saul's hungry muzzle.

Stetson broke away from the kiss, and Matt licked instinctively toward him, trying to renew it, but Stetson shook his head and pressed his nose to Matt's chest, burying it in the fur, pushing it in the canyon that had formed between those pecs. He inhaled deep as he nuzzled down. Matt tugged at his chained arms, trying to reach forward to take his boyfriend in his arms, but this only made his chest squeeze at Stetson's muzzle. The rabbit gave a shuddering giggle at that and nuzzled lower, his soft, whiskery nose drawing down the otter's abs until he was right up against Matt's thigh, cheek to cheek with the tabby who was gagging slightly as he moved back and forth. The rabbit waited until Saul drew back a bit and then flicked his tongue across the base of Matt's shaft. Matt caught his breath, realizing he could feel the difference in texture between Saul's somewhat coarse tongue and Stetson's silky-smooth one, and his hips bucked again, hard, his thigh bumping against Stetson's cheek. Saul made a sudden gurgle of protest.

"Sorry," Matt managed to groan, but he felt his cock flex again—*it* wasn't sorry at all. Stetson ignored him, nuzzling lower, his muzzle sliding alongside Saul's as the tabby moved back and forth and slurped up and down Matt's cock. Eagerness had apparently overwhelmed expertise for Saul.

Stetson was suffering no such handicap: he let the tip of his tongue glide along the length of Matt's sheath, and then, twisting around on his paws and knees, somehow managed to rotate upside down to lean backward between webbed paws—gods, even *those* looked larger—without ever breaking the kiss against Matt's sheath. Matt's sac tickled as his boyfriend's breath puffed against its short fur. Stetson kissed slowly downward until he was bathing the otter's larger balls, already drawing up in preparation for climax, with broad, smooth strokes of his tongue.

Matt's breath came in short, hungry gasps—his balls felt bloated, straining with cum, and Saul's teasing had driven him near the edge as it was. His body tensed, his paws yanking ineffectually at the clinking chains as he tried to reach down, to seize the cat's head and press it hard up against the top of his sheath, to squeeze one or two more of his hidden inches into that tight gullet. When he groaned, his voice echoed loud in the basement. His shaft throbbed, strained. And then pleasure and relief washed through him as he shot his seed deep into Saul's throat.

The cat gagged in surprise, his teeth pricking lightly at Matt's flesh. He tried to draw back, but then stopped, his tail lifting behind him, and pushed forward again, tongue massaging with greedy swallows. Matt's hips bucked again and again, each burst of seed feeling too voluminous to squeeze through the end of his shaft, seeming to stretch it wider. He strained, every muscle tensing hard… and then he felt himself grow.

His forearms thickened in the manacles, biceps swelling outward as he tugged at the restraints. His shoulders tensed, strength filling them as they pushed apart, a little broader than before, his traps mounding up behind his neck as it thickened. He felt his back widening, and, looking down, could see new layers of muscle bulking his chest as it swelled outward. Below it, his abs tensed once, again, three times, each time the lines between the hard muscle there growing a little deeper, the bulges rounding out a little larger. His thighs widened, and behind him he could feel his tail thickening as well. His calves balled up rounder, and he suddenly felt oddly light on his feet, as if he'd lost, rather than gained, weight. And then Saul gagged again, struggled, and pulled back, his jaws pushing apart slightly as the column of flesh pushing between his teeth widened perceptibly. Below the cat's chin, Matt felt his balls pulse, strain. He groaned again, tugging at the chains, feeling the new strength in his arms as they pulled the manacles tight to dig into his wrists. His hips bucked twice more, and then his climax waned to a drooling close. Saul made faint whimpering noises as he slowly slid backward off of Matt's cock. Then the cat fell backward, panting heavily, his hand rubbing at his stomach, which looked slightly bloated.

"Oh my God," Saul said. The cat's own cock was dripping cum; Matt had no idea how long ago he'd climaxed. He looked down to see his own shaft listing forward heavily, leaking a thick, viscous cream onto Stetson's belly as the rabbit grinned up at him. Matt's cock was slightly but perceptibly larger, and from what he could see of himself, he'd gone from underwear model to proper amateur bodybuilder. Every muscle bulged and strained through his fur, exuding strength and power and raw sexual attraction. He wasn't sure, but he thought he might be gorgeous now. He looked like a porn star.

"Oh my God," Saul said again. "Oh my God, oh my GOD."

Matt looked down at the cat and rabbit at his feet, both of them still erect. The relief that had flooded through him just a moment ago gradually dissipated, replaced by incredible need. His desire hadn't waned at all. His cock flexed, sending a string of seed arcing across the basement. The smell was intense, rich, and alluring. "Unh," he groaned. "I need to fuck. I need to fuck so *badly*."

"Again?" Saul gaped.

Matt's stomach growled, the sound gurgling in the room.

Stetson immediately got to his feet and began putting on his jeans.

"Wait, Stets!" Matt called toward him, tugging on the chains as he turned in the rabbit's direction. "Don't leave! I need… I need…" His cock ached, and then pre spilled from the end in a shining cataract. He stared down at it in amazement, and saw the plum-sized balls below it pulse in their stretched pouch. "I *need*," he finished lamely.

Stetson began pulling on his shirt again, ignoring the pink spire of flesh that jutted up above his waistband. "Since Saul," he said, his voice calm and confident, "is so eager to have fun with you, he is going to let you fuck him while I go to get you food. Aren't you, Saul?"

The cat nodded, biting his lower lip.

Stetson gave Matt a reassuring grin. "Do you want to fuck Saul, Matt?"

Matt's gaze shifted over to the tabby, tracing the lean lines of his waist, his round, soft-furred rump, the slow wave of his tail, and realized that even though all these things were incredibly appealing, none of them mattered too much. He needed to fuck, and he needed it badly. The mating instinct raced through his mind. If his hands were free, right now he'd be snatching the cat up, sinking his tip up under that switching tail into tight, hot warmth. Pre shot again from the end of his cock, spattering the floor.

Then he looked back at his boyfriend, covering up that gorgeous, white-furred body with clothes that almost seemed an affront to it, and he realized that as much as he wanted to fuck Saul, he wanted his boyfriend that much more. "Yes," he said. "Yes, I want to very much." He gave a low, urgent groan. The need boiling in his balls was actually rising. "But I'd rather fuck you," he murmured.

Stetson came forward, fully dressed now, and patted Matt, his paw feeling smaller on Matt's forearm than it used to. His eyes shone. "I'd rather that too, Matt. And maybe that's fair, since Saul's the reason you need food so badly."

Matt nodded, his breath huffing from his nostrils as he turned back toward the frowning cat. Saul's erection had not diminished at all, but his ears were folded back.

"That's fair," the tabby mumbled his agreement. He looked at Stetson, then back at Matt, and whimpered. "But he's just so… *so*…" He turned his gaze back to the rabbit. "You can't blame me for this, right? You know I couldn't help myself. How could *anyone* help themselves with him?"

Stetson ignored the question, pulling off his shirt again. "It'll be hard to buy food when you're naked, Saul." He looked Matt up and down. "And I think he's going to need a *lot* of food, don't you?"

Matt puffed up a little as the cat stared at him. His muscles seemed to *want* to show off.

"Yeah…" Saul breathed slowly. His tail tip twitched back and forth excitedly. "He sure will." Apparently forgetting his clothes, he began climbing the steps naked, his slender hips swaying back and forth, pink erection conducting his way. He looked back over his shoulder. "You'll let me have him when I get back," he pleaded. "At least once. Won't you?"

Stetson's expression darkened. "That would be up to Matt," he said. "Now hurry. My boy is hungry, and he's hungry because of *you*."

The cat mewled and then hurried up the stairs, shutting the door behind him. Stetson watched him go with a cold expression, then turned back toward Matt and a smile lit up his face. He unbuttoned his jeans again and slid them to the floor, nestling up close.

Matt groaned as his slick tip pushed up against the rabbit's silky-furred, hard stomach. His cock was straining so hard, it felt as if it might burst. Stetson slid his paws across Matt's chest. The sensation was strange to the otter. His skin felt tight, the weight of his pectorals heavy and full and oddly pleasant under his pelt. He felt *strong*. He looked down as the rabbit traced his fingers under the bottom of Matt's chest, able to conceal them under the solid shelf of pecs that had once been flat.

His boyfriend looked up at him, that smile still wide, but with a trace of sadness. "Are you sure you want this?" he asked. "If this keeps happening, it might be permanent. You might not be able to go back. And who knows how big you'll get before it wears off." He walked his fingers down Matt's abs a few inches and curled them around the otter's slick head, squeezing it. Matt groaned as pleasure and need lanced through him. "And this." Stetson said. "I can take a lot—an *awful* lot—but you grow this thing enough, you're gonna get too big for me. Maybe too big for anybody. You understand that? Are you okay with that?"

There were two answers here. One of them led to sweet, mind-blowing pleasure and relief. The other led toward endless, aching increase of the pressure. "Yes," Matt said without hesitation. "Please. It doesn't have to be a lot. I just need to let off a little of the pressure. It's too much. Please, Stets."

The rabbit sighed heavily, then smiled up at him, biting his lip. "You know, I honestly doubt I could have left if you'd said no." He looked Matt over, then winked. "I don't think we should unchain you, though. Can you crouch a little?"

Matt nodded eagerly, feeling the unfamiliar thickness of his thighs as he slid into an easy squat, the chains jingling with his lifting arms. His boyfriend's huge and solid erection jabbed forcefully against the bottom of his chest as he slid down as far as he could. "Lube?" he asked.

Stetson barked a laugh at that, and rubbed his paw all over the slick surface of the otter's cockhead, making him groan again. "Hon, you make more natural lube with that thing than I could ever need." The huffing in his nostrils betrayed his eagerness as he reached back with the coated paw, leaning forward to rub up under his flicking spade tail. He shuddered and stood up, his tip poking Matt in the chest again. Matt inhaled the heady, masculine odor of his boyfriend's cock, and leaned down, sticking his tongue out to try to lick at it.

"Hon, don't," said Stetson. "You'll make me cum before I'm ready. Just smelling you, looking at you, is almost putting me over the edge." He reached his paws up and gripped Matt's shoulders. Matt couldn't believe how different those fingers felt on his shoulders. More delicate, unable to dimple his skin. He rolled his delts back, feeling them bulge under his pelt.

"Oh yeah," Stetson said, his voice shaking a little. "I think you can handle me, no problem." And with that, he dug his fingers in, and then hoisted himself up against Matt, bracing his broad leporine feet against the wall behind the otter. Matt grunted, his thighs flexing as they were suddenly required to support the rabbit's not insignificant weight. But even though Stetson was heavy, he found himself able to hold him up. His traps bulged, engulfing the sides of his neck as he lifted his shoulders, pulling Stetson higher with their might alone.

"Gods, you're strong now," the rabbit gasped. He reached behind him, one arm and both legs straining to support his weight. His fingers found Matt's cock and pulled it up toward him.

Another groan escaped Matt as his shaft flexed. The sound of his pre arcing to the floor several feet away accompanied the wave of pleasure. The soft, matted fur of Stetson's muscled rump pressed against the achingly taut skin of his cockhead. He felt a squeeze of muscle as the rabbit carefully lowered himself against it until Matt's tip pressed against something quivering. Then Stetson let go, gripping his tip there between his glutes, returning his hand to Matt's other shoulder where it left a warm, sticky smear. It was all Matt could do not to buck his hips upward. His cock pulsed again and the slipperiness of his pre flowed up around his tip.

"Unf," Stetson said. "Good boy." And then he relaxed, letting himself slide down, the heat of his insides slowly swallowing the thickness of Matt's cock. Matt gave a low, urgent growl and this time his hips did buck. He pushed a few inches into the rabbit, and Stetson yelped suddenly. "Careful!"

"Sorry, sorry," Matt said. Distant in his psyche, guilt flickered, barely registering amid the waves of pleasure and need crashing through him.

Stetson's grip on his shoulders tightened as he slid down farther and farther onto Matt's cock, his exposed tip furrowing down the newly deepened groove between Matt's abdominals, and then the rabbit lowered first one foot, then the other to the floor, standing impaled by his crouching boyfriend. "Oh gods," he muttered between clenched teeth, and let go of Matt's shoulders. He gripped Matt's waist instead, and leaned back. "Okay, lift up a little, but *slowly*."

Matt nodded. It vaguely occurred to him that crouching for such an extended period of time, especially while supporting a heavy weight, would once have been tiring, but he barely felt exerted. He began to push his hips upward, still keeping them angled forward. He had to bend his knees more, and the manacles bit at his wrists as he began to depend on them for support, but he didn't care. The pain was distant, barely noticeable. His thighs bulged against his boyfriend's as they supported his weight and he pushed up, deeper and deeper.

Stetson groaned loudly, his head tilted back, and Matt felt the rabbit's ring squeeze firmly around his girth. He paused.

"No," the rabbit said. "More. More."

There wasn't much more to go, though. Stetson must not have been kidding when he said he could take a lot; Matt already felt, with his new size, as though he'd sunk *two* cocks into his boyfriend. The pleasure was lengthened, extended. He felt his shaft surge with pre inside Stetson, and the sudden, urgent bliss made him push up firmly. Stetson's hips connected with his thighs, his cock swinging forward to thump him heavily against the stomach as he gave an almost shrill rabbit cry, burying those last two inches deep inside his rump, his heavy sac sprawling over the top of Matt's shaft.

Instinct was quickly consuming Matt's focus again. He rocked his hips toward the floor and then thrust sharply upward again, making Stetson gasp as he lifted him briefly into the floor. The manacles bit

sharply against his wrists, and without really thinking, he twisted his paws around to grip at the chains, his forearms and biceps bulging at either side of his head as they hefted his weight. Stetson squeezed firmly around him, his fingers digging into his sides as the rabbit clung to keep his balance. Matt lowered and thrust again, and again, not so much sliding in and out of the gripping heat as he was almost bouncing it, stretching it with his flexing cock. With each thrust and squeeze, Stetson's eyes widened slightly, his breath shuddered out in sometimes groans, sometimes cries. The rabbit's cock spattered pre, and then abruptly cum, musky-smelling ropes arcing across Matt's chest, one hitting his chin.

Seconds later, a huge wave built inside the otter, a tide, a flood in his balls, and then they squeezed almost painfully. He bellowed then at the sudden crash of pleasure, feeling his cock surge into his boyfriend, feeling almost as if he were pouring out of his own body, down the length of his cock, and into Stetson. And then the now familiar tightness entered his limbs, his whole body tensing, squeezing, his skin feeling about to split. His body, and the rabbit astride it, seemed to grow lighter, his grip on the chains hefting his weight far more easily.

He could actually feel himself thickening, new layers of muscle forming across his chest, his abs swelling. His thighs tensed once, twice. Then the muscles swelled to meet each other, his inner thighs touching, then pressing together firmly, then forcefully. His biceps, stretched up in the chains, pulsed, strained, and touched his ears; his back pushed more firmly against the wall.

Then the tenseness flooded into his cock. Stetson cried out again as he seemed to slide down just a little deeper upon it, though that was impossible; Matt was hilted in him already, but even so he sunk deeper and slightly tighter. The otter felt his sac, aching with relief, swell against his thighs and the rabbit's rump, oddly crowded for room, and then the tenseness passed.

Stetson was shuddering, leaning against him and panting. "Oh, Matt," he said. "Oh, Matt. Oh, Matt." He leaned up to look at the otter.

Matt grinned down at him and flexed his cock once more, making the rabbit yelp in surprise.

"Yeah, otter, you definitely grew," he said. "I can feel it." He groaned, and gripped Matt's shoulders again, carefully beginning to lift himself up off the cock. "Gods, I feel full. How much did you have in there? Can you crouch down again, please?"

Matt nodded and crouched, his biceps pressing firmly against his head as he extended his arms. His cock made a sticky sound as his boyfriend hefted himself up, slowly sliding up off of it.

"Gods," Stetson said again, moving awkwardly as he stepped back. "That was great, but let's never repeat that position again, okay?"

Matt stood upright and nodded. "Okay," he said. "Are you all right?" His voice sounded strange. It was rich and resonant, and definitely deeper than before.

Stetson wrapped his fingers around his erection, which was beginning to droop slightly, and squeezed, then lifted them to his muzzle, licking the white drops from their tips. "Oh yeah," he said. "I've taken way bigger than you, hon, like I said before." He eyed Matt up and down, his expression strange. "Though I think you're definitely a contender for the beefiest I've ever had."

Matt looked down at himself, but most of what he saw was just two heavy slabs of muscle and the slick, pink tip of his cock poking out in front of it. His erection hadn't flagged, but his stomach growled again. Now that the lust was fading, he was aware that he was acutely hungry.

Stetson's ears flicked at that sound. "Oh!" he said, still keeping his gaze transfixed on Matt, "You must be starving by now. I'll go get cleaned up and see if I can find out what's keeping Saul. You going to be okay down here?"

Matt thought about that a moment. The relief he'd felt a couple of minutes before was already beginning to subside, but he was definitely hungrier than horny now. "Yeah," he said. "I'm just—I think I'm going to need food badly really soon."

Stetson nodded, and crouched down to pick up his clothes, his muscular, naked body gleaming with pre and seed. "I'll be back as soon as I can. You try to relax, okay?"

Matt nodded back. "Stetson, about earlier, when Saul came down here—"

Stetson shook his head. "Hon, don't say anything. When I took him upstairs before, it took every ounce of willpower I had to leave that room so I didn't do anything. You were stuck down here, chained up in a cloud of your own pheromones. I'm amazed you lasted at all. Don't blame yourself, okay?"

The otter sighed, relieved. "Okay."

Stetson smiled broadly at him, and climbed the stairs, careful to keep his clothes free of any fluids clinging to him. "Be back in a flash," he said, and as he went through the basement door, his paw went to the light switch and flicked it off.

"No wait, Stets, you—" Matt began, but it was too late. He sighed. The rabbit was always doing this. He was kind of anal about power conservation, and turned off lights more out of habit than anything else by now, not even aware he was doing it. Matt couldn't count the number of times he'd been reading in a room when Stetson left it, leaving the otter to grope for the switch in the darkness. Oh well. Probably just as well he couldn't see anyway; looking at his chest and cock for who knows how long wouldn't do anything for restraining his libido.

Libido. He felt his cock throb. It felt so different, so heavy. He could feel the new weight of it between his legs, and when it bobbed, it bobbed lower. Why wouldn't his erection go away yet? He could feel his sac hanging heavily against his thighs, with what felt like a pair of goose eggs inside it, stretching the flesh. His thighs, too, rubbed against each other when they moved, a new and strange feeling. He shifted up and down, feeling the muscle rub, waiting for his eyes to adjust to the light. Time passed, but all he could see was a faint line of light under the door at the top of the basement steps.

His cock strained urgently, the need to mate ratcheting up again. A slow, constant pleasure came from his tip, and then he felt a line of warmth slide down his underchannel, steadily, centimeter by centimeter, moving down. He gripped the chains with his hands, enjoying the small but delicious sensation, the new power in his arms evident as he tugged at them. He thought of how incredible it had been to have Stetson ride him a few minutes before, and shivered. He imagined the line of heat drooling down the bottom of his cock was the rabbit's delicate tongue, moving farther and farther down toward his balls, and his cock jumped. The sound of liquid spattering against the floor reached his ears, and then the warmth spread farther down his length and began to kiss at his balls. He groaned, hearing the strange, deeper sound of his voice, feeling it vibrate in his chest. He wished Stetson were there now, tongue sliding up and down his cock, huffing hot breath into his short, dense fur, perhaps taking each of his oversized balls between his teeth and suckling lightly at them, curling his tongue around them.

Matt shuddered at the thought, his cock straining again, this time making a heavier splat. The warmth of his pre tickled at his balls and began to soak into the fur of his thighs. Maybe having the lights off wasn't such a good thing after all. His imagination was running wild. He gasped with pleasure, cock flexing a third time, another spatter of his pre trickling against the floor. He needed to think of something to calm down.

What was it he'd focused on before? Oh yes, the office, that was right. Horrible, dreary work. Was it today or tomorrow he was supposed to go back? He couldn't remember. Not like he could go back like this, sit there in his chair while dealing with assholes like Jim, a bully of a rhino who thought that being confrontational and demanding meant everyone else would do his work. Of course, one whiff of Matt's pheromones, and Jim would be likely to do whatever Matt wanted. Matt could strip one of those stupid Hawaiian shirts off of Jim's thick, rough hide, bend him over a desk, drop his slacks and bury himself deep into that—no!

He tore his thoughts away, but the pleasure at the end of his cock had increased; the line of warmth going down it had broadened. The slick wetness of his pre was soaking halfway down his thighs by now. Not Jim, no, Jim was kind of hot in his own way.

How about his boss, Gomez, a dreary, unimaginative lion who just wanted to save his own skin? It'd be really interesting to strip him down, see if that mane connected all the way down his chest with his crotch, see if he was hung—almost certainly—smaller than Matt himself, and then plug that platitude-spewing muzzle with a thick, throbbing length.

Matt caught his breath, his hips thrusting upward, his pre splashing on what must be, from the sound of it, the far side of the room. Oh gods! How could he find everyone at work hot? But now he was unable to stop thinking about it, his fingers buried in Gomez's mane as he tugged the lion's head toward his hips, bloating his belly with cum and then turning to Jim and fucking him up against the wall so hard that cracks jumped outward like lightning bolts. He could feel a pressure building in his balls, his cock straining.

Pre was trickling down between his paws, and he didn't care. He was lost in the imagery. After the smell of that, the whole office would be hooked, desperate for his body, for his seed. They'd hold him down on a table and begin to lick him all over, Casey, the labrador, eagerly lapping between his thighs, a couple of the weasels from accounting matting the fur on his thick pecs while he flexed them hard to awe them. Phil and Toby lapping at his shoulders and neck, Gomez roaring as he rode his cock while Stetson bent over him from behind and kissed him deep... deep...

A thick pressure pushed at the base of his cock and then built upward. He couldn't believe it. Unable to touch himself or see himself or anything else, he was about to cum, and he couldn't stop it. His hips bucked upward hard, and he held back, tensing, trying to stop the orgasm, but then it was spewing out of him. He heard a splat hit the ceiling and he cried out, arms tugging violently at his chains as he tried to break free, to plunge his cock into anything, a towel, the drywall, anything, just to get the satisfying sensation of *contact*, but the chains didn't even begin to give, and so he just kept thrusting at empty air, growling and crying out over and over, feeling as if gallons were pouring out of him, hearing the splattering sound as it coated the basement floor. And then his body went tight again, straining, his shoulders pushing up at the sides of his head, thighs pressing each other apart as his paws spread across the floor. Then the wall seemed to slide downward along his back, and his arms didn't have to reach quite as high anymore. He felt the heaviness of his pulsing cock increase before him, bowing forward slightly, still spitting his seed into the air.

And then finally it was over, and he was alone in the dark, the only sounds his own deep-voiced, bestial panting and an occasional drip as something from the ceiling plopped down to hit the floor.

# Chapter 7

"Matt?" Stetson opened the door to the basement and winced. The lights were out. Had he switched them off when he left? He must have, unless they'd burned out. Even through the menthol-scented surgical mask covering his face, the reek of his oversexed boyfriend hit him squarely in the face. The air in the basement was almost stifling.

He fumbled for the light switch. The light flickered on, but it was odd, dim. Stetson frowned, reshifted the bags of food in his arms, and stepped carefully down the stairs.

"How is he?" came Saul's voice from behind him.

Stetson stopped halfway down the stairs to stare agape at the room. The ceiling, the wall, the floor—all were painted with a viscous white fluid. The light glowed a baleful yellow through the substance spattering it. It couldn't all be cum. It *couldn't* be.

His eyes wandered to the left. A hulking figure hung slumped in the chains, apparently unconscious, knees buckled nearly to the floor. Before him jutted his erection, huge and thick, and, Stetson realized, finally rivaling his own. Perhaps just a *bit* smaller. It flexed from time to time as if trying to erupt, but there was no seed or even precum dripping from it anymore, and Stetson was not surprised. It was all spattered about the room. There was no way the otter's balls could have held anymore. He glanced down—sure enough, Matt's sac was pulled up tight between his thighs.

Matt suddenly took a deep breath, looking up, lifting. He was massive. Not Mr. Olympia, but definitely a seasoned bodybuilder. No one looked like that without taking steroids, Stetson suspected. The otter groaned. "Is it—is it morning yet? I'm so… so hungry. So… horny. Please, please, I need to fuck so badly."

Stetson shook his head. "No, you definitely do not. You need to eat and sleep. We brought you food. And a sedative. We'll help you sleep your way through this until the drug wears off, okay?"

A look of relief washed over the otter's face. "Thank you," he breathed. "This is too much. And I'm so tired."

Stetson stepped closer, his long ears picking up the sound of Saul coming down the stairs behind him. The closer the rabbit drew, the larger Matt seemed. Something was definitely off. "Are your wrists okay?" he asked.

Matt shook his head. "Chafed," he said. "Sore. They really hurt."

"Oh my *god*," Saul said, his voice muffled by his own surgical mask. "This isn't *possible*." He came up beside Stetson, also wearing a surgical mask. "He's a monster."

Matt flinched, his eyes opening wider despite his obvious fatigue.

"Don't exaggerate," Stetson said. "He's just a reasonably big guy now. Come on, get the keys, help me get him down."

The otter shook his head. "No," he mumbled. "Don't wanna… wanna…"

"He has a point," Saul said, stepping back. "I mean, look at him. If he gets loose, he could—he could do whatever he—" He flicked his ears. "On second thought, maybe we *should* let him go."

"Keep it together, Saul," the rabbit snapped, irritated. Saul hadn't always been the wisest of friends, but Stetson had always thought he was reliable, trustworthy. Tonight had proved differently, and the rabbit found himself very disappointed. "He's in no condition to do anything. Look, he's bone dry, see?" He waved his paw toward the erratically flexing cock. "And anyway, he's tired. Let's just get him down, give him the sedative, and let him sleep this off."

Saul nodded. "You're right, of course. I'm sorry, it's just…" He sighed. "Never mind." He walked toward the otter, paws *splitching* in the white puddles on the floor, leaving trailing strands behind his toes when he lifted them. "Good god, there's so much…"

Stetson caught him inhaling deeply, and was grateful once again for the menthol-scented masks. The cat pulled a small key out of his pocket and reached up to the manacle. "Er, better give me a hand with the beefcake, huh? He looks like he weighs well over two hundred by now."

Over two hundred? The rabbit found himself, for the first time ever, wondering if he'd be able to support the weight of his own boyfriend. He stepped across the floor, trying to avoid the puddles,

which were already cool. He wondered how long Matt had been hanging there, exhausted. He stepped in front of the otter, careful to avoid the still erect (and presumably tender) shaft. "Here, hon," he murmured. "Lean on me."

The large otter groaned and nodded, shifting forward, the weight of his thick chest falling heavily against Stetson's upper back. There was a scraping sound as Saul unlocked the right manacle. Matt slumped forward, putting his arm around Stetson, who braced his large paws on the slick floor, widening his stance to support the otter's weight. Another scrape, and he was free. "God, you're heavy," Stetson grunted. He strained to keep his balance, thighs complaining, and settled back. His ears pushed to the side as he nudged his head under Matt's chin.

Odd. From this position, his boyfriend actually felt… taller. There was a conspicuous jut into the small of his back; Matt groaned, his hips giving a push up and forward.

"Uh-uh," Stetson admonished him. "Let's go, big guy. Come on, walk." Carefully, he led Matt over to the mattress in the corner of the room—fortunately, it was still quite dry, though a bit musty-smelling—and helped him lie down. Matt sighed in relief, huge chest swelling massively.

Stetson gaped under the raspy fabric of the surgical mask. "We figured you mainly need protein to support all that growth," he told Matt. "So we brought you tuna. Saul, could you go upstairs and get it ready."

"Yeah," the cat said. His voice was hushed, almost awed. "Okay. Back in just a few minutes. Don't do anything without me."

The otter's stomach gurgled, rounded abdominals rolling as he clenched it.

Stetson felt a pang of pity for him, and took a pitcher from the bag. "And protein shakes," he said. He filled the pitcher with powder and milk, then opened the package of sleeping pills. The dosage suggested two pills before bed, but Stetson wondered, as active as Matt had been lately, if that would be enough. He decided four would suffice, crushed them with his claws into the mixture, and stirred it up. It didn't blend well, filled with nasty, chunky-looking brown lumps. Chocolate mocha, the container of protein said.

Doubtful. But Matt snatched the pitcher away from him with both hands—even his fingers looked thicker—and guzzled its contents within seconds, the pink smear of his tongue greedily licking away the clumps on the inside of the glass pitcher.

"More!" he pleaded.

Stetson nodded, filling the pitcher again, and starting to wonder if, with as much as they'd bought, it was enough. It had cost a pretty penny. Matt watched intently as Stetson stirred the mixture. His stomach made a loud, protracted gurgle. Stetson handed him the pitcher and then, as and he began to drink again, his still spasming cock actually began to ooze clear fluid once more. Stetson couldn't believe it. Was it possible Matt had metabolized the shake that quickly, and was already using it to produce more precum? The notion would have seemed utterly ludicrous a few days ago, but now…

Matt shoved the pitcher back into Stetson's hands and he began to fill it again. The otter's belly growled again and again, and that ooze of lubricant from his tip gradually turned into a stream. Matt looked down at his bobbing shaft, and his tongue curled out and licked at his nose. "Just once," he said, looking to Stetson. "I just need to cum once more, and then I can rest, I think. Please. Please, I need it so badly." His voice shook. "Got to fuck, got to mate, got to—got to *rut…*"

Pity plucked at Stetson's chest, mingled with desire. Even through the mentholated mask, the scent was urging him to lean down, run his tongue up that impressive shaft, cradle those huge orbs, swallow the glistening nectar spilling down from the tip, lick the furred abs clean of it. He shook his head, forcing himself back to focus, aware that his own erection was pressing painfully into his trousers. "You need to sleep first," he said. "Then we'll see." He handed another pitcher to Matt, wondering how long the soporific would take to affect him. Matt guzzled it down, and three more after it, before Saul finally came downstairs with a plate stacked with seared tuna.

"Oh my god," repeated the cat, staring at the clear puddle filling in the lines between Matt's abs, filling his navel, streaming down his sides. "He's ready again." His gaze turned to Stetson, intent above the mask. "Let him fuck me."

Matt nodded eagerly, taking a fillet off the tray and cramming it into his eager maw. "Yes," he managed around the fish. "Let me fuck him!"

Stetson scowled at the tabby. "No! We talked about this, Saul!" He turned to Matt. "And you, be careful of bones." The otter began working on a second fillet by way of response, not looking any more careful than before.

"But just *look* at him," protested the cat. "He's a sex *god*. He needs to fuck. He's made for it."

"He's overdosing," snapped Stetson. "And you're trying to take advantage of him."

Saul shuddered. "I'm sorry, I just… when I'm away from him I feel fine, but when I see him there, so… so…"

His voice trailed off as Matt slumped backward onto the mattress, half a fillet of tuna still clutched in his webbed fingers, his eyes closed. Stetson sighed in relief. "There, he's asleep. Finally. Poor guy. Hopefully by the time he wakes up, this stuff will be out of his system."

"Yeah," muttered Saul. "Hopefully. So, you wanna sleep on the couch, I assume?"

Stetson shook his head. "I'll sleep down here with him, just make sure he's okay, make sure nothing happens to him in the night. Everything should be fine now he's passed out."

Saul nodded toward the otter, whose erection still jutted up above his belly, oozing steadily. "I wouldn't be so sure about that," he said.

"I'll be *fine*, Saul. Good night. And… thanks for your help, events of the evening notwithstanding."

"Yeah," the cat said, his voice sounding bitter. He looked at the plate of half-eaten fish, and the puddles everywhere. "God, this place is going to stink in the morning. Well, good night. I'm going to go jack off three or four times or however many it takes."

He crouched and picked up the plate of fish, and, just when he was near Matt, Stetson saw the paper of the mask dimple inward as the cat took a deep, heavy breath. Then Saul sighed, stood up, and headed up the stairs. "Light out?" he asked.

"Yeah," Stetson said, and then the room went dark. He sat next to Matt for a few minutes, feeling slightly sick to his stomach. Perhaps it was the odd mixture of arousal and deep worry for Matt. Perhaps it was the mingled reek of sex and tuna and the horrible menthol on the mask. Or maybe it was the unexpected betrayal of Saul, a friend he had thought he could trust and rely upon. Saul had always been there for Stetson, always been supportive of his relationship with Matt, and once or twice they'd even played together and really enjoyed it. Maybe you never really knew someone until you got between them and something they really, badly wanted.

Or maybe he was just really susceptible to Matt's pheromones. Otters and cats were genetically much closer to each other than rabbits. The chemicals might have a more powerful effect. Stetson shrugged. It was very dark in the basement. He didn't think there was a window, so his eyes didn't have much light to adjust to. A faint yellow line shone around the door at the top of the stairs, but nothing other than that.

Suddenly, he felt very, very tired. He climbed carefully over his boyfriend in the dark and lay down next to him on the other side of the mattress, most of which was spanned by the otter's broad frame. He lay one furred arm across Matt's chest and closed his eyes, nestling up against him. Within moments, he was asleep again.

\* \* \*

"Stetson." The voice was rich and angelic. Where was he? In every direction was bright, golden light and fluffy, white clouds. The very air seemed to shimmer.

"Yes?" he asked. "Who is this? Where am I?"

"You are dead," thundered the voice. It was frightening, yet soothing. "You have entered the afterlife."

"Dead?" he asked. "What do you mean, dead? How did I die?"

"You died of bliss," the voice said casually.

"So this is heaven?" the rabbit heard himself ask. The light was so bright, he could barely see anything.

"Yes," the voice answered. "But you were not good enough to go to heaven."

Fear gripped the rabbit's heart. "I'm going to hell, then? Please, I wasn't wicked. I don't deserve to go to hell."

"No," said the voice. "You were not wicked enough to go to hell."

"Then… what?" Stetson asked.

"Your life was filled neither with great piety nor with great evil. But it was filled with great eroticism. Therefore," thundered the invisible voice, "You will go to Sex."

Stetson frowned. "What?" he asked, and then the light went out, and he found himself in a strange room. The walls seemed to pulse, and tendrils slithered across the floor. The sudden smell of musk hit his nose like a brick; he felt his malehood jut up and press painfully against his trousers, and unthinkingly, he pushed them down. Tendrils snaked around his wrists and ankles instantly. Another thin tendril coiled around his neck, rubbing up under his chin. He gasped in shock, and immediately his lungs were filled with the thick, heady air. Then something pushed up under his tail from behind, wriggling easily into the hole there. He groaned aloud, feeling whatever it was sink deeper within him, pushing him up into the air, stretching him wider, making his cock ooze. It began to pulse in and out of him, rubbing with aching smoothness against his ring, jutting up against his prostate, and all he could think of was, "I have died and gone to Sex, and this isn't so bad, actually. It's wonderful! And if this goes on and on for eternity, I will be the luckiest rabbit…"

And then his eyes opened, and he realized that his hands were braced against two firm pectoral muscles, his feet on the floor and mattress, and oh god he was being fucked by Matt in his sleep. There was enough dim light coming from around the door that he could faintly see in the dark. Matt's eyes were closed, and he was breathing heavily through his muzzle, still plainly asleep even as his hips thrust up into Stetson, filling him with aching perfection.

Stetson's mask was dangling around his neck. It must have gotten pushed down in his sleep, and now he realized he didn't want to put it back. He breathed in deeply, feeling the adoration, the need for his boyfriend surge through him, and he pushed back against the hungry thrusts. His cock bobbed heavily before him, dripping down onto Matt's chest, between the white rabbit paws braced there.

This was right, this was perfect, this is how it should be, serving his otter, pleasuring him even while he slept. Matt's thrusts were powerful, his abs clenching like a giant fist, even as his shoulders and arms lay still and unmoving at his bulging sides. In the faint light, Stetson could see the otter's tongue curl out at the open air, and he leaned forward to take it between his teeth, tilting his head, suckling hungrily at it.

Matt made a low, rich groan in his sleep, and then the thick organ buried in Stetson's rump flexed once, twice, and then he felt the climax erupt into him with a palpable impact, so much so he pulled forward slightly. Matt mewled into Stetson's kissing muzzle, a plaintive, hungry sound, his cock throbbing again and again as it emptied, and then, beneath his fingers, Stetson felt the otter tensing beneath his fingers, his hands moved apart by swelling slabs of muscle, the ache behind him intensifying as what was within him slipped just slightly farther, stretched him just a little wider in the darkness.

With trembling fingers, he reached up and pulled the mask over his nose once more.

# Chapter 8

When Matt woke, he still felt sluggish, drowsy. His head was swimming, and his limbs felt heavy. He lay for a while with his eyes closed. The mattress beneath him didn't feel like his bed. It felt different: sort of hard and lumpy. He licked his nose, turning over. No one was next to him. Stetson must be up making breakfast.

Breakfast. The thought made his stomach growl. He was really hungry. He sniffed the air hopefully for the scent of it and wrinkled his nose. The room was pungent with the stench of cum. Awareness began to glow in his mind. What had he done last night? And then he remembered. The sex had poured out of him; he had been like a monster, like something made to rut. Even now his sheath felt fat and ready, but it lacked the desperate urgency of before.

He opened his eyes. The cement ceiling hung over him. The room was dark, but the stairway door was open, and light streamed down from it into the basement. Shifting his weight experimentally, he leaned up on one arm. He felt the bulge of his biceps pressing against his lats, the tightness of his triceps. The mound of his traps pressed up on one side when he leaned, squeezing against his neck, nudging the back of his head.

His mind tried to race, but his thoughts were still slow. For a moment, he began to panic, wondering if the drug combinations had caused some kind of brain damage, but then he remembered, vaguely, Stetson giving him something to help him sleep. That was probably still affecting him somehow. Still, he didn't want to lie down anymore. He rolled to his feet and almost fell forward, the push of his legs lifting him into a small jump. His paws hit the floor heavily, and his muscles tugged all over his frame as he landed, gravity pulling at his chest and arms and back.

He looked down at himself. The twin swells of his pecs pushed out in his vision below him, and poking out just beyond that, the end of his sheath, pink tip nestled just inside it. He brought his hand forward to give his package an experimental heft and gaped at the thickness of his arm. Powerful cords of muscle rolled beneath his pelt. He wouldn't be the biggest guy at the gym, but he was definitely approaching their class now. His fingers curled around his sheath, and for the first time in his life, it more than filled the cup of his fingers. He felt its contents stirring and, recalling the previous night, decided messing with it might not be such a good idea.

Carefully, he took another step, feeling the odd weight of his leg and simultaneously the new springiness in his gait—the thick ball of his calf pushed him up into the air more than he wanted, and he came down heavily on his paw. He stepped again, using a little less force this time, and this time he felt like he got it mostly right, but his toes set down in something wet and tacky. The scent in the room told him all he needed to know about that.

He peered down in the dim light, but couldn't see where the puddle was; he stepped again, and his other paw came down into it. Oh well. He made his way across the room, finding most of the way dry, his paw pads leaving smears against the floor, and when he got to the stairs, he wiped first one paw, then the other, against the wooden lip of a step, looking down to see the bulging breadth of his thighs as they lifted. His paws looked broader too, somehow, the toes a bit larger and thicker. The stairs creaked their complaints as he made his way up, still having difficulty taking normal steps and not bouncing into the air.

At the ground floor, he squinted in the daylight, peering around Saul's living room, which had been furnished with aggressive tastefulness. He could hear Stetson in the other room humming to himself, and followed the sound. "Stets?" His voice was deeper, more resonant. He walked into the kitchen, bumping his shoulder on the doorframe. The rabbit was at the kitchen counter, and on his right was a large heap of empty plastic wrap and foam containers. To his left were several plates piled high with food.

"Oh hey, hon," he said. "I was just about to come wake... you..." His voice trailed off as he turned around and looked at Matt. He looked a little shorter somehow. "Good god," he breathed. "It's one thing to see you lying down, but standing there, in the light..." His eyes flickered up and down, tongue licking at the corner of his mouth. "It's lucky I'm so drained, or I'd want to jump you now. How are you feeling?"

Matt lifted an arm to scratch the back of his head and watched Stetson's gaze follow it, the rabbit's brown eyes widening. "Pretty good, I guess. Still kinda sluggish."

Stetson shivered. "Your voice— This is going to take some getting used to, hon." He nodded his chin upward. "Turn around, lemme see."

Obligingly, Matt made a slow spin, his thighs sliding against each other, jostling his sac. When he turned back, he noticed the front of Stetson's shorts bulging out, drained though the rabbit claimed to be.

Stetson shook his head. "Damn, Matt. I hardly recognize you. Do you still feel like you want to—like you have to… cum?"

Matt shook his head. "No," he said, though just the mention of it made the tip of his shaft peek from his sheath. "I mean, I feel ready, definitely, but not like I *have* to."

Stetson slumped in naked relief. "Good to hear. You're hungry, I guess?"

"I could eat," Matt said, nodding, and as if in response, his stomach gurgled.

"Sit down then." Stetson gestured toward the table. There was a large, white plastic tub there, a pitcher of water, and a glass full of a brown liquid. "I figured you'd need more protein more than anything else."

Matt walked over, briefly forgetting to control the strength of his legs, half-bouncing across the room. Stetson chuckled. "Don't be too eager now."

Matt shook his head. "No, it's…" he trailed off. Why try to explain? He lifted the glass to his muzzle and gulped down the chocolate-flavored protein. The stuff tasted better than he remembered. The flavor of protein shakes tended toward the vile. Maybe his body just knew he needed it. The liquid in his stomach gurgled, and he poured a second glass, and then a third.

Stetson watched him quietly, and in the middle of Matt's fourth glass, brought over a plate of chicken and tuna fillets. Matt realized he just felt hungrier than ever and began gulping them down in huge bites, hardly pausing to chew. His stomach still didn't feel satisfied, nor even bloated. He guessed he was digesting the food quite quickly.

"Matt," Stetson began slowly. Matt looked up at him, chewing on a huge bite of chicken. "Are you okay?" the rabbit asked.

Matt kept chewing for a moment, thinking about the question, then swallowed. "I think so, yes," he said. "I mean, it's a lot to get used to, but you know I always wanted to be bigger." He grinned broadly. "And it's hard to argue with intense, mind-blowing pleasure, huh?"

Stetson smiled weakly. "Yes, but, you know… what if it doesn't go away?"

The big otter paused with his fork halfway to his mouth, briefly distracted by the feeling of his large biceps balling up on his arm. "I don't want it to go away," he said. "I really like being like this!" The question puzzled him a bit. Surely the rabbit knew this was a dream for him.

Stetson shook his head. "No, I mean… suppose it doesn't stop? Suppose for the rest of your life, every time you climax, you grow even more?" He stepped closer, putting a paw on Matt's round shoulder, fingering the new separations between the lobes of muscle there. "I've spent over four hundred dollars on food for you just over the weekend. And I mean, that's all right. We're not bad off. We can afford it. But if this keeps up, it might be hard. Not to mention finding clothes for you, transporting you around. And did you notice that you're taller now? I don't know how much. Maybe only a couple inches. But this is after only a couple days. What about in a year? What about in ten years?"

He nodded toward Matt's plump sheath. "How long before you can't fit that in me… in anyone?" His fingers slid down over the curve of the otter's biceps, and Matt instinctively tensed the muscle, watching as it jumped to steely roundness against the rabbit's paw. "What if you grow too thick to move?"

Matt shook his head. "Anything like that is a long way off, Stetson."

The rabbit nodded. "Yes, hon, but we should start thinking about it now. We need to find a way to stop this before… before it's too late. And you should see a doctor to make sure your tendons aren't going to snap or your heart give out from trying to pump blood to you."

Matt wasn't sure why, but he really didn't like the idea of seeing a doctor. How would he ever convince them what had happened? Who would believe him? All the same, he nodded. Stetson had always been the more level-headed of the two of them.

"I think you should start by going to the nutrition store," Stetson said. "Find out what all the products you swallowed are. Then maybe the doctor can figure out what happened and if it's going to be harmful for you. I'll call and set up an emergency appointment for you tomorrow."

Matt nodded again, continuing to gorge himself on the plates of food, washing them down with thick glasses of the chocolate-flavored protein. He was finally starting to feel sated, but his balls felt fuller, too. The Wholebutrin might be out of his system finally, but his body was energetic and virile. The urge to mate was always on a low simmer. He looked up at Stetson. "Thank you, love. I don't know what I would do without you."

The rabbit laughed. "I do. You'd spend all night jerking off and it would take a wrecking ball and a vacuum pump to get you out of the basement."

Matt looked around. "What happened to Saul, anyway?"

Stetson's expression darkened a little. "He went out to a brunch or something. Got tired of waiting for you to wake up."

Matt looked at the tuna on his fork and put it back down on his plate, finally feeling full. "You're pretty pissed at him, huh?"

The rabbit sighed, his brow furrowing. "Not… exactly. I mean, it's not like you were very resistible last night, you know. It's just disappointing that he didn't even seem to try. I thought I could count on him a bit more. I've known Saul for a while now—even before meeting you, and while he's always been a bit shallow, I never pegged him for the type to go behind my back just because he wanted something bad enough. Last night, you know, I tried. *You* tried. Saul didn't try at all. Whenever we were out of the room, he was begging me, pleading with me to let him have you more." He looked down. "I probably shouldn't say it, but he even offered me money…"

Matt gaped. "What? You mean, like, he tried to pay you to have sex with me? Like a pimp?"

Stetson shrugged. "I don't think he saw it that way. He just saw it as, well, demonstrating to me how much it was worth to him. Still, I almost hit him."

"So." Matt grinned. "How much am I worth?"

Stetson gave him a long look. "Twenty-five grand. For until he wanted to quit or you did."

"Seriously?"

The rabbit nodded. "Honestly, if there were any way I could have left with you then and there I would have. That's really... not right. I don't know what he wants with you, but it's not just a horny guy wanting to get his rocks off. I don't care how hot someone is. You don't pay that kind of money for sex. You pay it for something specific." He walked over to the counter and leaned back on it. "I don't like the idea—like I said, he's an old friend—but I don't think we can trust him."

Matt nodded. "It *is* pretty creepy, now you mention it. Okay, I'll be on my guard. And anyway, we'll be out of here today, so it shouldn't be an issue." He stood up from the chair, patting his belly in satisfaction, his fingers thumping against the unfamiliar lines and curves of his furry abdominals, rounded out from his gorging. "Thanks for breakfast, Stets. Should we head home, then, and then I'll go over to the WNC and talk to them?"

"Sounds like a plan," the rabbit smiled.

"Okay, then." The otter took his plates to the sink and dumped them in. "I figure after trying to buy me, making Saul do a few dishes isn't a crime."

Stetson chuckled. "No, I expect not, but we'll want to grab the rest of the tubs of protein and the food."

Together they scooped up the remainders, threw out the trash, and then Matt headed for the front door, a protein tub tucked under each arm.

"Uh, Matt?" Stetson said, staring at him pointedly.

Matt turned around. "Yeah, what?"

"You heading outside?"

"Uh-huh."

The rabbit nodded. "You maybe want to put on some clothes first? I mean, you cut a nice figure and all, but..."

Matt blinked, looking down at himself. "Huh. I just feel so different anyway, I guess I didn't notice. Um. *Are* there any clothes for me?"

Stetson tossed him a large tank top and some gym shorts, and Matt pulled them on. They hung loosely off his frame. "Wow," he said. "I grew huge and you still managed to find clothes too big for me."

The rabbit raised an eyebrow. "I didn't want to have to buy a second pair tomorrow," he said.

* * *

Matt paused outside the sports nutrition store. He wasn't even sure if that raccoon—What was his name? Harry? Perry?—would even be there. Hopefully whoever was would still be able to help him out, anyway. The drive over had been strange. His car's seat fit oddly, its edges digging into the swell of his back, and he kept bumping his elbow into the car door. He'd had to adjust everything: the seat, the mirrors. Even the steering wheel dug into his legs before he raised it. And when he sat down at first, he'd squashed his sac between his thighs, sending a sharp pain up into his gut. This was definitely going to take some getting used to.

He pushed the door open and walked through, bumping his arm rather hard on the frame. The raccoon was at the counter again. He glanced at the nametag. *Terry*, that was it. Right, with the arms that nicely filled out the shirtsleeves. Matt felt a habitual pang of envy before recalling that he probably couldn't fit his arms in those shirtsleeves anymore.

"Can I help you, sir?" the raccoon asked, looking up at him. He had an almost deferential look in his eyes. Do people treat you differently if you get big? Matt considered. He couldn't remember the last time anyone had called him sir without being snide about it. But then, he probably looked like a regular customer here.

"Terry, it's me," Matt said.

There was no recognition in the raccoon's eyes, but he forced a broad smile anyway. "Hey, man, great to see you."

Matt shook his head. "No, me, Matt, from the other day. I fell into the display case, swallowed a bunch of stuff by accident. Remember?"

The raccoon's expression went shifty and defensive. He backed away a step. "Dude, I don't know what that little guy told you, but it's all lies. Nothing happened. He was—he was trying to get free stuff, and when I wouldn't give it to him…"

Matt sighed. This was going to be more difficult than he thought. "No, I don't want to… sue you or get you in trouble if that's what you're thinking. I just need to know what was on that shelf. Everything that fell. Every package you threw away. For medical reasons."

The raccoon scratched at his chin warily. "For medical reasons?" he said. "I dunno, man, that sounds like it… uh… violates doctor-patient… privilege."

Matt rubbed at his forehead, feeling his biceps press against his forearm. "Yes," he said, "you might have a point, if you were a doctor. And if I were someone else entirely. Look, I'm the guy."

Terry shook his head. "Don't even, dude. Don't even. That guy was, like, half your size. Scrawny, high voice. You do look like him, I guess. Big brother, maybe?"

"No, look, I swallowed all that stuff, and it mixed funny, and now I'm—well, I'm growing. I know it's hard to believe, but—"

"Try impossible," the raccoon said, rolling his eyes. "Nobody grows like that in two days. It's a fantasy. Do you have any idea how much shit we'd sell if anything actually worked like that? Sorry, man. Play your games somewhere else. There is absolutely no way I'm going to believe that you've just been growing like that. No way."

A surge of frustration flooded through Matt's chest. He planted one arm on the counter and leaned forward. "Now look here, you little—" he paused. Terry had backed away farther from the counter, lifting his arms in front of him and squeezing his eyes closed as if about to be hit. Matt could feel the thick bulge of his sheath sliding against the delightfully slick fabric of the gym shorts. He looked back at Terry again. The raccoon was young, well-toned, lithe. His tail switched behind him nervously, pulling Matt's eyes toward it. The otter felt his sheath pulse. This wasn't a good idea, he told himself.

But still, if it worked… "What if," he said, trying to keep his voice reassuring, "I could prove it to you?"

The raccoon's folded ears swiveled partly forward. "Prove it?" he asked, opening one eye. "How?"

Desire churned in Matt's loins, rising upward with his scent. Mating would be good. And he even had a good reason for it—it was the only way to get the information he needed. "What if I could grow a little bit for you now?" he said.

The raccoon sniffed at the air suddenly. "You can't…" he began. "I mean, that's impossible."

Matt leaned farther forward on the counter, feeling his triceps thicken under his weight. "Not impossible," he said. The squeeze of the counter against his sheath pushed a few inches of his shaft out against the rough elastic of his waistband, making it bulge. "Do you have a back room?"

The raccoon sniffed the air again. Matt inhaled deeply, but couldn't smell anything different. Terry shook his head. "No. I mean, we do, but it's full of stock. There's no room." His fur was beginning to stand on end. "I could take a break," he said. "I mean, lock the door and close the shutters."

The otter nodded. "That will work." Excitement was beginning to course through his veins; he felt his cock push out a few inches more, jutting obscenely up under his tank top.

Terry quickly opened the counter and moved to the front door. He locked it, looking over his shoulder almost hungrily at Matt as he did so, and closed the blinds. "You know, dude," he said, walking slowly back over to Matt, scanning him up and down, "you didn't have to make up some story for me. If you wanted this, all you had to do was say so. I'd have dropped everything for you." He stood close, and, watching Matt's face for any warning signs of disapproval, put his fingers on the otter's chest, slowly sliding them down until they rested atop that rising tent. "God, how big does this thing get?" he murmured.

"That," Matt said, lifting up his shirt and pulling it up over his shoulders, "is what I'm trying to find out."

Terry crouched down, his whiskers twitching as his breath huffed over the rising spire. He inhaled deeply, black mask peering up at

Matt over the twin swells of the otter's pectorals, then shuddered. "I think I can get it in me, dude," he breathed. "Unless you want me to lick?"

Matt shook his head. He was hungry to feel Terry's tightness around him. "I think you can get it in you too," he said.

Terry bit his lip, nodding, and slid his hands down to unbutton his pants, letting them drop down to his ankles, revealing toned, grey-furred legs, and, Matt was amused to note, Spiderman underwear. He pushed those down as well, quickly stepping out and stripping off his shirt to reveal his lithe torso, with a light swimmer's build, his somewhat smallish grey sheath straining with the pink cock already thrusting up from it.

"Lube," he said in a sudden, hushed voice, remembering, and then he looked down at Matt's cock. The end was already gooey with pre, a long rivulet sliding downward. "Never mind!" he breathed. His eyes were wide. Matt followed his gaze and immediately pushed his gym shorts down over his thighs and kicked them away—he couldn't afford to mess them up here.

Terry turned around, crouching on hands and paws, arching his rump high, his striped tail swaying above it. "Hurry," he pleaded, biting his lip again. His cock was already dripping onto the floor.

Matt crouched behind him, the raccoon's thick-furred brush swishing against his pectorals. He planted his tip up under Terry's tail, sliding it between the slim, rounded cheeks of his rump. His pre made a sticky sound as he pushed forward. "Relax," he advised the raccoon, and then, gripping at Terry's hips with his right paw, he increased the pressure.

"Oh gods!" the raccoon cried out, his voice going high. He was tight, very tight, around the head of Matt's shaft, but spread open slowly. Matt accidentally gave a little growl. He didn't want to go easy on the raccoon. Terry had wanted proof, so Matt would give him proof. He gave a little thrust with his hips, making Terry cry out again. "Gods!" The store clerk lost his purchase, sliding across the floor toward the shelves a little, gamely pushing backward with his feet and hands. Matt tugged again at the raccoon's hips and felt the satisfying tightness close behind the head of his shaft. He flexed inside the clerk, looking down past his chest to see the thick pink pole of his erection stretch where it slid under the striped tail. The raccoon gave a wordless cry this time as Matt's pre splashed into him, then panted. "Did you… did you already…?"

Matt chuckled, stroking his claws up through the fur on Terry's side. "Oh no," he said. "We're just getting started." And with that, he began to push deeper into the raccoon, sinking in inch after inch, his low, lustful growl joining the clerk's groans. He paused once he was nearly all the way in, not wanting to hurt the little procyonid, and then his cock flexed on its own, flooding Terry's gut with another wash of precum. He drew back a bit and begin to thrust, provoking loud groans in response, Terry's claws scrabbling as the thrusts pushing him across the smooth linoleum of the store toward the shelves.

Matt was taking his time this time, no longer under the control of the hyperactive drive of the previous night, feeling in charge of the situation and wanting to enjoy the raccoon who had so eagerly offered himself to him. He thrust again and Terry's nose bumped into product on the shelves. The raccoon lifted his paws to brace against the shelves, and now there was satisfactory resistance; Matt made smooth but forceful thrusts against the tight rump, sinking in a half inch deeper, and then another, as the raccoon began to climb the shelves with his hands, changing the angle with each of Matt's thrusts. Soon Matt was standing upright, pinning the lithe, squirming frame of the moaning raccoon up against the shelves as he thrust upward into him, each push rattling the contents of the shelves, protein jugs and vitamin bottles thumping, clattering, bouncing as they toppled to the floor.

Terry's arms were above his head, his arms braced against the upper shelf, his teeth clenched as he pushed down against the thick spear thrusting into him, and Matt let him go, gripping the shelves to either side with two strong hands and tugging at them as he thrust a couple more times, still unable to hilt entirely, and then his climax burst into the raccoon with ecstatic intensity. He heard the gurgle of it in Terry's gut; the raccoon groaned, his belly tight, and Matt's hot seed begin to squeeze out around his shaft and run down to drip from his sac. Again and again he came, the puddle spreading to touch one broad lutrine paw. And then, just as the urgency of his climax

began to fade, he felt the familiar tenseness seize his body once more, every muscle squeezing in contract, his head arching back as he tried to keep a groan from becoming a roar. He could feel it more acutely this time, feel his biceps mounding up, the spread of his lats, his traps rising like hills, neck thickening, his spread quads pressing into each other again. And then Terry yowled, his fingers gripping tightly at the shelves. He pulled himself upward as Matt felt his cock pulse thicker and longer inside the raccoon, as the shelves to which his webbed fingers squeezed seemed to lower just a bit.

Then it was over, and they were both panting in the conspicuous quiet of the store. Matt waited a bit, neither of them saying anything, as he waited for him to soften up so he could pull out without causing Terry too much discomfort, but apparently his balls' growth had just refilled them. He wasn't going to get any softer planted inside this exhausted raccoon; far more likely, lust would take hold of him once more and he'd go for another round. So carefully, slowly, he pulled himself out, seed spilling onto the floor. With strong hands he gripped Terry and helped him back down to the floor.

"There, you see?" he said finally. "I told you I grew."

Terry nodded wordlessly, his eyes wide and apparently a little frightened. "Dude," he finally managed. "Dude, that was amazing."

Matt chuckled. "It was pretty good, yeah. So, now you wanna tell me what was on that shelf that got spilled? I'm happy now, but if I keep growing…"

Terry shook his head. "Why would you ever want to stop? Nearly every guy who comes here would kill for what you have."

Matt scratched at his chest, noticing how it pushed out a little farther. "It's good up to a point," he said. "But if I grow every time I cum, that sort of limits the amount of sex I have in my lifetime, yeah? So I need those ingredients." He paused, a mischievous smile crossing his muzzle. "And can you hook me up with a jug of protein? Seems like I've earned it, huh?"

Terry nodded dazedly, not even questioning the request. "Sure thing, man." He turned around. "Geez, this is gonna be a mess to clean up. Again."

# Chapter 9

Matt squinted at the papers in his paw. The task of noting down everything he might have swallowed had been more daunting than he'd anticipated. Seventeen different mass building products had toppled off the shelf; fourteen of the containers had come open for certain—apparently the shelf above them had slipped down and crushed the containers, spilling their contents everywhere. Who knew which—or how much—of those he had accidentally swallowed. Carefully, he'd copied down the product names and the ingredients from each of the labels. There were hundreds of ingredients in total, some of them suspiciously vague. What was "herbal cellulose," for example? He wondered if the doctor would be able to make any sense of this, but perhaps one of the ingredients would stand out to her. Shrugging, he opened his car door and stepped in.

The act of squeezing into the unexpectedly small space made him grunt. His knees were pressed up against the steering wheel, his chest hunching forward. He could just feel the brush of his ear tips against the car ceiling. Driving over had been a bit uncomfortable on the way to the store, but now he could really feel the difference. He reached under the seat, his thighs squeezing at his sac as he did so, and found the lever to adjust it. Pulling it slid the seat back only couple inches, but it was still more comfortable, so he started the car and pulled out of the lot.

It was like having to learn to drive all over again. The weight of the pedals was different, the height of the steering wheel. That, at least, he could adjust, along with the mirrors. But his shoulders bulged taut, rippled when he turned. His chest crowded his arms for space. His back was a bit wider than the driver's seat, which was made for a person with a normal frame. Now the edges of the seat pushed into his lats. It wasn't uncomfortable, exactly, just an ever-present reminder that he was larger than the auto manufacturers planned for.

He headed down Roxburgh Avenue, a main thoroughfare with lots of shops and restaurants. His stomach rumbled. He'd downed a good third of the jug of protein, but apparently his body craved more. He eyed the jug sitting there in the passenger's seat. No good dry. Inedible, even. Up ahead was Cobee's Fish Shack. Matt swore he could smell it from where he sat.

Twenty minutes later he was back on the road with a bucket of cod. The clerk had stammered at him when he ordered his food. She had kept looking away. He was pretty sure that the others in the Shack hadn't, though. He could practically feel their eyes crawling over him while he stood there. When he had looked over his shoulder, they all stared at each other, or down at their food. It had unnerved him a little, even though it was a thrill. He wasn't even that big! Muscular, sure, but hardly excessively so. There were plenty of larger guys at his gym. Did all guys this size get that kind of treatment?

He shrugged mentally, and pulled onto the freeway, reaching over into the passenger seat to take another piece of cod from the bucket. As he accelerated into the merge, the slippery fish slid from between his fingers and landed in his lap. Swearing, he pawed at it, trying to catch it before it soaked into his shorts or slipped down onto the floor, and just as his eyes followed it, he heard the loud honk of an SUV.

Immediately alert, he looked up and over and jerked the wheel to the side just in time to avoid sliding into the other lane and plowing into a truck twice the size of his little car. His arm pulled the steering wheel farther to the side than he meant to, sending his vehicle skidding to the side and onto the gravelly shoulder.

His heart pounded for a moment as he tried to straighten the wheel, hearing tiny rocks spray out from under his tires and rattle against the undercarriage, and then the tires caught the asphalt again and he lurched forward, only to be rewarded by an annoyed honk from the vehicle behind him. Yeah, I know, he muttered to himself. The previous honk and the nearly barreling into the guardrail sort of tipped me off that I fucked up, but I appreciate your input, asshole.

He felt the brief surge of adrenaline flooding out of his chest as he steadied his vehicle and accelerated back up to speed, but it was too soon: there was the *wup-WUP* of a siren behind him, and the flash of blue lights. Great. Great, great, great. He waited for a broader part of the shoulder and slowed onto it. The car pulled in behind him, lights flashing.

His stomach growled again. He reached down and picked up the fallen piece of cod and, feeling guilty, crammed it into his mouth. He was still chewing when he sat upright and saw the police uniform outside his window, a hand capped with the thick black nails of a horse tapping at the glass. He rolled down the window. "Officer, I can explain," he started.

"License and registration," the horse said, leaning down to peer at him. He was wearing those stereotypical mirrored sunglasses you always saw cops on tv wearing. Great.

Matt reached in his pocket for his wallet, his fingers grazing against the bulge of his thigh. He took out his license and handed it to the cop—the horse's thick nails clicked on the plastic as he took it—and then reached across to the glove box for his registration.

"You having any problems with your vehicle today, Mr. Stafford?"

"No, sir."

"No engine trouble, tires, other mechanical problems?"

"No sir, I just… my paws slipped on the wheel for a second."

"Have you had anything to drink today?"

"No sir."

The cop leaned down again, peering at the license and peering at Matt again. "Sir, is this your vehicle?"

"Yes, sir."

"If I go back and look this up in my computer, is it going to say this car is registered to Matt Stafford?"

"Yes, sir."

"Are you Matt Stafford?"

Matt was beginning to feel a bit panicked now. This was not how this situation was supposed to go. "Yes, sir, that's what my parents told me." He tried a laugh. It sounded pathetic.

"I'd like you to step out of your vehicle now. And keep your hands where I can see them."

There was no emotion in the horse's voice other than Routine Procedure. Matt, on the other hand, couldn't stop his knees from shaking. He fumbled for the door handle. His fingers were slippery with oil from the fish, and the handle didn't seem to be where he remembered it being. Clumsily, he managed to open the door and stepped out, keeping his hands on the door frame.

"Sir, I want you to keep an eye on the traffic and walk around to the other side of the vehicle. I'm going to follow you. We're going to walk toward the back so that you can see the cars as they're coming. Do you understand?"

"Yes."

"Okay, let's go."

The cars roared as they went by, the gusts of hot wind from them tugging at his fur, reeking of partially burned gasoline and smoke. He stopped at the other side of his car.

"Turn around."

When he turned, the horse took off his sunglasses. His eyes were large and brown, with long lashes, and stared intently into Matt's. Probably looking for dilation or other signs of intoxication, Matt figured. The cop put his sunglasses back on, and Matt looked down. The nametag on his uniform read COKIE. Officer Cokie, really?

"You're a big guy, aren't you?" Officer Cokie asked.

Matt looked back at him; the horse was at least three inches taller than him, and pretty broad-shouldered. "I guess I am, sort of."

"Your license says you're five foot ten."

Oh shit. "Yes, sir."

"My wife is five foot ten."

Matt scrambled in his mind for a way out of this. "Well, that's what I was when I was twenty. Maybe I've grown a little since then?

"And it says you weigh a hundred and fifty pounds."

"Sir..."

"I'm going to ask you this one more time, and I want you to think very carefully before you answer me: are you Matt Stafford?"

"Yes, sir, I swear, sir, you can call my boyfriend and ask him..." No sooner had the words slipped out of his mouth than he heard his mistake.

"Your boyfriend?" The cop's voice curled in disgust.

"Yes, sir."

"Please turn around and put your hands on top of the vehicle."

Trembling properly now, he obeyed.

"Are you carrying any weapons?"

"No, sir."

"Is there anything in your pockets or on your person that might endanger me?"

"No, sir."

"I'm going to frisk you now. Remain still and keep your hands on top of the vehicle."

The cop's hands were at his sides, then, sliding down his lats. He actually had to reach forward a bit to cup around the front of them, and then he breathed a low, quiet whistle. His hands moved down to the otter's waist, and then down over his thighs. Despite his fear, the otter felt a little shiver of excitement run through him, and when the cop's hands slid up between his thighs to where the thick muscles pressed together, it amplified.

"Sir, please spread your feet a farther apart."

He did so, and the policeman's hands slid higher, until they bumped into the bottom of his sac. He felt the contents of his sheath swell and rise, pushing up under his waistband, below the bottom of his shirt. *Really?* he thought to himself. *Now?!* The horse's blunt-fingered hands reached around his waist to pat his stomach and then across his protruding tip. He felt the cop stiffen and back up.

"Do you have a weapon in your waistband?"

Despite his fear, he felt a sudden urge to snicker and quickly suppressed it.

"No, sir."

"What was that, there? What did I feel?"

"Sir, it's, uh… it's" —he felt his cheeks flush hotly— "me."

There was silence behind him for a moment. "Bullshit."

"I swear, sir."

The cop's arms reached around his waist again; he could feel the horse's breath against the back of his shirt. Fingers gingerly groped at the bulge rising up under his shirt, squeezing at the tip and then farther down. His cock instantly pulsed and swelled thicker in response to the touch; despite himself, his libido was beginning to charge through his veins once again.

"Turn around," the cop said.

He turned, and Officer Cokie looked down at the tent comically jutting out the front of his shirt. Reaching down, the horse took the bottom of Matt's t-shirt and lifted it up, exposing a pink pillar which, as if on command, surged higher, a viscous trickle of pre running down to stain the front of Matt's shorts. Matt felt suddenly, acutely aware of the traffic roaring by just behind him.

The horse breathed in sharply, his jaws gaping. "You weren't lyin'," he said, shaking his head. He seemed to try to compose himself. "Well, you ain't as big as a horse, of course, but damn, boy." He breathed in again, and then sniffed at the air. He looked right and left, as if to convince himself no one was watching. "You said you have a boyfriend."

Oh, great. Matt nodded.

"So you—you have sex with guys then."

He resisted the urge to make a sarcastic reply. "Yes, sir." There was a thin pattering sound coming from below; his tip was spilling pre onto the ground, the drops rolling up in little dusty balls.

The horse's voice was hungry now. "You ever fucked a cop before?"

"Sir, I—I can't." But he wanted to, all of a sudden. He couldn't deny that.

He saw the horse's jaw tighten in anger. "I could always take you in on suspicion of a stolen vehicle. Would that be better?"

He couldn't believe he was actually hearing this. "Sir, are you saying?"

The cop nodded. "You can go to jail today… or you can stick that pole in me." He licked his lips, staring down again.

*Stick that pole in me?* Who *was* this guy?

"Are you—are you even gay?"

The cop spat. "Fuck, no! That's disgusting! I told you, I got a wife! Now what's it gonna be, son?" His fingers toyed with his belt buckle.

Matt could tell himself he didn't have a real choice here, but to be honest, it wasn't as if he didn't want to. "Where do you want to do it?"

The horse's voice quickened with excitement. "Here," he said eagerly. "Up against your car." He was already undoing his belt.

Matt frowned in confusion. "But… the traffic. People will see!"

"Shit, son, you're on the *other* side of the car. What you think they're gonna see?" He dropped his pants, revealing thickly muscled legs covered with sleek, dark brown fur, a pair of heavy, orange-sized balls held tightly in their sac, and jutting above, an already rising erection that, Matt had to admit, was significantly bigger than his own.

"Well," Matt said slowly, "at the very least they'll see some guy pinning a cop up against his car."

The cop hesitated. "You got a good point. Here." He took off his hat and sunglasses and handed them to Matt. "Put these on. That way it'll look like you're the cop, and you're just frisking me."

This couldn't be for real. "Seriously? This has to be some kind of trap."

The cop reached down for his discarded trousers, where he'd left his handcuffs and, presumably, a pistol. "Son, I swear to god…"

"Okay, okay!" Matt put the hat on his head, feeling the grip of the band around his ears, and then the shades, dimming the world into brown. He allowed himself a grin. "Turn around slowly and put your hands atop the vehicle."

To his astonishment, the officer actually bit his lower lip and made a faint mewl of excitement. His black-haired tail raised and swished back and forth against his uniform shirt as he leaned forward against the car, arching back and pushing his rump outward, looking back over one shoulder at Matt. He had a hungry, eager expression.

Matt's shoulders swayed with confidence as he swaggered up behind the cop and nudged his dripping tip between those roundly muscled buttocks. He slid in smoothly, easily, the cop relaxing for him as if experienced. And as he began his short, urgent thrusts, making the horse groan and scratch at the paint of Matt's car roof with his heavy nails, making that cop's thick horse cock smear up the glass of his windows with pre, making the whole car shake with the force of his movements, all the while, the officer's expression was plain, serious, that of Routine Procedure.

Finally, he finished, panting, feeling the heat of his seed floating around his shaft, buried deep within the groaning horse's ass, and started to slide outward, when he felt the cop's easy grip around his

cock suddenly grip tight, the cheeks of his rump clenching. "Hold on there, son," the horse said. "I ain't done yet. Now let's go again."

Matt shook his head, and felt the new thickness of his neck, felt the way his arms pushed against his chest just a little more, felt the way the horse was just a little tighter around him than before. He'd grown again. "I can't," he said. "I really can't."

No sooner had he said it than his shaft twitched, flexed as if of its own accord.

"I dunno," said the cop. "It feels to me like you can. Anyway," he turned to look over his shoulder, and his eyes took on a pleading expression, "I didn't mean it, Officer, I swear. I'll never do it again. Sir, please, Sir, couldn't you just let me off with a warning? I'll be extra good from now on." His rump clenched again, squeezing deliciously down Matt's length again. "Please, Sir, let me go?"

Matt's voice came out in a low, wicked growl. "I'm sorry, son," he said. "But that would be against the Law." And with that, he pushed his hips forward, sinking just a little deeper than before.

\* \* \*

He knew Stetson would be upset when he got home, but there wasn't a lot he could do about it. The door to their house actually looked smaller; he had to reach down a bit for the knob. His arm and shoulder hit the doorframe pretty hard as he entered, but it didn't hurt at all.

Stetson was lying nude on the sofa in the living room, reading a book, and his jaw went a bit slack when he looked up. "I'd ask how it went," he said, "but the answer is either 'not good' or 'very good,' and I'm not sure which one I want." He sighed and got up from the sofa. "I guess you're hungry again; I figured you would be. There's a roast in the oven."

Matt's stomach growled. "Stetson, there was nothing I could do. The guy at the store wouldn't tell me what was in the stuff. He didn't believe it was me. I had to prove what was happening to me. And then on the way home this cop pulled me over and... he actually *made* me under threat of arrest." He couldn't stop a half-smirk from creeping across his muzzle.

Stetson gave him an appraising look. "Yeah, I'm betting you didn't take much convincing. But look at you now! You're—you're huge. You've got to be at least three inches taller than when you left this morning, and have you weighed yourself? I'm betting you're in the upper two hundreds." He tapped at his chin with a paw. "You could compete now, you know?"

Matt stuck out his tongue. "Like bodybuilding? No way, it's just too weird, getting up there and flexing in front of people."

"It might be weird, but it could be lucrative," Stetson said. "And we're gonna have to feed that appetite of yours somehow."

Matt sighed. "So you're not mad that I...?" he trailed off.

Stetson got up from the couch, setting down his book, and walked over to Matt. He looked so small now. He actually had to look up at Matt, his chin at the otter's chest. "Of course I'm not mad," he said. "Look at you, you're *built* for sex. How can I blame you for doing what you're wired to do... and so clearly enjoy? Besides, you were so unhappy as you were before. I'm glad that you've gotten what you wanted." He hesitated. "I'm just worried. And we've talked about why. I don't want this to become something you *don't* want."

Matt cupped the rabbit's rump and thighs in his webbed paws, hefting him up against his chest. His thick sheath pressed against the rabbit's own, but for now, he ignored the twitching, ever-present desire in his cock, resisted the urge to slide his fingers between the rabbit's glutes and heft him higher. Instead he pressed his muzzle to Stetson's, closing his eyes and kissing firmly, enjoying the tickle of the rabbit's whiskers against his cheeks. He barely even noticed the way his arms never seemed to tire holding his boyfriend aloft, nor the way his tongue felt just a little bit bigger between Stetson's teeth.

\* \* \*

Stetson woke in the middle of the night to a familiar and compelling scent. There was a persistent sticky sound coming from his right. Blearily, he blinked in that direction. Matt lay there, apparently asleep, his eyes closed, his breathing slow and steady, huge, muscled chest rising and falling in the dim light of the room. Jutting up from his loins was a huge erection, bigger now than Stetson's, nearly a foot in length, too big to get a paw around. It reached nearly to his chest. In his sleep, Matt had curled his torso forward—still flexible despite his increased bulk, and was slowly licking at his own tip, cleaning away the clear, salty flow. Stetson gaped for a moment at this sight and then leaned over the other side of the bed and rummaged beneath for their video recorder—Matt would never believe this otherwise. He set it recording on the nightstand, and then rolled over, leaning up to assist, his tongue lapping at the oozing tip and the otter's tongue in smooth, peaceful strokes, for the first time kissing his boyfriend in both places at once.

\* \* \*

It wasn't fair.

Saul paced back and forth across his living room. It wasn't fair and it wasn't right. He'd had his eye on the otter first, right from the beginning. He'd pointed him out to Stetson at the restaurant that time, back when the rabbit used to wait tables. And then Stetson had hooked up with Matt and left him out of the equation! All right, so that's the way it goes, that's fine. But then to bring the otter, this being of pure sex, *back* to his place and deny him access? To treat him like—like some kind of imposing rapist after he'd offered his basement and services and help? It was ungrateful, is what it was. No, it was beyond ungrateful. It was spiteful. Stetson didn't want him to have Matt just because he knew because Saul wanted him.

"It's not even," he muttered, "like he can handle him—that is way too much otter hunk for one person. It's selfish. And greedy. And wrong. Matt's a free person. He should be able to have sex with the people he wants to."

"And he's going to want to have sex with me." He looked down at his paw, his fingers curled around the little orange pill bottle there. "He's *really, really* going to want to."

# Chapter 10

The raccoon really wanted it again. That was the only excuse, Matt figured. Otherwise, how could he have tracked him down from the health supply store. The little health store clerk nestled up against Matt's front, and Matt went instantly and immediately stiff.

"Matt!" Stetson's voice said sharply.

He looked around to see his boyfriend standing in the doorway. "What's up, Stetson? You want in on this too?"

"Matt!" Stetson said again.

The raccoon—Gary, he thought it was—wait, no... anyway, the raccoon pushed on his side, but it wasn't a raccoon after all. It was that husky— What?

Matt opened his eyes. The room was bright and sunny, and he was lying in bed, with Stetson pushing at his side. "You have to get up. We forgot to set the alarm."

"What?" He spoke the word lingering in his mind out loud. His erection pulsed. He wished briefly that he could go back into the dream, but then thought better of it, and reached for Stetson instead. "No—no we didn't. It's..." He squinted into the morning light.

"It's Monday morning."

Monday! Matt sat up, scrambling out of bed, and his erection pulled the sheets halfway with him, making him wince. He staggered dizzily, still not used to seeing the floor so far away. It felt like he was standing up on a platform or something. He stared down at himself, looking past his broad chest, trying to will his morning wood away. It couldn't be Monday. "No, because last night was..."

"Sunday night," Stetson said, pulling his slacks over his broad feet and buttoning them. "And the night before, you spent at Saul's, and the night before that was Friday night, when all this started. Remember?"

"Crap crap crap," Matt said. Monday morning already. He went to the closet for his clothes.

"I know, I forgot too," Stetson said. He was already buttoning up his shirt. "But I did pick up some clothes for you yesterday. I hope they fit."

Matt saw them immediately, hanging in the left of the closet with the tags still attached: a blue dress shirt and chinos. He gave Stetson a grateful smile. "What would I do without you?"

Stetson nodded. "Just be prepared, you know, for some questions. You don't really look the same. I've got no idea how that's going to go."

The shirt was tight around Matt's arms and shoulders. His chest fit into it okay, but his back seemed to stretch the fabric even when it was unbuttoned. It wasn't going to look good no matter what he did. "Maybe I should just call in," he said.

The rabbit wiggled his tail through the back of the beltloops and buckled his belt. "It's not like you're going to be smaller tomorrow, Matt. You've got to go in sometime."

His thighs were too big for the pants. He tugged them up anyway, but they looked like ill-fitting tights around his quads, and fitting his sheath and sac into the front required some strategic arrangement and tucking. He hardly looked presentable. He turned and shrugged at Stetson, whose ears drooped backward at the sight. "Well, it's still better than going in gym clothes," the rabbit offered.

Matt nodded. "See you tonight, Stets." He stepped over and reached down for his rabbit, still amazed that he had to reach *down* to put his arms around him. He hefted Stetson up against his chest for a kiss, and his still plump sheath pulsed against the belt that he'd tightened across it. Stetson was so light in his grip, so easily lifted. He could strip those clothes away now and rut the rabbit up against the bedroom wall….

He pushed the thought from his mind. No. Time for work. Reluctantly, he broke the kiss and eased his boyfriend back to the floor.

Stetson gazed up at him for a moment, breathing heavily, his nostrils flared. Then he shook his head as if clearing it. "Might want to take a jar of that protein to work with you in case you get hungry again. Are you seeing the doctor after work?"

"Going to try to," Matt said. "Hopefully they'll be able to tell me if anything is weird about what I took."

"I think we can safely say there is." Stetson patted his arm. "Try not to have *too* much sex today, dear."

Matt laughed. How had this ever become a consideration in his life? "I'll try."

* * *

Pilaris Industries was built with personal motivation in mind. As soon as you walked in the front doors, you felt like you were on your way up. And you were, because as soon as you entered, you had to go up a set of stairs or an elevator. Matt had no idea what was on the ground floor, behind the stairs. He assumed that, much like the various inspirational platitudes lining the walls, that there was nothing behind it at all.

He swiped his ID badge to get into the elevators and tried to ignore the stares of the security guards, which he felt more than saw. He wished now he had called in after all. It would at least have given him a day to pick up some better-fitting clothes. Had he not been late to work, though, the elevator would have been full of people crowding to squeeze in, so he was somewhat grateful for his tardiness.

It wasn't until he entered the office that the reality of his change really hit him for the first time. Here he was, in the place where he'd spent countless tedious hours typing away at his computer, shut up in a little cubicle. Only now, he was not the same otter anymore. He could tell by the way he could see over the tops of all the cubicle walls. They were five feet, eight inches high, just tall enough so that, before, if he stood up on the tips of his webbed toes, he could barely peer over their edges into the cubicles. Now he towered over them, the pathways through their labyrinthine arrangements easy to see, their occupants' semi-private lives laid out before him.

Casey looked up at him as he paused by the chocolate lab's cube, and grinned up at him. "Spyin' on me, huh, buddy? Come on, get off the chair before you fall."

Matt felt his ears go hot. "Yeah, okay, Casey. Have a good weekend?"

Casey frowned at him. "You feeling all right there? You sound a little weird. You shouldn't come in if you're coming down with something. I got enough to do here without having to take sick days."

Matt knew his voice had been a little deeper and rumbling lately, but if it was bad enough that people noticed immediately...

"I feel okay," he said. "But if I notice any symptoms, I'll let Gomez know I'm going home. Thanks, Casey."

There was no way this was going to work. How was he going to explain himself? It had been stupid to come in. He ducked his head down and quickly hurried past the rows of cubes to his own. He tried to dart inside so that no one would notice, but his shoulder struck the edge of the doorway hard and made the whole row shudder. "Sorry!" he called out hastily, hoping it would keep anyone from popping out to check. He sat down heavily in his chair, and it creaked in complaint with his weight. He felt like he was squatting: his knees were sticking up, and the arms of the chair were digging into his lats.

"A little late this morning, Matt?" Janelle's voice floated over his cubicle wall.

"Yeah, a little," he called back. He tried to make his voice sound higher. Janelle apparently found her tech writing job tedious, because she could be overly concerned with her coworkers' affairs sometimes. With one arm, he reached over the side of the chair and fumbled for the lever to elevate it. His fingers finally found it and he gave it a tug. The chair made a loud *clock* sound and collapsed to the floor. "Damn it," he muttered under his breath.

"Mr. Gomez was looking for you," Janelle said, an admonishing tone to her voice. "I told him I hadn't seen you all morning."

"Thanks, Janelle." Matt gritted his teeth as he said the words. "Appreciate that." He stood up, pulled the chair's lever, and elevated it all the way. He could see Janelle's antlers poking up inside her cubicle, and then her brown eyes and mussed fur as she blinked dully up at him.

"Having chair problems?"

The otter winced and ducked back down. "Yes." He adjusted his chair's arms so they wouldn't dig into his lats as much and sat down in it again. It creaked once more as if it were going to collapse.

"You know, you should have made that appointment with Terrell for your ergonomics assessment. We were all supposed to." The noise of her nails clattering away at the keyboard began its machinegun fire again.

Arguing with her would never get you anywhere. It was best to just keep agreeing until she forgot about you. "That's a very good point, Janelle."

"Anyway, he wanted to see you when you got in. Mr. Gomez, I mean. He's not pleased that you've been tardy so often, Matt."

"Thank you, Janelle," Matt sighed. He slid his chair under his desk and then nearly yelped as his knees slammed into the desktop.

"What is the problem over there?" the reindeer demanded, her tone growing more strident.

Matt bit his lip, hunching over, trying not to swear out loud at her. "Nothing. Just... banged my knees." At least, he thought, there was no chance at all of getting aroused today.

"What the hell are you doing in here?" came a voice from behind him.

Matt turned in his chair—gingerly avoiding the desktop this time. Marc Gomez stood in his doorway, shirt sleeves rolled partway up, powerful arms folded across his chest. The otter blanched. "Mr. Gomez, I'm so sorry I was late; I just forgot to set my alarm this morning."

A series of expressions shifted across the lion's face: recognition, then shock, then confusion, and then suspicion. "And just who the hell are you? A brother, I suppose?"

With a worried shake of his head, Matt answered, "No, sir, it's me. It's—it's Matt, sir."

The lion's jaws gaped in laughing incredulity. "Do you think I'm an idiot?" he spluttered. "It'd take three of that little runt to make up one of you."

Janelle came around the corner, peering in at him with narrowed eyes. "I thought he sounded funny, Mr. Gomez. There was something wrong the moment he came in, and he's been making all kinds of racket."

"Back to your desk, Janelle," Gomez said.

"And he was spying on me," Janelle continued, as if the lion had said nothing at all. "Over the top of my—"

"*Now*," he roared. She squinted malevolently at Matt and then bustled around the corner.

Matt stood up from his chair, and now there were heads poking up over the tops of the cubicles, looking toward the commotion like a colony of curious prairie dogs. "Sir, if you would just allow me to explain."

The lion looked around at the growing crowd of unproductive workers peering toward them. "In my office," he growled in a lower tone. "Let's go."

His ears folded back as he followed his boss through the cubicle aisles to his office. The room was windowless, the walls white and austere, except for a picture on one that said SUCCESS, and showed a lion sailing through high waves on a yacht. The caption below read, "Winning is having the strength to take courage in your own vision." And a yacht, Matt always thought whenever he saw it. The furniture was utilitarian, brown. There were barely any decorations on the desk: just a few photos of a lioness and two cubs.

Matt's eyes strayed toward the lion's rump as he moved around the desk, the ropey tail switching above a muscled butt that his tailored pants couldn't quite hide. Matt had always been jealous: lions always had naturally great builds, and Gomez, despite his desk job, was no exception. The glance made him recall his fantasy of the night before, the one that had made him paint Saul's basement, and he felt himself stiffen in his pants, the belt strapped across his sheath starting to dig in a bit. Oh gods. Not here. Don't have sex in the office, not here, in this horrible, lifeless place. Not with Marc freaking Gomez.

The lion sat in his chair. "Close the door." He stared up at Matt. "It is amazing how much you resemble him."

"Sir, it's me." Matt reached up to rub at his head with one hand and heard the seams in his shirt begin to complain. He quickly lowered it again. "I know it seems strange, but something happened to me after work last week. Since then I've been growing. I swear it's me. Ask me anything about my job. Anything."

Gomez's yellow eyes narrowed. "Just how stupid do you think I am?" He leaned across his desk, his claws unsheathed, pitting the desktop. His tail lashed behind him.

Matt had never seen him angry and threatening like this before. Gomez had always been imperious, but he'd never seemed dangerous. He waited for the lion to continue, and when he said nothing, he finally said, "Mr. Gomez, I—"

"Be quiet!" the lion snarled. "You look a *little* like that little milquetoast otter, sure. Around the face and the eyes. But you honestly expect anyone here to believe some cockamamie story about how you're him? What's your game here? Why the story? You some relative trying to help him get a day or two off? That it?"

"No, sir, I told you—"

"I said be *silent!*" The lion's mane bushed out as he roared, his claws digging into the desk. The walls shook with the sound.

Matt bit his lip, barely daring to breathe. The yacht picture tilted to one side and then dropped to the floor, making him flinch. He was incredibly frightened… wasn't he? He reached down inside himself. There, true, some part of him was frightened. It quailed in terror, wanted to run from the office, to tear out without even packing up his things, just race away and never return. But now he found there was another part inside him, a part that was saying, *This lion is smaller than you. Weaker. He should be put in his place.* He felt himself straighten up, and his gaze locked with that of Marc Gomez, steady, unfazed. His shoulders spread a bit wider, and for the first time, he saw uneasiness flicker across the lion's face.

His name badge was clipped to his belt, attached by a retractable cord. He reached down and lifted it up, extending the cord to hold it up to Gomez's muzzle. "Look at my badge. Look at my face. It's me. I don't have any other way to prove it to you."

The lion's gaze flickered over to the badge and then back to Matt, then returned to the badge again. His ears went back, and his jaw slackened. "The badge," he muttered. "That's what this is about. They needed someone who looked like the badge to get into the building." He stood up from his chair, backing away from the desk a pace, his tail switching faster now. "This is industrial espionage, isn't it? That careless little whelp left a badge lying around and you found someone who looks like him to get into the building."

Matt tried not to laugh out loud in utter disbelief. He couldn't be serious! "What? No! Industrial espionage, are you kidding? You think I'm some kind of… giant spy?"

Gomez leveled a thick finger at him, the claw still extended. "Of course, your company had no idea from the badge that Matt is just a tiny little runt, so you just stuck some hired goon who looks like him in some office clothes and sent him in here to steal company secrets! Well, the joke's on you, buddy. Your little otter clone knows nothing. You hear me? Nothing!"

He grinned, showing a row of predatory fangs. "Because that pathetic, simpering little faggot is the worst employee in our division. Always needs supervision, never takes initiative, never challenges anyone, never moves on his own. He's a whining, submissive, passive little suck-up. We keep him working with the lowest level data we've got—I wouldn't even give him keys to the break room. So this little breaking and entering scheme you've got going on here is utterly useless. You understand? You get nothing. And don't even think of trying this again, because as a result of this little stunt, he's fired. Gone, kaput. I'm revoking his access just as soon as I have security drag you from this office."

Matt could hardly bring himself to move as the lion reached for the phone. The words were like repeated kicks in the gut. He'd always known Gomez hadn't liked him, but this? *Pathetic, simpering faggot.* The words were cruel, crushing. Of course. He should have stood up for himself more. He should have spoken up in meetings, should have taken initiative. He should have done more than what he was told. And he should never have put up with all the crap heaped on his head every day. He should never have tolerated Jim, all the times that he'd dropped a heavy file of vendor forms on his desk and told him he'd be finishing those up, while the rhino went off with everyone else to an early Friday at the bar. He should have never have tolerated Janelle's miserable, meddling whining from the next cubicle over, week after week after week. And most of all, he should never have put up with that vicious, backstabbing, credit-stealing, unimaginative, arrogant, pompous…

"Gomez," he said. His voice was deep, and commanding.

The lion froze, one hand on the receiver of the phone.

Matt reached across the desk and grabbed the phone in one paw. He yanked it away from the wall and squeezed. The plastic crushed easily in his grip, his forearm bulging so thickly with the squeeze that it ripped his shirt. A torn edge of the plastic cut his paw, but he didn't care. He tossed the useless piece of junk aside. Gomez gaped at him and backed away from the desk, his eyes stretched wide with shock.

"You're right," Matt said. "I was not a great employee. I did what I was told and no more. And when people told me to do something the wrong way, I did it the wrong way, just because I didn't want to argue."

He strode around the desk, shoving it out of his way, the furniture skidding across the floor as if made of cardboard. The lion fumbled in his pocket for his cellphone, and then pawed at it uselessly, forgetting in his panic how to use it. Matt snatched it from his fingers and tossed it aside. Gomez looked back and forth in panic and backed up against the wall, his ears flattened against his skull.

"But you know what?" Matt continued. "A good manager recognizes his employee's strengths and encourages them. He recognizes weaknesses and helps his employees to work past them. I had all these strengths, Mr. Gomez, that you never saw. I'm smart. I'm creative. And I'll work my heart out for someone who respects what I do. It's not that I was a bad employee. You're just a really bad boss."

The lion crouched lower against the wall, the tuft of tail lying on the floor between broad feet. "What—what are you going to do to me?" he stammered.

Matt stood over him, cornering him. He suddenly realized his paws were clenched into fists, his arms straining his shirt. His boss was afraid of him. Never, in his whole life, had anyone been afraid of him before. He felt both powerful and awful at the same time, some part of him yearning to punish the lion for every miserable hour he'd worked here in the office, for every ugly comment. The other part felt sick at the very notion.

Gomez breathed in deep, close to his body, and then suddenly his ears went up. "What do you *want* to do to me?" he purred, his voice very different. He reached out with one paw and placed it on the front of Matt's trousers, right against the obvious bulge. He pawed higher and higher, trying to find the top of the bulge. "Oh my god," he said.

Matt took a step back. He didn't want this, he told himself. He didn't. His cock thought otherwise, though. How long had it been since he'd had sex? Half a day almost? It felt like a week. His sheath plumped, the belt digging into it. He could feel his tip sliding up, pressing against his shirt. A wet spot soaked the front of his shirt, the smell of his musk filling the office. He could feel his balls aching with sudden need.

Gomez stood up and stepped closer. "You want me," he purred, lower than before, a hunger in his voice. "I can smell it." His claws fumbled with the top button of his shirt.

It was true. Matt did want him, desperately. His cock slid higher in his shirt. The belt was digging into his flesh so painfully, so he reached down, almost unthinkingly, and unbuckled it. Gomez's gaze followed his fingers with rapt attention. Then the lion's gaze drifted across his desk, lingering on the photos of his wife, his cubs. He looked back to Matt with an expression of horror. "Oh my god," he said, taking a step back. "What are you *doing* to me?"

He couldn't do this. He couldn't. He forced his fingers to buckle his belt over his sheath again, albeit looser than before. Just the brushing of his paws against his sheath made him shudder. But all the same he stood up straighter, ignored the pulse from his loins. "Mr. Gomez," he said. "I quit."

Then he turned, opened the door to the office, and stepped out. His coworkers were staring as he walked out, but he ignored them. He tried not to think of the obscene picture he posed, walking through the office, his pants straining, shirt ripped, the front of it soaked with the spreading stain of his musk. Too, he ignored the sounds of sniffing and groaning as he walked by.

He stopped back in his cubicle and looked around. There was nothing he really wanted to take; just a framed photograph of Stetson. The rest was facile, superficial. Work documents he'd never need again, computer books that were outdated, desk toys that would only ever remind him of all his time working there. He took the photo of Stetson and left, walking right past Janelle who gaped at him as though he were something astonishing and loathsome, like a serial killer.

He took the elevator down to the lobby, headed through the security station, and down the stairs to the parking garage. He felt sort of numb and floating. He was free. He'd hated this job, always hated it, and now he was free of it. There was a terrifying dizziness to the feeling, as if he'd just leapt over a precipice—perhaps not floating after all, but falling. What would he and Stetson do? They needed the income. How was he going to break it to the rabbit? As quickly as the anxiety appeared, it vanished. He'd just tell him the truth, that's how. Stetson wouldn't hesitate to support him. He'd tell him they'd find another way to work it out. He'd always been amazing like that. Yes.

Matt breathed a sigh of relief as he reached his car. Everything would be all right. He reached down to open the door.

"Where do you think you're going?" a voice rumbled. Gomez stepped out from behind a pillar, his tail switching predatorily behind him. His eyes had a hungry look to them.

"I'm going home," Matt said. "I quit. Remember? I don't work for you anymore."

"Yes." The lion stalked closer. Matt could see now that his dress pants were bulging in the front. "I remember that. But there's also that little matter of the industrial espionage. You didn't think I was just going to let that go, did you?"

"Oh, for cryin' out—I told you, I'm *Matt*."

"It's a ridiculous story," Gomez said. "And no one will ever believe it. Especially not the FBI."

Matt froze. If the FBI got involved, there would be no way they'd believe he was the same person. Not without DNA tests or something. And who was to say that stuff he'd swallowed hadn't done something crazy to his DNA, anyway? Not to mention, if they were poking around, they'd probably find out something about the highway cop he'd fucked. And if they talked to Saul, what would the cat tell them? "What do you want?" he asked.

"Fuck me," the lion said, through his hungry grin.

Seriously? His pheromonal effect seemed to be getting stronger. Or maybe Gomez had just actually been gay the whole time. He felt his cock stiffening again inside his sheath. "You can't do this," he said. "It's sexual harassment."

"No, it isn't." Gomez stepped forward, one foot in front of the other, tail swaying lazily behind him. He started unbuttoning his shirt again, revealing a broad, tawny, powerful chest, a thick line of dark brown fur running down it. "You quit."

Matt stared, feeling his resolve weakening. The tip of his cock poked between two buttons of his shirt, pushing into the cool air of the parking garage. "Then... then it's blackmail!"

"Uh-uh. The whole office saw you leave my office with an erection. They *smelled* you leave it. Everyone knows you want it. *You* know you want it."

He did want it. He wanted it so badly. "But you've got a wife, two cubs!"

Gomez scowled. "They hate me," he said. "Paula's had the kids in our summer house for two months now. She won't take my calls." He seemed to dwell on that thought for a moment, and then breathed deep. "But don't think about them. Think about yourself. What do *you* want, spy?"

The lion unbuttoned his shirt and shrugged it off his shoulders. That brown line of fur went all the way down into his pants. He had a lean and powerful build, his golden fur short, accentuating the heavy set of his pecs, the ridged, inward curve of his abs.

"Hey, get a room!" someone's voice echoed across the parking garage.

"Mind your own business, Max!" the lion snarled. "Or find a new job!"

He padded right up to Matt, who backed up against his car nervously, and unbuttoned the shirt buttons around his cock, which jutted up proudly in front of him. "This tells me you want it," he said. "So what's it going to be, spy? You going to deal with the FBI poking around your life? Going to deal with investigation, courts, prison?" He turned around and unbuttoned his trousers, letting them fall around his ankles, exposing the heavy, masculine globes of his rump, his tail pushing up his dress shirt as it lifted high. "Or are you going to take something you want?"

\* \* \*

"Oh god!" the lion roared, gripping at the hood of his Porsche with both paws. His breath fogged the windshield as he panted. Matt's thrust squeezed pre out of the lion's rump as he pushed in hard. His own paws squeezed the front fenders tightly, the force of his hips making the car's tires screech as they skidded backward with his push. "Oh god!"

Another thrust, and then a crunching sound as the car's rear bumper hit the concrete wall. The sound filled Matt with a visceral satisfaction; he thrust again, and heard the crash of a tail light breaking, mixed with the yowl of the lion.

"Oh, my car," Gomez moaned.

"Fuck your car," Matt growled in his ear. His biceps strained as he lifted the front end of the Porsche and then shoved forward with his hips again, rewarded by another shattering sound.

"I'll have you –oh god!" Gomez's rump squeezed tight around Matt a few times, and then he sprayed his seed across the hood of his Porsche. "—have you arrested for this!"

"No, you won't," Matt groaned back through his teeth. Thrust, thrust, thrust. Crash, crash, crash. It was more the grip of his arms and the push against his thighs that was smashing his car against the wall. Gomez was just along for the ride. Atop his ridiculous, unnecessary car. "Security cameras. On the. Ceiling."

He shuddered, hesitating for a moment as he felt the unstoppable rise of his climax, and then pushed forward as hard as he could. There was a dull crumpling sound, and then the hood dented in, the bumper of the car coming off in his grip. The front of the car dropped to the ground, bouncing, and at the same time, he came, his cock jerking convulsively as he erupted into his former employer, flooding into him. He collapsed across the lion's back, panting, crushing him into the hood of his car with his bulk, his hips spasmodically twitching into the beefy cat beneath him.

Then, before the climax was even over, the change came. Gomez actually seemed to shrink beneath him. Matt's arms slid a little farther over the edge of the car. His muscles strained with the new power surging into them, his toes slid against the ground. Then his shirt and pants tightened around his limbs, and began to tear.

Matt had always loved the Incredible Hulk as a cub, and those iconic scenes of the scrawny fox tearing his clothes apart. But it turned out that the show got it all wrong. That wasn't how clothes tore at all. With the Hulk, clothes split across his biceps and chest and back, diamond-shaped tears opening across his thighs, his calves splitting the material apart. Instead, Matt's clothes bunched up into all the narrowest places—elbows, armpits, around his knees and crotch, and dug in deep, painfully. Then the material tore, down his forearms and between his knees. Stitches pulled apart, the sleeves of his shirt separating from the sides, buttons ripping away. He winced as the fabric of his pants suddenly squeezed at his sac, cramping his balls, and was grateful he had unfastened his belt.

The lion's ass was uncomfortably tight around his cock, and he was whimpering with the sudden new pressure, so Matt carefully and slowly pulled out of him. As he withdrew, backed-up seed spurted out of his tip in a few sudden arcs, soaking Gomez and his car even more. Matt stood there, erect and dripping, rings of fabric clinging around his limbs.

Panting, Gomez lifted up his head and turned, his own tip still dripping. His eyes widened. "You… you were telling the truth," he gasped. "You grew."

Matt looked down at him, lying in a puddle of seed on his damaged car. Had he done this? Did he even feel bad about it? He tried to cover his erection with his paws. "I—I have to go," he stammered.

He ran back to his car and fumbled with the keys, unlocking it, then ducked down, trying to get in. He bumped his head. He hunched his shoulders, turned sideways, and squeezed through the door, working himself into the seat. There was no question about it. He'd grown more than last time. The effect was getting stronger.

# Chapter 11

Matt crouched in the chair of the waiting room, trying not to look around. He was acutely aware of people looking over at him. He'd changed into his gym clothes shortly after his encounter with Gomez—and had actually had to use a pocketknife to strip the bunched shirt and dress pants away from his joints, where the clothes had cinched painfully tight. He'd crouched, naked, behind a couple parked cars in the parking garage and sprayed deodorant liberally across his chest and down his shorts to try to mask his scent. Then he'd tugged on the new, baggy gym gear, only to find out they clung to him like they were a size or two too small. The black clothes gripped and hugged every contour of his newly grown body. It was embarrassing.

He figured he looked like a jackass trying to show off. Some people had stared agape when he'd walked by them in the hospital, and he'd picked up the smell of lust from one or two others, but more than one had rolled her eyes after he'd passed. A burly, late-middle aged bear had muttered, "asshole," just in earshot as he walked by, and he'd heard a couple of receptionists giggling to each other with a few well-timed, "Oh. Mygods," sent after him.

He felt self-conscious and uncomfortable. Worse, he found that the situation was turning him on in spite of it. If he didn't look around at the other people in the waiting room, the sight of his own powerful, new body bulging into his lower vision made other things start to bulge.

Which, obviously, he had to keep from happening. There would be no way he could hide it in those shorts. His sac and sheath obscenely swelled out the front of his gym shorts even without arousal. He tried his best to keep his mind away from it. This time he knew better than to think of work; he dug deep into his memory for moments of grief or shame, and these served to keep his mind away

from sex. For the first time since swallowing all those supplements—
it felt more like three years ago than three days—his condition really
had begun to feel a bit like a curse; he was reduced to thinking of lost
pets to try to avoid humiliation in a hospital waiting room. Not how
he'd hoped things would end up.

"Stafford?" A young ram wearing a nurse's uniform looked
around the office. "Matt Stafford?"

Matt stood up, his thick tail nearly knocking the chair over.
"That's me."

"Whoa," the nurse said amiably. "Back this way, big fella."

Matt followed him back through the door behind reception and
over to a scale.

"Hop on up here and let's get your height."

He stood patiently as the ram reached up and adjusted the height
bar up over his head, having to stretch to reach up. He was grateful
again for having thought to spray his deodorant down below. The
ram was small, but kind of cute, and he didn't want to have to deal
with the nurse coming onto him. He wasn't sure he could say no.

"Hmm." The ram frowned. "What's your name again?"

"Matt Stafford," Matt answered.

"Can I see your patient ID card?"

With a sinking feeling in his stomach, Matt reached into his
pocket and pulled out his wallet with his patient ID card. The nurse
took it and peered at the card, then back at Matt, then down at his
clipboard. "This is weird. It's your chart, for sure, but… they've got
the height down here at five ten, and you're pushing six and a half
feet easy. And your weight says one fifty." He peered at the display on
the scale, which Matt couldn't easily see from his angle. "You're more
than twice that. Three twenty."

He couldn't really be over three hundred pounds, could he? Matt
suddenly felt dizzy. "It must be some kind of typo," he suggested.

"Well. Could be," said the nurse. "We started switching from
physical to digital records a couple of years ago, and sometimes we
get weird little errors. You know how it is."

Breathing a sigh of relief, he nodded and stepped down off the
scale.

"All right," the cute little ram said, smiling up at him. Will, his nametag read. "Why don't you sit down here, and we'll get your blood pressure?" He patted the back of a large chair.

"Okay." Matt threaded his tail through the hole in the back of the chair and sat, wincing as his thighs crammed against each other and pushed his sac up in the shorts. He grinned apologetically at the nurse, who, if he noticed, pretended not to. He must see a lot, working in a doctor's office. Matt's eyes flickered down his body, wondering what he looked like out of that uniform, tight white curls covering his chest, his ass... No. Focus.

The nurse lifted a wide, black Velcro strap to Matt's arm and then paused. "Hmm. Better break out the bigger cuff I guess." He set it down and crouched to rummage in a cabinet.

He looked lean. Matt probably could pick him up with one hand. Hold him against the wall—Crap! No!! *No!!*

"Normally we break this out only for our patients who are... uh, having dietary issues," the nurse said, holding up a strip of black fabric that looked like could wear it around his waist. He fastened it around Matt's bare arm. "You must be able to bench press a lot, huh?"

"Actually, I..." The otter hesitated. He had no idea what he could lift now. He hadn't been to the gym since the day this whole thing started. The thought of finding out sent an electric thrill through him. "I dunno," he finally answered.

"Oh, come on," the nurse said, flashing him an amiable smile. "You don't have to be modest with me. What is it?" He connected the cuff to a machine and pressed a button. With a hiss, the cuff began constricting around Matt's upper arm.

"I'm not being modest. I honestly don't know," he said. He gave his arm an experimental flex in the cuff, and the Velcro gave a tearing sound as it started to separate.

"Just relax," the nurse said. He looked a little disappointed.

"I'm on an unusual program. It... I haven't really tried bench press since I started it."

The nurse brightened. "Curls, then? You curl a lot?"

Was the ram hitting on him? Matt couldn't tell. Maybe big guys just got asked these kinds of questions all the time. Maybe it was something he'd have to get used to. He thought of lifting Stetson up onto his cock down in Saul's creepy little dungeon basement. "Yeah, you know, around one seventy-five, I guess, for a max lift."

Will—he decided he liked that name—stared at him. "You're shitting me."

"No, seriously," Matt said. "It's probably more." Wait. Could that be right? He thought back to the other day at the gym. What had he curled? Sixty? And that had been high for him. Was curling that much normal? He didn't think so. "Oh, but that's really loose form," he amended. "You know, getting the shoulders in there, swinging and everything. Strict form it's probably like one forty-five."

The ram gave a low whistle. "That's nuts," he said. "You could almost curl me."

"Would you like me to?" Matt heard himself ask.

At that moment, the blood pressure machine beeped, and Will dropped his clipboard on the floor. "Oh!" he said loudly. His ears turned pink beneath his wool. "Startled me. Uh…" he looked at the machine. "One… one twenty over eighty. That's… that's perfect." He scrawled the numbers down on the sheet.

Matt wished he could melt down off the bottom of his chair and slide down into an air conditioning vent or something. *Would you like me to?* What the hell was that? Where had that come from? His condition was going to his head. His face burned with embarrassment.

"Why don't I show you to the examination room?" the nurse said, not meeting Matt's eyes.

"Okay." Matt stood up, followed the click of the ram's hooves down the hallway, and sat in the proffered room. At least, he thought, his utter mortification had killed his wood.

"The doctor will be along shortly," said Will. He hesitated at the door. "I have a break in about half an hour." The words came in a sudden rush, and then he closed the door.

Matt gaped after him. He could hear hoofs moving at a very rapid pace down the hallway. It could happen. He could take that cute little nurse in an isolated hallway, or across the table in an unused examination room. His sheath thickened with interest, straining at his shorts, and he sighed, and tried to think of horrible things again.

* * *

When Dr. Jann entered the room, Matt was flipping through an index with colorful images of various foot diseases. He set it down hastily. "Hello, Mr...." She looked down at her clipboard and back up again. "...Stafford?" she said. "I'm sorry, I guess I have the wrong room."

He shook his head. "No, that's me," he answered the lemur. "Matt Stafford." This again. He was growing tired of it already.

The lemur frowned. "I think we must have your charts mixed up with someone else's." She waved the clipboard at him. "I saw Mr. Stafford last Friday, and he is perhaps half your size."

Matt held out his paws. "I know it's hard to believe. But it's really me. I saw you last Friday, and then what happened is, I stopped in a weightlifting supplements store, and there was this accident, and I accidentally ingested a lot of stuff, and then, well, I started growing."

The doctor stared at his face, and then her face tightened. Then laughter bubbled up out of her. "That is... utterly ridiculous," she said. "For any number of reasons. I don't know what you're trying to pull here, but committing medical insurance fraud is a serious offense. You could go to jail. Do you understand me?"

Matt rubbed at his head with both paws, but that only made his shirt lift up and expose his abs. He wondered, embarrassed, if it had looked like he'd meant to. "Isn't there anything I can do to make you believe me?"

The lemur snorted. "That one of my patients grew half a foot and over a hundred pounds overnight? What you're talking about is medically impossible. Even if muscle *could* grow that fast, it would probably kill you. Your skin would rip, your bones would fracture, your tendons would tear, and the metabolic change necessary would probably burn you alive. If what you are saying were true, you'd be dead right now."

He blinked at her, confused. "But it *is* true. Can't you do a DNA test or something to prove it's me?"

She sighed. "I could order up a DNA test if I found it medically relevant, but it would still take two weeks to get results. It's not like on CSI."

"I don't know how to convince you, then," Matt said. "But please, can you help me out anyway? It's important. You're a doctor. You can't—you can't turn down someone in need, right? It's the Hippocratic oath."

"Not exactly how that works," Dr. Jann said. "But why don't you tell me what you want."

Matt dug the crumpled-up piece of paper out of his pocket and held it out to her. "This is a list of everything I used," he said. "I was just wondering how long this stuff would be in my system."

The doctor looked disappointed as she took the piece of paper. "You mean you've injected yourself with steroids, and you want to know how long it will show up on a drug test."

"What?" Matt almost shouted. "No! I haven't used steroids."

"Honey, I'm a doctor. Nobody gets that big without steroids. Not without a myostatin deficiency or some other genetic condition." She perused the paper, and her brow furrowed more and more. "You said this is all you took?"

Matt nodded.

"This… none of this is steroidal. There are a few esoteric herbs. Most of this is just junk." She flicked at the paper with the backs of her fingers. "If you honestly haven't been injecting anything besides what's here, then maybe we *should* do a DNA test. It could identify a genetic disorder that might have caused this. I don't know what your own medical insurance situation is, but it's a crime for you to be using Matt's ID card to get medical assistance. There are free clinics."

"Can you… will you run the DNA test for me? If you do, I promise I won't do it again. No one has to know."

The lemur looked reluctant. "I shouldn't… but we do have his DNA on file from a prior screening. All right. If only to prove that you shouldn't be receiving medical assistance under Matt's account."

Matt slumped in relief. He could get medical proof that he was who he said he was. "And what about the ingredients on that list?"

Dr. Jann frowned again. "Like I said, I don't see anything in here that could be causing muscular development—at least nothing that's been proven to. But since you asked, some of these chemicals look like they're fat soluble."

"What does that mean?"

"They get stored in your fat cells. You may think you're nice and lean, but everyone has fat cells. And when your body stores stuff in there, it generally takes about thirty days to clear out. Longer, if you've been consuming the stuff regularly."

Matt's eyes widened. "Thirty days?"

"Or more."

\* \* \*

Thirty days or more. His gaze was distant in thought as the nurse in the lab filled several vials with his blood. He didn't know why they needed so much. Wasn't a DNA test just a swab? He guessed they were also doing steroid tests or something like that. Thirty days or more. In a tenth of that time, he'd grown more than half a foot and doubled his weight. He could barely stuff his balls into a pair of underwear, and his sheath was up above his waistline, climbing toward his navel.

The nurse affixed a liquid bandage on his arm that sealed in around his fur. He thanked her, vaguely, walked back to the lobby, and plopped heavily into a chair, thinking. How many times had he climaxed in the last three days? Ten? Eleven? He couldn't recall. And thinking about sex made him stiffen up again. He had to hunch forward awkwardly to keep it from showing, and that just put the enticing smell of his tip uncomfortably close to his nose. It was so easy to lick himself now. He was doing it in his sleep. Hell, even if he didn't touch himself at all, he would climax.

So even if somehow, *somehow* he could restrain himself from touching himself or sucking himself or fucking any of the guys that wanted him, it wouldn't make any difference. His body was built for sex. He'd climax on his own, with just the touch of the fabric against his cock while he was awake. Or he'd suck himself while asleep. Or his scent would drive Stetson wild. It didn't matter.

There was a hand on his knee. He looked up. Will, the nurse, was sitting next to him. "Bad news?" the ram asked. His voice was soft and concerned.

"Yeah, I guess so," Matt answered. He sat up. His erection was no longer a threat, at least for the moment.

Will nodded. "You want to go someplace quiet?"

The otter's gaze flickered over him. He felt like he could almost see the lean, lithe body through the uniform. "I don't know if that's a good idea right now."

"We don't have to do anything," Will said. "If you just want to talk."

Matt hesitated. The only other thing was to go home, and Stetson was at work. He didn't think he wanted to sit by himself with his thoughts for five hours. "Okay."

The ram took his hand, and he stood up. They walked down through the medical offices, past elderly people huddled alone in chairs, past people on crutches or with arms in slings. One old bear had an eye patch with damp fur beneath. They turned the corner into an isolated corridor and then Will dug into his pocket for a ring of keys and unlocked a door. The window was dark, and the sign next to it read, *Physical Therapy*. He clicked a light switch and pale fluorescent lights flickered on in the room. Matt followed him inside, noticing the odd, inclined cots, weight machines, treadmills, mirrored walls, and a set of waist-high parallel bars running down a platform in the middle of the room.

"People come here to learn to how to move and walk again," Will said. "After something happens, like a stroke or something. But it's okay. We don't have any sessions scheduled for a while." He braced the heels of his hands on one of those inclined cots and hefted himself up, his hooves swinging above the floor. Matt sat down on one opposite him, his webbed feet firmly planted. "So, you want to talk about it?" The ram gave him a shy, encouraging smile.

Matt shrugged, feeling his heavy shoulders cramming his traps for room. "I just... found out that I have a condition. From now on, my life is going to have to be... different... than it used to be."

Will blinked his amber eyes with sincere concern. "Is it terminal?"

That was a good question. Could it be? He thought about what Dr. Jann had said, about all the negative side effects that he should have experienced. If whatever was going on with him was going to kill him, it probably would have already. "No," he answered, feeling relatively certain that was true. "But I don't know what's going to happen. Everything's changing."

Will nodded, and said nothing.

"So, I've already lost my job, and my boyfriend's really worried, and, well, I can't really talk about the specifics, but... things are just going to be different."

The ram smiled at him again. "Does different mean bad, in this case?"

Again, Matt hesitated. Did it? He thought about all his worries. He'd lost his job. People looked at him funny. He had some unusual social difficulties. Maybe he wouldn't be able to do all the things he wanted to do. But he could do different things now. He thought of the people he'd seen in the hallway with broken limbs, missing eyes, rashes, or alone and infirm. Maybe their lives were just different, too.

What was wrong with him, really? He was big. He had powerful sexual urges. These were all things he would have given anything to be a few days ago. Granted, he hadn't expected his condition to go this far. Granted, there were difficulties he hadn't anticipated. But he was fine. Great, even. He just needed to accept that things were going to change.

"I guess it doesn't," he finally said. "Just different."

Will nodded. "A lot of people figure that out in here," he said. "Just usually not so fast. You know, even when bad stuff happens, it changes you, and that means a new perspective. It's a new way to look at the world. It can make you a stronger person."

Matt laughed out loud at that. "It sure can."

Will leaned forward and put a hand on his knee. "It was nice to meet you, Matt." His fingers kneaded there, and Matt let out a slow, easy sigh, feeling the stress drain away from him. "But if you have a boyfriend..."

"It's okay. We're open. But I don't really know if it's a good idea for me to..."

Will's hand slid higher, up his thigh. "You got something I could catch?" he asked.

"No," Matt said. "It's just that..." He trailed off then as the ram's fingers brushed at the side of his sac, an almost electric surge going through his loins. "Gods," he groaned. His sheath thickened instantly at the touch, the bulge of his tip pushing up his athletic shirt. *These are your only clothes*, his brain warned him, and he immediately stripped off his shirt before it could get any of his musk on it.

Will's eyes widened, looking him up and down. "Holy Toledo," he breathed. His eyes lingered on Matt's cock, rising with his heartbeat up to jut up before his pecs. "You're enormous." He hastily half-unbuttoned his nurse's uniform and then pulled the rest of it over his head, the fabric catching on his horns. His chest was lean, the slight swell of his pecs covered with tight, woolly curls. He hopped down off the cot and stepped up to Matt, putting his fingers on Matt's shorts and giving him a questioning look.

Matt nodded and pushed up his weight with both arms, his triceps flexing against his sides, his pecs bulging out.

The ram stared in astonishment for a moment at that and then pulled Matt's shorts down, working the stretched material over his thighs to expose the rest of his sheath and his full, bulging sac. He paused then, reaching forward to heft Matt's balls in his hands. "I've never seen," he said, almost to himself. "Each one is a handful by itself!"

His touch was electric; the otter's cock flexed hard, and then a rivulet of pre ran down his channel. Almost absently, he kicked his shorts away.

Will leaned down and caught the stream of lubricant with his tongue and traced it back up to Matt's tip again, and Matt groaned and redoubled the volume with another flex of his cock. The ram shook his head. "I can't fit that inside me, big guy."

That was the first time Matt had ever heard that! He wondered, distantly, if he would ever be able to have sex with guys in the future. But no, there were still some species that were plenty bigger than him. "No, it's okay," he said. Still, he thought. Plenty bigger for now. But after thirty days?

The thought was pushed out of his head by another stroke of Will's smooth tongue on his aching flesh. "Why don't you lie back?" Will said. "Just relax. Close your eyes."

Matt nodded at him and turned, reclining on the cot, his cock thumping against his chest as he did so. His back was thick enough that his head tilted back when he rested normally, so he lifted his arms and crossed them behind his head, letting his eyelids close.

He felt Will's gentle touch slide across his thighs, thumbing over the lobes of his quadriceps, moving up toward the pulsing center of his lust. He lifted his hips, straining, and then hot, slippery fluid spilled out of him and into the cleft of his chest, slowly running up to pool in the hollow of his neck. With his eyes closed, his low groan sounded different: bestial, and almost predatory.

Will's touch moved up his hips, tugging lightly at his waist. He felt the padded material of the cot compress near his thighs; it must have been Will climbing up onto the cot with him. Wooly fingers slid up his belly, thumbs stroking at the outer edges of his abs, and then hands gripped at his pecs, squeezing them. He felt the light touch of the ram's woolly chest against his glans, and his hips twitched upward; he wanted to take him in both paws and lift him up to bury his cock deep under the ram's tail—but of course, that would hurt him, so he kept his paws where they were and lay still.

"God," the ram whispered. His breath buffeted Matt's tip agonizingly, and he pushed his hips up again. It would feel so good to take him, to sink deep into him.

He felt the cot padding press down at the sides of his head, and then there was a musky smell right near his nose. His eyes blinked open; he saw the bright pink spear of Will's lust above his nose. His knees were on either side of Matt's head, crouched upside down above him. When had Will even taken his pants off?

The ram wiggled his hips meaningfully. "This isn't all just about you, you know," he said impishly, and then he leaned down and dragged his tongue over Matt's sac, opening his jaws and taking one orb in his mouth, suckling at it. Matt thrust again, groaning—it felt like when they grew, almost, and his shaft ground up into Will's wool, the sensation coarse but enjoyable.

Will had said something important just now, he felt, but right now he couldn't focus on it. He unfolded his arms from behind his head and gripped Will's hips, lifting them upward so that he could get at the shaft jutting out over his muzzle. His chest bunched up as he lifted, pushing toward his chin, but he ignored it, as he also ignored the feeling of his sac being released by Will's jaws with a *pop*. Leaning up, he took Will's cock in his mouth, pushing it deep into his throat, privately delighted as the ram squirmed in his grip. He curled his tongue around it, suckling. Otters had an advantage: they could hold their breath a long, long time.

Fingers groped at his cock, tugging at it, trying to heft it upward. Will twisted in his grip, moaning out loud, and Matt rewarded him by pushing the ram's tip deeper into his throat and swallowing repeatedly. He felt the broad, smooth strokes of the ram's tongue against several inches of his cock, painting it down toward the base with eager strokes, and his hot pre splashed out against his neck and chin, rivulets running down either side to pool on the cot. They were going to have some work to get this stuff clean. He wondered absently if his scent would affect people even after he was gone.

He bobbed his muzzle, curled his tongue all the way around Will's stout pink shaft, swallowed again and again, and then he felt the ram twitch and tense in his grip. Hips spasmed toward his muzzle, and fingers tightened on his cock. Will gave a series of helpless groans, and then his cock started flexing hard in Matt's mouth, but the tip was buried too deep into his throat for him to taste any seed, so he just swallowed a few more times, and was rewarded by the sound of Will crying out and tugging urgently at his cock.

After a moment, the ram relaxed in his grip, and began panting. "Uh… sorry that… that happened so quick. I don't usually." He sounded embarrassed.

Matt gently released Will's cock from his muzzle, feeling him squirm with oversensitivity as he did so. "No worries."

"Er… I can… help you a little more easily if you… could set me down?"

Matt opened his eyes. He realized suddenly that he was holding Will up in the air, above his head. No wonder the ram had been struggling so much to attend to him. "Sorry," he said, letting Will down.

Will shook his horned head. "No, it's just… damn! You didn't know you were lifting me?" He took a few steps back. "Maybe you should sit up after all."

"Okay." Matt hefted himself upright again, his thick tail curling around the other side of the cot. Spilled pre started soaking down through the fur on his pecs. He was going to smell like it; there was no escaping that.

Gazing up at him with wide yellow eyes, Will reached up and curled his fingers around Matt's cock, which looked over three inches thick by now, and pulled it down toward his face. Matt shivered in delight at the sensation, felt himself clench, and then his pre splashed across the ram's muzzle, soaking it. Will gasped in surprise, breathing in deep, and then shuddered, his eyes squeezing closed. He crouched there for a moment, nestled between the otter's thighs, the point of his erection nudging against one.

The otter reached forward and brushed his fingers through the ram's curled head fur. "You okay there?"

Will gasped again, spluttering, his nostrils flared wide. "Yeah. It's just that... usually after I climax, I'm kind of less interested, but... there's something... I can't..." He trailed off, staring at the otter's dripping tip as if he were starving, and then, opening his jaws wide, he stuffed Matt's tip between them. He groaned around it, his slippery tongue sliding against the glans. His breath puffed heavily through his nostrils, his brow setting determinedly. He gripped at Matt's shaft more tightly, fingers dimpling the surface, and pushed it deeper into his mouth.

Matt felt himself squeeze another jet of precum out, and was gratified to see Will's eyes widen again as he almost choked on it. The ram looked up at him questioningly, as if to ask, *was that it?* And Matt just shook his head, took Will's curved horns in both hands, and pulled him forward on his cock again.

The ram couldn't fit much of Matt's erection into his mouth, but his tongue was soft and firm, his suckling so eager and hungry, that it didn't take long at all for his arousal to build. Then Will pulled back, wrapped both slender arms around Matt's aching length and hugged it to his chest. With fervent, rapid strokes he painted the otter's tip with his tongue, licking over it as if it were candy, groaning with urgency. He inhaled deep and then looked startled, and started bucking against the cot. To his surprise, Matt felt a second hot climax from the ram splash against his thigh and sac, but he barely had time to register this before Will dove down around his tip again, cramming it as deep into his muzzle and throat as he could.

The squeeze of the ram's arms and the unexpected softness of his muzzle and throat pushing steadily down around Matt's cock drove him almost immediately over the edge. He gripped the ram's horns and tugged, hips twitching. Through the blaze of intense pleasure, he distantly recalled that his strength was not as feeble as it used to be, so he tried not to tug too hard, but focusing was difficult.

His cock seemed to bulge with his climax as it rose up much farther than it had ever had to go before, and then he cried out with the pleasure, his voice almost a roar, his feet and legs moving together to squeeze at the ram nestled between them. Will pulled back, drawing in deep, alarmed breaths through his nares, and then Matt tugged his horns forward again, pushed his cock into his throat, sending another wave of his seed into it. At the third load, Will spluttered and drew back, pulling his horns free of Matt's grip. Cum was already drooling from the corners of his mouth, soaking his chest fur, and Matt sent a few more volleys into his muzzle and across his face.

Will slipped backward and fell onto his haunches on the floor, gasping. "Oh gods!"

"You okay?" Matt asked through a mixture of elation and concern.

"I… yes, amazing," Will began.

Matt barely heard his answer, though, because that now familiar feeling of intense and rising pressure was building once more. He turned toward the mirror, and for the first time, really saw it happen. His body just seemed to expand all over, like a balloon inflating, gradually increasing evenly all over in size. The effect was subtle; he might almost have been faking it by stretching out his posture and puffing out his lungs, but arms and legs grew in length and size as well, his knees rising up with his feet braced on the floor.

"What in the hell…" Will breathed.

Then, all over, his muscles began to contract of their own accord, flexing. His chest, shoulders, back, traps, arms, legs, even abdominals and obliques, all tensed and bulged with power. Each lobe of muscle stood out now, clearly and plainly defined, his short, lutrine fur unable to conceal even the smallest detail. The feeling was almost as orgasmic as the sex. He watched his whole body contract and flex, and then relax, and when it relaxed, each muscle was larger than before: biceps swollen out, triceps hanging off of the back of his arms like hams, his neck wedge-thick, traps hulking up to either side of them. Shoulders the size of bowling balls, each of the three heads of muscle crowding the others for space, swelled out wider. His forearms thickened nearly as wide as his upper arms; his chest pushed out even heavier, a split down the middle of each pectoral, his nipples pushed down out of his normal view. In the mirror, he could watch his abdominals contract and push out into cobblestones, the space between each looking deep enough to wedge a pencil into. His back flared even wider, bulging with power, pushing his arms up and forward. His legs pulsed, his calves growing into thick, split globes of power, massive thighs nudging each other as their lobes grew more defined. Even his tail thickened and developed, easily as big around as his waist.

The contractions of his muscles ceased, and he panted in ecstasy, only to have his respite interrupted as his cock flexed hard a few times, spitting another rope of his seed across the floor, visibly pulsing larger with each flex, his balls straining as they filled out his sac even more, seeming to refill as if he had never climaxed at all.

Once he was sure everything had stopped, he stood up from the table, having to adjust his stance to accommodate his larger thighs and sac, his heavier cock dripping on the floor as it bobbed. He was massive. He stared at his reflection, transfixed. It was impossible that the otter in the mirror could be him. He wasn't at Mr. Olympia levels of development, but he wasn't too far off, and he was freakishly tall. Besides, the winners of those contests tended to be bulls, horses, big cats, or bears. He was pretty sure no otter had ever been his size before. It was his dream. He lifted an arm and flexed a biceps, watching it swell into a massive ball of power half as large as his head.

"What..." Will's voice came from the floor, trembling with astonishment. "...what *are* you?"

Matt turned around and crouched, reaching out a paw to help up the ram lying in the pool of musky fluids, his cock still straining with apparent lust. "I told you," he said. "I have a condition."

The ram nodded, staring. "I'll say. You just... I did see you grow just now, right? I mean, that's not my imagination. I did see that."

"Every time I climax," Matt said. "Which it's getting harder and harder not to do."

"Every time?" Will shook his head, walking in a little circle. "You serious? This is crazy." He looked up—*way* up—at Matt's face. "For how long? I mean, when does it stop?"

The otter shrugged, feeling his traps squeeze against his neck as he did so. "When it stops, I guess."

Will looked at the floor. "Wow, that's... it's kind of cool in concept, but no wonder you were freaking out." He paused. "You could take something, probably. There are drugs that kill libido, or, you know, make it really hard to... to... pop."

Matt had not considered this possibility. "There are? Um. Any I could get without a prescription?"

Will shook his head. "And you'd have to make sure you weren't on... anything else. You know?"

"Oh." Matt looked around for his clothes—they were, fortunately, still dry—and tried to pull them on. They looked comically small on him. He had to wait a bit for his erection to go down enough for him to squeeze his sheath into his gym shorts. "That's no good, then. Doctor's cut me off from medical services. She doesn't believe I'm me." He looked at the mess everywhere. "I can help you clean this up."

Will nodded at the suggestion, then looked up at Matt again and breathed deep. His naked cock flexed as he did so. "Um. I appreciate it, but maybe that's not a good idea. If you're around, I think we're gonna get up to stuff again. And my shift is gonna start soon."

"Okay." Matt was careful to step around the puddles as he made his way back to the door. He looked back at the little ram standing there, shaking out a shirt that had not escaped the events unscathed, still panting. "Thanks, Will," he said. "Not for the sex. I mean, yes, for the sex, but mostly for talking. You know? It helped."

Will's face lit up in a bright smile. "I'm really glad. Will I... will I see you again?"

Matt grinned back at him. "I'm hard to miss," he said.

\* \* \*

All the way back through the hospital, he felt more at ease. His situation wasn't any different than before; he was going to keep growing and who knows what else for quite some time. His future was uncertain. But he felt better all the same. Whatever shape it took, it was *his* future. He would embrace it, accept it, own it. He passed a couple of young interns and, when they giggled at him derisively as he passed, he turned and gave them a broad, cocky grin. They could laugh, maybe, but he was finally comfortable. He could feel the swagger in his walk now as he made his way back to the lobby, the way his thighs rolled around each other, the way his shoulders swayed from side to side. He could feel his stomach growling. He was *starving*.

He hurried to his car in a swift, loping pace, his legs propelling him with a speed and power that surprised him, and pulled open the trunk. Inside was his bag of protein bars. He greedily wolfed down one after the other. They tasted horrible, as usual, but it didn't matter. Only when he was finished, his belly uncomfortably full, did he realize he had downed about thirty of the things. He'd have to go pick up some more at some point.

He knew he was in trouble when he stepped up to his car door and realized that the top of his car barely reached the bottom of his chest. It took some doing to fit himself inside: he leaned the seat back a bit, adjusted the steering wheel, and then wedged himself in. He tugged at the door and couldn't close it; his shoulders were too broad. Finally, he leaned to the side and managed to yank the door closed.

Driving was an ordeal; the steering wheel was mashed up against his chest and difficult to turn, and hunching over to look out the windshield only made things worse. To top everything off, his shorts kept riding up into his crotch, his shirt climbing up his abs. It was just uncomfortable. And his stomach was growling with hunger again.

Demigods Gym was coming up on the right, and on an impulse, he pulled into the parking lot and found a spot, taking the opportunity to pull himself out of his tiny car and stretch his legs and shoulders.

He leaned on his car, resting his elbows on the roof. He shouldn't go into the gym. It was asking for trouble. A locker room full of naked, muscular guys? Raw displays of power? All the stuff that got him excited in one place? If he went into that place, if he walked into Demigods, he was going to get in trouble.

On the other hand, he reasoned, he didn't *have* to get into trouble. He could focus: just head on in, find out just what he could lift now, see how he measured up to the other lifters, and get out. Also, they had clothes there that were designed to fit guys like him. He could get out of the barely-decent clothes he had on and find something more comfortable.

Yeah, he told himself, you don't *have* to get into trouble, but you *will*. You know it. You're even hoping for it, heading in there.

But they also had protein bars and protein shakes. His stomach growled urgently. That cinched it. He closed his car door and headed for the front door of the gym. He could behave himself. He would. There were too many people there at this time of day, anyway. No chance to get into trouble. Everything would be just fine.

His balls pulsed with lust.

# Chapter 12

The car creaked in relief as Matt stepped out of it, rising up and bouncing a little. It looked like the struts were going. He looked back over his vehicle and realized that replacing them probably wasn't worth it. He didn't fit in the car anymore. He'd probably have to sell it. He felt a twinge of sadness at the thought. The old car had been with him through college, road trips, vacations with Stetson. But now he'd outgrown it.

Well, like he'd told Will, his life was going to be different now. This was just one more way. He grabbed his gym bag from the car and locked it.

Matt had always hated the name of Demigods Gym. It sounded cocky. Ostentatious. The mascot wasn't great, either: a glowing logo of an overly rounded, stylized wolf doing a clean and jerk with a loaded bar. Something about the overly circular proportions made it look really stupid. But the gym itself was a good one: light on the machines and treadmills and heavy on the free weights. Serious lifters worked there.

It'd taken Matt a few years before he'd gotten the nerve to cancel his membership at Family Fitness and get a membership at Demigods. Many of the guys who lifted there were huge and intimidating, and Matt was, well, just not at all. They chatted casually in the locker room about prison time and steroid use, and had a generally gruff demeanor that had always made Matt's ears flatten. Still, after he'd been there a while, he'd found that nobody really gave you shit as long as you were lifting, no matter what condition you were in. Some of them had even helped him out with his form. But all the same, every time he'd come to the gym, he'd always felt just a little shy and nervous.

This time, he did not feel shy and nervous. He couldn't help pushing his chest out a little, letting his shoulders sway with an easy swagger as he walked up to the door. He had to reach down for the handle, and when he stepped through, the tips of his ears brushed against the top of the doorframe. If anything unexpected happened while he was inside, he'd have to be careful on his way out.

He scanned his card at the entrance and suppressed a grin as the stocky cougar behind the counter did a double take, glancing briefly up at him, looking away, and then immediately back. "Heya" —he paused as his eyes glanced down at the screen— "Matt. Good to see you again. How's it going today?" He flashed his white fangs in an ingratiating smile.

"Just fine," Matt said. He resisted the urge to roll his eyes. The staff had never greeted him before. They must think he was a pro, someone who would bring the gym a little extra cred. He checked the cougar's name tag, but it just had a T, O, exclamation point, and a triangle. He tugged with his thumb claws at the chest of the sleeveless tee currently painted onto his upper body. "So these clothes aren't really doing it for me. You have any gear in my size?"

"Shrunk in the wash, huh? I feel you. I keep runnin' those things through the dryer by mistake, you know, and they come out lookin' like they're for babies or something."

"Something like that. You have anything?"

"Hey, yeah, we can totally help you out. Lemme check the computers—it'll just take a minute." The cougar looked down at his computer and began typing. It seemed to be taking an unnecessarily long time, whatever he was looking up. They must be using really old systems. Matt leaned onto the counter with both elbows and looked into the gym. It wasn't too full. Nobody was really staring in his direction, and he sighed in unexpected gratitude. It felt nice, just for a little, not to feel out of place.

"Sorry, brah, just a minute more," the cougar said, apparently mistaking Matt's sigh for impatience. "Oh. Yeah, we still have a few things from our Olympiad line in stock." He pointed to the wall just beyond the drinks machines, on which were hanging a selection of black exercise gear with DEMIGODS written on it in an obnoxiously large, bright red font.

"Are you serious?" Matt said.

"Yeah, dude, right over there. You can see it from here. Anything in that line should fit you okay."

"Then why did you have to—" Matt shook his head. "Never mind. Thanks."

"No prob, brah. Just bring over whatever you pick out."

"Right." Because until you said that, I was just going to run off with it, he thought. This cat was about as sharp as a wet paper towel. He went over and grabbed a couple pairs of exercise shorts from off the rack, a tank and tee that looked like they might still be loose on him, and, thinking ahead, he grabbed a few jugs of protein, as well as a few drinks from the fridge. It was all ridiculously overpriced, and he couldn't stop thinking about the job he didn't have anymore. But he was pretty skilled; he shouldn't have any trouble getting another. And he had a healthy savings account, still. He dumped all the items on the counter.

"That's a lot of gear, huh?" the cougar said. He rummaged through the clothing, trying to find the tags, scanning the items one by one.

"Yeah, I guess," Matt said.

"Whoa." The cougar stared at his screen. "You don't have a pro discount with us?"

"No, I— What's that, like a rewards program?"

"Yeah," the cougar nodded. He stared at Matt. "Exactly." He kept looking, and didn't say anything.

"Well… why don't you tell me about it?"

"Oh, you know. It's like a discount. For pros. You just bring in your certificate from any local or national competition—first or second place—and you get free membership *plus* a twenty percent discount on gear."

Matt rubbed at his head, the motion of his shoulders yanking his shirt up above his abs, exposing the top of his sheath. His ears heated as he tugged it down again. "I don't… I don't really compete in anything."

The cougar blinked. His brow furrowed, ears going back. Then he laughed hesitantly but loudly. "Come on, brah. Course you compete. You ain't gonna juice up like that for nothin', right?"

Matt sighed. "Can you just ring me up please?"

"Hey, sure thing man." He poked at the register with one finger like he was attempting to stab a wandering ant. "That'll be $543.09."

His jaw dropped. He thought again of his bank account, with only one more paycheck to be deposited before the money stopped rolling in. "Are you serious? Five hundred—I can't afford that!"

TO!▲ shrugged. "Hey, this is quality gear. Guaranteed not to rip or tear. And, you know, not many companies make stuff in your size. So… you should totally compete! Free membership plus twenty percent off couldn't hurt, right? Come on, you could win a local competition easy." His gaze flickered down Matt's frame again.

Matt saw his nostrils flare and groaned inwardly. Not *this* guy. Never. Still, not *everything* he said was dumb. The idea of competing was embarrassing. He couldn't really imagine himself doing it. But on the other hand, a cash prize and a free gym membership were nothing to sniff at. Maybe it wouldn't be so bad. He could just get up there, flex a few times, and see what happened. He sighed, and looked down at the clothes and protein. "I guess I'll just take the one pair of clothes," he said. "And two jugs of protein."

"You got it, brah. You want me to set the rest of this stuff aside for you?"

"Sure."

The cougar stuffed the clothes, along with the protein, and even the drinks under the counter.

"You don't have to…" Matt began, and then decided it wasn't worth it. "Never mind."

"One eighty-five even," the cougar announced.

Still painful. Matt surrendered his credit card, signed, and made for the locker rooms on the other side of the gym. The cougar called after him, "Hey, if you can bring in your cert in the next thirty days, you can still get the discount on the stuff you bought."

Sure, Matt thought. Why not? Worth a try. The worst that can happen is complete humiliation, right? He wondered what would happen if he tried to squeeze his new sheath into a pair of posing briefs and shuddered. Probably impossible.

He had to pass through the weight room to get to the locker rooms, and once again he was conscious of his new height. Many of the machines and benches looked like ridiculously small now. He doubted he could use some of them. There weren't too many people here, either. A huge bear, definitely pro, working the cables. Horse doing squats. Couple of rabbits swapping off on the pullup bars. And—

He cringed. He recognized the two wolves working at the bench press. They were the two who had come into the locker room the other day, after he'd gotten a blow job from that husky, Devon. A twinge of guilt went through him as he remembered leaving him in the locker room to those two. They hadn't seemed friendly. Queerboy, they'd called the husky.

They were, he was unsurprised to see, really obnoxious lifters. They had to be pro bodybuilders, definitely juicing, but they were really interested in letting everyone know how hard they were working. Granted, the one was pushing up 385 on the bench, which was phenomenal, but still. He was roaring with each push like he was attacking someone with a broadsword, and at the end of his set he *slammed* the bar down onto the rack and leapt to his feet with a whoop and a loud, "Yeah!" Then his buddy got down on the bench and growled at the bar the whole time while his spotter shouted, "You're the man! You're the fuckin' *man*."

Matt rolled his eyes and hoped he'd be able to ignore them while lifting. Lifters like that tended to distract and bother everyone else, but when they were as big as these two wolves were—neither was as tall as he, but they were both thicker, one with a stocky, compact build, and the other as massive as anyone he'd ever seen—the gym tended to turn a blind eye.

"Hey!" the larger wolf shouted, staring right at him. "What're you lookin' at, homo?"

"Nothing," Matt mumbled, feeling his ears go down, his tail curling between his legs. He never knew how to handle confrontation like this. He could feel his face burning under his fur.

The smaller wolf sat up on his bench. "This gym's getting full of faggots," he said. "They ought to ban 'em."

"Or shoot 'em," the larger one said.

Matt couldn't help himself: he looked over his shoulder at that. Both wolves had lolling grins. That was pretty close to an outright threat. If there were anyone else up at the counter, he'd have thought about reporting it, but he didn't have a whole lot of confidence in TO Alarmed Triangle.

"Walk away, homo," the small one said. "Just walk away." He sniffed the air, and a strange look crossed his face. He said something in a low voice, and the larger one sniffed too, and then nodded.

Matt made a beeline for the locker rooms. He could feel the adrenaline surge, hot in his veins. Why would they call him a homo? He wasn't mincing or anything. He didn't... he caught his reflection in the bathroom mirror.

The clothes Stetson had bought him earlier were skin-tight, gripping every curve, sinking deep into the cleft of his ass, outlining every muscle. It looked hot, but... not exactly straight. Still. It shouldn't matter. They shouldn't be allowed to threaten him like that. This was not a good situation; it sounded like they were looking for a fight.

He should just change and go. That would be best. The unfairness of it all ate at him. Why should two assholes be allowed to just push everyone around? Why should they get away with it? No. Best not to think about it. Life was unfair sometimes. People were jerks. That's just the way things were. You could get worked up about it, or you could let it go, move on.

He sighed and peeled away his shirt, enjoying the sudden coolness as his fur was allowed to relax and fluff out a bit. He caught his reflection in the mirror again and turned away. It was embarrassing that the sight of his new body excited him. Was he narcissistic now? Was that wrong? He pushed the thought from his mind.

"Matt?" a voice said hesitantly. "It's you, isn't it?"

He looked around and saw a short husky standing near the lockers, towel around his waist, his lean chest bare. No. The husky wasn't short. He was average height. Matt frowned. "Devon?"

The husky's ears flicked nervously, his curled tail giving a slow wag above the top of the towel. "I knew it was you. It's impossible, but it's definitely you."

Matt rubbed at the back of his neck, and Devon's jaw went slack, his eyes shifting focus. "How did you know it was me?" he asked. "No one else seems to."

The husky took a few nervous steps closer. "I'd know your smell anywhere," he breathed. "The rest of you looks different, but that hasn't changed. Well. It's stronger. A lot stronger. But it's

151

unmistakably you." He sniffed at the air, and Matt winced. Don't do that. "How are you so much bigger now?" he asked, stepping closer again. "I mean, what *are* you? Are you like some kind of shapeshifter or something?"

Matt couldn't quite suppress a laugh of disbelief. "What? No! I just, I took some supplements that seem to be having a weird effect on me, is all. I don't really know what happened."

Nodding, Devon looked down at his paws. "I had to tell my girlfriend what happened. That I—that I blew a guy in the gym showers. We're on a break now."

"I'm sorry—" Matt began, but Devon interrupted him.

"Am I gay now?" he asked, his voice plaintive, almost frightened. "Is that what you did to me? Did you make me gay? Am I gonna have to—have to get a... *boyfriend?*" He actually shuddered at the word. He looked back up at Matt, desperation written across his face.

Shit. Somehow he had wrecked this guy's life without even realizing it. He'd told him, he'd said to him there in the showers, "I'm not gay," and Matt had let him do what he did anyway. And now the poor guy was falling apart. Was it wrong if you made someone want it? He didn't even know how to answer that question.

"Look," he said, "you're not— at least, I don't think you're gay. This has been happening with me. It has something to do with my scent. It's got extra strong pheromones in it or something. When guys smell it, they want me, bad. That's what happened with you. It's not what you want, you know? It's just... chemistry."

Devon frowned for a moment, as if sorting his thoughts out. "Wait, your scent makes guys want sex with you? Does that mean you have female pheromones?"

"What?" Matt almost laughed. "No!" At least, he thought, I don't *think* so. "No, I mean, it doesn't matter what species you are or anything. It just works. Maybe it works on women too. I'm not sure. I'm not really interested that way, you know?" Although, he thought, maybe it'd be worth a try. He discarded that thought for now. He was getting plenty of sex as it was. Too much, even.

"So the only reason that I did that is... because you had some kind of weird pheromone thing? I could tell my girlfriend that? I mean, I don't think she'd believe me, not at first, but... but I've been thinking about you ever since." His gaze was fixed, intense, almost hungry. "It wasn't enough. I wanted you again." He breathed in deeply, his well-built chest expanding. "I still want you."

With that, he tugged at the fold at the front of his towel and it dropped away. He was naked in front of Matt, his red cock already rising with urgency. Matt stepped back in shock as Devon stepped forward and grabbed at his stretched shorts, pulling them out and down around his oversized sheath. Unbidden, his shaft started to rise upward, a pulsing pink pole as big around as his wrist. Devon reached for it, jaws opening, and Matt pushed him back. "No," he said. "You don't want this. Not really."

The husky's ears went back, his eyes large and soulful and pleading. "Yes, I do," he breathed. "I've been wanting it since you left me in the showers the other day."

Oh yeah, he thought. When those asshole wolves came in. "Those wolves, did they… you know, did they give you trouble?"

Devon shook his head, keeping his eyes fixed hungrily on Matt's cock, which hung forward out of his shorts like a salami. "I think they were gonna, but then they started to get all hard, and I think it freaked 'em out. They decided to take cold showers instead." He hesitated, one ear tilted to the side and then turned around, leaning forward onto a bench, his rump round, tilted up, the curved tail wagging hopefully above it. "You can fuck me if you want. I've never had anyone take me before."

Matt stared at the soft-furred rump, perfect round buttocks arched upward for him, eager. His cock throbbed, rising higher and higher, aching with instant and intense desire. He paused. "I'm too big for you," he said. "It would hurt."

The husky was panting with desire now, digging his fingers into the bench in anticipation. "Only at first," he said. "I can relax, I promise." He looked back over his shoulder, his eyes wide and earnest, full of yearning. "Please, Sir," he said. "Please fuck me. I need it."

Gods! Matt tensed with arousal, his cock flexing and spilling a trail of precum across the floor. Barely thinking, he pushed his shorts down, the cuffs rolling up into rings as they stretched around his huge quads, his balls grateful for the sudden relief of pressure as they bounced against his thighs in the open air.

Devon breathed in again and groaned, his red cock jutting down toward the bench below his lean belly. His tail began wagging. "Fuck me, Sir. Fuck me hard."

It was going to feel so good. Matt crouched down, nudging his tip under that wagging tail, the soft fur teasing the sensitive flesh. Devon keened in anticipation, pushing back. Yeah. Matt would just fuck him this one last time, and then he'd have what he wanted, and go back to his girlfriend, and… no.

Devon nudged again, his ring twitching against Matt's tip, already slick with precum.

Matt pulled back. "I'm sorry," he said. "I can't do this."

Devon's ears drooped. He turned, leaning on the bench, looking back. "What?" he asked, confusion in his voice.

"Listen to me," Matt said. "You're not gay. You understand? It's just… it's the pheromones. They're sticking with you a little, making you think you want things you don't." He sat down on the bench next to Devon, his cock slapping up against the bottom of his chest as he did so. Devon reached for it and he swatted at the husky's paw. "You don't want this."

"Yes," the husky said, nodding urgently, "I do want it! I want it so much."

"No," Matt replied. "You want your girlfriend. You want your happy life you had. Go and explain things to her. Give her my phone number if you have to—I'll write it down for you. Get her back. You give it a week or so, and you're going to be wondering what the heck you were doing with me, I guarantee it."

Devon looked up at his face, and then down at his aching cock. He could feel it drooling hot pre all the way down to his balls. "You think so?" His eyes were suddenly uncertain.

"Yeah, I'm pretty sure. Tell you what: give it a couple weeks. If you're not over it by then, and you can't work things out, then come find me here and we can have some fun, okay? But I know you're gonna feel weird about it after a while. And I don't want to wreck your life, Devon."

The husky wasn't wagging anymore. "Okay," he said, his voice slow. "Okay, I'll give it a couple of weeks." He stood up, his shaft still jutting up eagerly. "I guess I'll go get my clothes on," he said. He leaned over and picked up his towel, his tail giving another wag, and it was all Matt could do not to grab that perfect rump and push into it right there. Instead, he turned away, squeezing his eyes closed and counting to ten. When he turned back, Devon was heading for the lockers. He looked back over his shoulder at Matt. "Thank you." Then he disappeared.

Immediately, Matt headed for the showers and turned one on at cold blast. The frigid water streamed down onto his fur and across his aching, needful flesh. He leaned against the wall with one arm, groaning as the cold sensation fought his aching, urgent libido. After a moment or two, his erection finally began to go down. Only then did he remember he didn't have a towel to dry off. Oh well. Thank god he was an otter; most of the water would just bead off his fur.

He turned off the shower and shook off against a wall, hindquarters and tail vibrating. His sac slapped uncomfortably from thigh to thigh as he did so, his lemon-sized orbs jostling in their overcrowded space. He was mostly dry, at least. He went back to his bag, dressed in the new clothes, which actually fit him surprisingly well, and headed out of the locker room. He felt oddly light and relaxed. He'd done the right thing, he was sure of it.

When he exited into the weight room, he looked instinctively toward the bench where the two wolves had been working out, but they weren't there. His shoulders slumped in relief; he had been afraid they would hassle him coming out. But no, they weren't by the bench anymore, or anywhere else in the gym.

In fact, there seemed to be no one here. Everyone had gone. It was only early afternoon on a weekday, but still. Had they closed? He looked around. No, the cougar was still up there at the counter, and plus, when they were about to close, they turned off some of the lights. The gym was still lit, the music still playing—some metal track or other that was supposed to get your pulse pounding. Must just be a lull.

This was a welcome turn. At least now he could try to find his new lifts without worrying about getting into a messy situation with someone. He took another look around and then headed for the Smith machine, a large rack with an attached bar and regular pegs up and down the columns to either side, good for doing presses and other lifts when you didn't have a spotter. If you rotated the bar while lifting, a couple of hooks would turn over and catch the pegs, securing the bar in place so that if you ran out of strength or energy, you wouldn't drop the bar on yourself. He figured it would be a good way to get some idea of his maximums without getting into trouble.

He dragged a flat bench under the bar, and then considered a moment. He'd been lifting ninety pounds with the press before, but he knew he was way stronger than that. One thirty-five should be no problem. He put a 45-lb plate on either side of the bar and sat on the bench. It felt small beneath him. His knees jutted upward. Leaning back, he braced both of his webbed paws on the bar and gave it a push upward. It shot upward and bounced at the top. He actually had to catch it. It felt like it weighed nothing at all. He couldn't believe it. He rotated the bar to hook it in place, stood up, and added another pair of 45s. This would make the total weight 225 lbs, more than twice what he'd lifted two days ago. He sat down and gave the bar another push, unhooking it. At least he could feel the weight this time, though it felt pretty light. He lowered the bar until it touched his pecs and then raised it again, feeling them bunch with strength and power, pressing against each other, pressing against his biceps. It felt great, but the weight was still no problem. He got up and added a third pair of plates, bringing the total weight to 315. This was a standard benchmark weight for pro lifters; if he could lift that, he was legit.

Again he lay back on the bench, feeling his lats bulge out to either side of it, and gripped the bar. He lowered it, feeling the stretch in his chest, and pushed upward, pecs and triceps bulging out hard. Unbelievable. It was easy. He did couple more repetitions, definitely noticing the stretch and strain, but not tiring at all.

Then the wolves walked up, standing over him. Matt froze mid-lift. "Look at this, Trav," said the bulkier one. "The homo thinks he can lift."

"Three fifteen ain't that bad. It's decent. Maybe he's not a homo after all, Ray."

Matt hooked the bar into place, his heart beating faster. "You guys want something?"

The big one, Ray, nodded at him. "Sorry for givin' you a hard time earlier, man," he said. "We didn't know you were serious. You had on those faggy clothes and everything."

Relief flooded through him. "Oh, yeah, well, they shrank. You know. I didn't realize until it was too late. That's why I bought new ones." The answer felt cheap, cowardly. He *was* a fag. He shouldn't be frightened into submission by these guys. But no. There was a time to stand up for yourself, and that time was not when two guys wanted to beat you for the wrong answer. That was just stupid. Better to get out of this safe and sound.

The wolf jerked his head toward the bar. "Three fifteen, that's what you do for reps? Looks like you can handle it okay." His voice was warmer and friendlier now.

Proud, Matt answered, "Naw, this is just a warmup weight. I haven't found my max in a while. You guys want to throw another plate on each side?"

The smaller wolf's brows raised. "Four oh five? You sure?"

"Yeah," Matt said, feeling confident. Three fifteen had been easy. "Should be no problem." He couldn't believe he was about to do this. 405 lbs? That was crazy. It was almost ten times what he'd been lifting a week ago. But he was not the little otter he'd been a week ago. He was a beast. He was still suspicious of these guys suddenly being so friendly to him, but he figured it was better not to antagonize them. They put another plate on each side—that was eight big plates, total—and he braced his paws. He pushed upward, the textured metal of the bar digging into his palms. His chest mounded up thick, straining, and bumped at his chin, his triceps bulging hard at the back of his arms.

The strain and ache felt good. He lowered the bar down to his chest and pushed it up again. His chest and arms pulsed with the effort, filling out with blood, muscle growing tight as he started to feel the pump. He lowered and raised again, and again, banging out a set of five. Gods damn. Four hundred and five pounds. It wasn't easy, but it wasn't difficult either. He hooked the bar again.

Trav whistled through his tongue. "Okay," he said. "We were totally wrong about you. You are fuckin' *pro*, man."

Feeling excited, almost amped, Matt urged them, "Put two more on."

Ray's tongue lolled in a grin. "You got it, boss." The plates scraped as they slid onto either side of the bar. Matt braced his paws and pushed upward. It moved. The bar was visibly bowing now, the heavy weight on either side bending the ends downward. His muscles strained, aching with the weight of a quarter ton of iron, but he lowered down to his chest and raised again, breathing out heavily with the upward push. He was doing it. The sense of raw power sent an erotic thrill through him. He wasn't just strong, he was *fucking* strong. Not world record strong, not by half, but still. He lowered for a second rep, and then a third. His muscles burned with the effort, but it felt good. He felt his sheath thickening with excitement as he realized his own strength, his tip climbing slowly up under his shirt. He tried to ignore it.

At the bottom of his fourth rep, the wolves moved into his vision, and slid another couple of plates on the bar. "Hold up," he pleaded. "585 is too much." But maybe it wasn't, he thought.

"Come on, man, you're a pro," Ray said. "Got to find your max. Just give it a try."

Not like he had any choice. He pushed, the bar digging painfully into his pads as he summoned his resolve. He arched his back, his feet braced against the floor. The bar rose, nearly six hundred pounds of it. He felt a sense of elation, his shaft crawling a little higher up his belly. Unbelievable. He was giddy with the sense of his own strength. He lowered the bar for one final rep. "Last rep, guys. This is it for me." When it reached the bottom, he heard a couple of scraping sounds. The wolves had slid another couple of plates on the bar.

It was more than he could handle. He lost control of the bar—it sunk down and dug painfully into his chest. "Guys!" he croaked, "too much!" He tried to push the bar up high enough to lock it into the pegs, but he couldn't move it.

Ray leaned over the bar, grinning broadly at him, showing a wide array of predatory teeth. "Aww, really? Is that too much weight for you, fag? I'm disappointed."

Fear ratcheted through Matt. They'd done this on purpose. He'd been dumb enough not to leave immediately when they'd showed up, and now they'd trapped him. Desperately, he pushed as hard as he could. The bar moved up a couple centimeters at most, his chest burning, feeling like it was tearing apart, arms screaming for relief, but it was enough for him to rotate the bar and lock it in place, just barely. It was still pressing down firmly against his chest, holding his arms in place. From this position, he couldn't let go of the bar. He was stuck.

"I dunno, Ray," the smaller wolf said. "He might have somethin' left. You know, after he rests a little."

"That's a very good point, Trav. We better make damned sure he's not gettin' up, huh?" The wolves disappeared from view.

Matt thrashed his tail and kicked with his legs, trying scoot the bench back and slip out from underneath it, trying to squeeze out to either side, but it was of no use. The wolves came back, each holding a one hundred pound weight, which they slid onto either side of the bar. That was eight hundred and seventy five pounds. There was no way he was moving it. Only the very best powerlifters could lift that much weight, and he'd struggled with two thirds of that. His heart pounded. The bar was digging painfully into his palms and chest, his triceps aching with the stretch. "Please," he begged, "why are you doing this? You don't even know me."

Ray leaned over him, one paw on the bar. "Don't know you?" he growled. "I dunno, homo. I think we might have met you before. Two days ago, right here in this gym. In the showers, in fact. We came in and found you preying on some little husky pup." He wrinkled his nose. "Trying to get him to do fag stuff. Disgusting."

It was impossible. He pushed again uselessly at the bar, knowing he couldn't lift it. "I dunno who you saw, guys, but it wasn't me. Come on. This is… this is illegal. You guys could get in big trouble for this."

Trav wagged his tail. "Don't think so, pal. Gym's all emptied out. Everyone had to leave. Tom decided he needed to lock up early. So it's just you and me and my buddy Ray, here."

The larger wolf tapped the side of his muzzle. "You may think you have everyone else fooled, but the nose doesn't lie. May have been just a quarter of your size, but it was you. We smelled you. We smelled what you did."

"A quarter my size? Two days ago? That's impossible, you know it is."

"Yeah," Ray said. "It is. Least it should be. So you're gonna tell Trav and me what you took to get like this. What is it? Some new kinda juice? Some sorta DNA thing? Gamma rays? You the fuckin' Incredible Bulk? What is it?"

Anger was mingling with Matt's fear. He suddenly didn't want to get away anymore; he wanted to pound them into the rubber floor. He struggled again with the bar, trying in vain to raise it. "I told you," he groaned. "I don't know who you saw a couple days ago, but it wasn't me. You're talking crazy. You know you could go to prison for what you're doing here. You should just get out of here while you can."

"You know, Ray, maybe he's tellin' the truth," Trav said from Matt's other side. "It does sound kinda crazy that a guy could grow that much in two days."

"I know what I smelled, runt!" the big wolf snarled, turning toward Trav. "It was him!" He leaned down, putting both hands on the bar, his fanged muzzle inches from Matt's, his hot breath puffing in his face. "I don't like faggots. I hate your little fairy parades, I hate your bitchy attitudes, I hate the way you prey on straight guys who just want to be left alone, doin' all your disgusting gay shit with each other in public where the rest of us have to look at it. But I'm a reasonable guy. You tell me what you did to cheat your way into havin' a real man's body, and we'll let you go. If not..." He trailed off with a low, threatening growl.

Matt spit in his face.

It was not the smartest thing he'd ever done. In fact, he realized immediately afterward, it was positively, absolutely, the stupidest, most idiotic, brainless, suicidal thing he'd ever done in his whole life. And yet he couldn't bring himself to regret it.

Ray's face contorted in livid fury, his hackles lifting. "Now you listen to me, you mincing waterdog *twat*, if you don't tell me what I want to know in two goddamn seconds, me and Trav over there are gonna go grab another one of those hundred pound weights and drop it on your fucking head, you get me?"

Okay, *now* he could bring himself to regret it. His blood turned icy with fear. Ray really might kill him. "Okay, okay!" he croaked. "I'll tell you. It's… I don't know exactly what happened, but I swallowed a bunch of supplements all at once. They had a funny reaction on me. As you can see."

The wolf leaned upward again, his rage momentarily forgotten, ears perking in interest. "What supplements?"

"A whole list of them," Matt sighed. "It's in my car out front. In the back seat. It's unlocked."

Ray jerked his head toward Trav. "Go," he said. "Check it out. And don't forget to prop the gym door open so you can get back in."

"Okay, Ray," Trav said, his ears back. His tail was drooping a bit, too. He didn't look very happy with the situation. Matt wondered if they'd done this sort of thing before. And what had happened to the people they'd done it to.

As the smaller wolf hurried off, Ray began to pace back and forth beside the bench. "You better pray he finds that list." He shook his head. "Even if he does, it doesn't look good for you."

Matt strained again at the bar, uselessly. Again he tried to slide the bench beneath him, bracing his feet and using his thick tail to try to push it. It wouldn't budge. He didn't know what to do. Maybe the gym staff would come back for something. Maybe Stetson would come looking for him. He sighed, the adrenaline beginning to make him shake. Maybe they'd let him off with just a bad beating. If Trav could even find the list. Had he put it in the back seat after all? He suddenly wasn't sure.

"Wait," he said. "Trav didn't ask me about my car. I mean, there's not just the gym here. How's he going to know which car is mine?"

"Oh, don't worry about that," Ray said. He tapped his nose again. "You got a real unique stink, there, homo. Won't be no trouble."

That was true, he thought. Sooner or later, everyone was going to know where he'd been, just from his scent.

Wait. His scent. That was it. His mind suddenly raced. He wondered if he could get hard like this, trapped by a sociopath, nearly a half ton of weight digging down on top of him. But no, he had to. He pushed the thoughts of his situation out of his mind. He closed his eyes so that he couldn't see Ray. He made himself forget about what was about to happen, forget about the threats and the insults. He thought instead of a half hour ago, in the locker room, and that tantalizing husky rump arched upward for him, the curled tail twitching in eagerness. He thought of Devon looking over his shoulder, his eyes pleading as he begged to be taken, begged to be fucked, nudging his rump toward him, his white-furred sac visible between his lean-muscled thighs. He thought of the way he'd leaked as he pressed his tip up under that soft tail, feeling the hot flesh against it.

His cock throbbed in eager need, responding to his lust. It slid up his belly once more, stiffening. It felt so good. He thought of how it would feel to squeeze into the husky's tight rump for the first time. His sensitive tip pressed up against the soft fabric of his workout shirt. It felt good. He opened his eyes and gave a low groan.

Ray looked back toward him, and then down, his amber eyes widening. "What the fuck is that?" he demanded. "What've you got under your shirt?"

Matt shivered at the sensation of the fabric and flexed his cock, making it surge up an inch, lifting his shirt upward.

"The fuck," Ray said, his ears back, his hackles raised. He reached out toward Matt's shirt as gingerly as if he thought there might be a snake under it, and then gave it a quick tug upward, pulling it back and exposing the thick pole beneath to the gym air. Matt shuddered again as the smooth, synthetic material slid against it. "Oh man. Oh, man. You really are a homo. You get off on… on this?"

Matt didn't answer him. He didn't need to feed the lust with any more thoughts of Devon, it was accelerating on its own, now. He wanted sex badly. He needed it. His cock climbed higher and higher, and Ray stared at it with an expression of both horror and awe.

"That's you?" the wolf asked disbelievingly. "That's all you? Did the supps do that to you too?"

"Yeah," Matt groaned. His hips twitched upward, making his cock bounce and slap the tip against his belly. It stiffened again, a few drops of pre leaking from the end.

"Impossible," the wolf breathed, and then he paused and sniffed the air. Almost absently, he reached down and pawed at his crotch. "You do smell... really strange," he said. He sniffed the air again. Matt turned to look at him and saw his exercise shorts tenting out. "I mean, it's not exactly a bad smell. It's just..."

Matt gave his hips another twitch, flexing his cock again, and this time a rope of clear pre arched out and painted his chest and face. Ray stared at it, taking a step forward. He lifted up his shirt, exposing a thick red tip jutting upward. So much for any theory that he was compensating for something; he was seriously hung.

"The problem with you gays," Ray said, "is that you keep makin' other people ask themselves if they might be gay too. You make people think about doin' dirty, disgusting stuff. That's why you guys need to go. It's because of the sick thoughts you put in other people's heads." His gaze never broke from Matt's erection. "Like, if I weren't a real man, I might be thinkin' about climbing up on that right now, while I've got you trapped there."

Matt looked back at Ray. If it weren't for the horrible personality, he'd be amazingly hot. He was easily the biggest, most muscular guy Matt had ever seen in life, his massive swells of muscle barely concealed by his thick, shaggy pelt, which seemed only to make each bulge and valley stand out in increased relief. "Please," Matt said, in as neutral a tone of voice as he could manage, "don't do that."

Ray licked his nose hungrily. "Yeah, you'd hate that, wouldn't you, tough guy? Gettin' trapped by a bigger guy, shown up, threatened, and then he has his way with you?" The wolf's cock dripped a single drop that landed on his exercise shorts. "Yeah." His eyes were confused, but then he seemed to make up his mind. "I'm gonna teach you a lesson." With that, he gripped the bottom of his shirt with both hands and lifted it up over his head, exposing a heavy, powerful body that rippled and swaggered with his movements. He shucked his shorts in a few quick moments, his full sac jostling as it was freed. Naked, massive, and erect, he stood before Matt, still breathing deeply, his eyes hungry.

"You sure this is what you want to do?" Matt asked. Up until that moment, he wasn't sure that he wanted it either, but fucking this homophobic jerk hard was going to be really satisfying. "You can still stop if you want."

The wolf reached forward and curled his clawed fingers around Matt's shaft, making it twitch again reflexively. His tail wagged a couple times with eagerness. "I bet you'd like me to stop now, wouldn't you?" he grinned, and then he tugged Matt's shorts down with a couple of pulls. His tip dripped into the otter's fur as he lifted one leg high and stepped over him, massive thighs straddling the bench. He stood over the otter, tall and broad, a bulging specimen of hyper masculinity, and then reached down, with one hand, his lats on one side swelling delightfully as he did so, lifting the otter's shaft upward. Matt felt his tip bump against the wolf's thighs, and then slide up between the most thickly muscled glutes it had ever touched. Ray settled back a little, the squeeze of his rump settled around Matt's tip as it nestled deeper and deeper. "Uhff," Ray grunted. "That feels weird." He looked down and bared his fangs in a triumphant grin. "You can beg me to stop this," he said. "You can beg me not to fuck you."

Technically, Matt thought, I'm fucking *you*. "Please stop," he said aloud. "I've learned my lesson. Stop." He felt a hot splash as he soaked Ray's ass with precum.

"No," the wolf barked a laugh, and then pushed back and down, his tight ring spreading around Matt's cock. Almost immediately, his eyes widened, and he gave a little yelp. "Gods," he groaned. "So thick. It... It kind of hurts."

Deeper, Matt groaned inwardly. Deeper. "Mostly the first time," he said. "Only real men can take it."

Ray gritted his teeth. "I can take it," he growled, and then he pushed down and backward again, sinking a few more inches of Matt's length into his rump. He was tight, almost too tight, and Matt had to make a mental effort not to flex his shaft now; if he hurt Ray too much, he might pull off. The wolf leaned forward, bracing both paws on the bar next to Matt's his chest bulging broad, his massive thighs flexing as he pushed himself down and down and down around the otter's oversized cock. Finally his heavy sac rested down against Matt's abs; impossibly, he seemed to have squeezed the majority of Matt's foot plus of virility inside him. The wolf's cock was drooling with ejaculate that had been squeezed out of him by Matt's girth, but it was still hard and throbbing. "I did it," he grinned triumphantly. "Just like a difficult lift." He lifted up a little and sank down again. "That'll show you. That'll teach you not to fuck with me."

"Hey Ray, I found it," Trav's voice called. Matt and the wolf both looked over at the same time; the other bodybuilder was rushing in, waving a piece of paper over his head. "It fell under a seat, but I finally found… it…" He slowed to a stop, bewilderment written across his face, his ears to the side. "Ray? Ray, what's… what's goin' on?"

Ray grinned cockily. "I'm teachin' this little fucker a lesson, that's what."

Trav wandered forward, his brow furrowed, looking from side to side and sniffing at the air. "Ray, it kinda looks from here like you're lettin' him fuck you."

Matt gripped tightly at the bar, braced his feet, and pushed his hips upward, making the Ray widen his eyes and groan, making more seed and pre spill from his cock.

"Gah," the wolf growled. "No, I… it's just, he's trapped and helpless, see, so… this is me… showin' him I can do whatever I want to him. And he can't do nothin' about it."

Ears going back all the way, tail tucked, Trav came up to the machine. "Ray, are you… are you gay?"

The huge wolf growled, lifting up a bit, and then pushing down on the cock in his ass, groaning in apparent pleasure. "Course I ain't gay," he snarled. "Like I said, I'm just teachin' this little fucker a lesson." He began rocking up and down, giving little whimpers each time he sank down around Matt's shaft, his rump hot and slick and velvety-smooth. Matt groaned back, using the purchase under his feet and clenching his abs to meet Ray's motions, sliding up and down with an easy rhythm.

Trav sighed through his nostrils and breathed deep. "I guess you know best. But you shoulda let me do it for you, Ray. You shoulda let me take care of it so you didn't have to… do *this*." He breathed again. "Please let me teach him a lesson, Ray. Please let me."

"No!" the wolf roared. "He's mine!" He gripped the bar of the Smith machine, crouching lower over Matt, his hackles raised. He began sliding up and down around Matt's cock faster, now, with more urgency, a good half a foot of slick shaft pulling out with each movement before Matt slapped his hips against the huge lupine's ass again. The wolf's tremendous physique rocked and flexed above him with his movements.

An erection was plainly showing in Trav's his own shorts, and he began trembling as he clutched at it. "Please let him fuck me, Ray, please." He stripped off his shirt, revealing a physique that nearly rivaled the larger wolf's and a rising erection. "I'll do anything you want." He nestled up to Matt's side and pawed at the otter's shoulder and chest, and then caught sight of Ray's own drooling erection. "I'll make you happy." His jaws gaped as he leaned down and engulfed the bigger wolf's cock in his muzzle, licking at it with a tongue that slid out to stealthily drag against Matt's own belly.

Ray half groaned, half howled, his ring clenching around Matt's shaft a few times, and then he bounced, caught between thrusting back against Matt's hips and pushing up into Trav's muzzle.

Matt was too lost in lust to discern much beyond that. He barely felt the bar digging into his chest, the ache in his trapped arms. His hips hammered upward into the bodybuilder atop him, his thighs squeezing at his balls, and then he came, hard, shooting into the wolf riding him with what felt like terrific intensity. He cried aloud as he climaxed, unable to silence himself, and at the same time Ray made a gurgling sound, as if the volume of seed had filled him to the back of his throat. Instead, he felt it spray out around the exposed part of his shaft and soak his sac and the bench below him. Distantly, he was aware of Trav making a choking sound and drooling hot wolf seed across his belly. He pulsed again, making Ray cry out, "Oh gods!" and then again. He could hear his cum trickling down to the floor and feel it running back along the bench between his glutes.

And then the intensity of growth came to him again, surging through him, every muscle tensing. He could feel his cock stretching and swelling inside Ray, making the wolf whine, could feel his balls pulsing with new heaviness. And then strength spread throughout his limbs. The bench slid along his back, which widened so much

that the breadth of it nestled between the wings of his lats. His ass scooted down along the bench as his height increased. He felt the sinews in his legs thicken and crowd each other even more. His abs pushed out, his traps mounded up, pushing his head higher. He could see Ray and Trav both staring at him in awe as his arms and legs thickened dramatically, his chest barreling out... and making the bar dig into it even more. He cried out in pain as nearly half a ton of weight dug into his chest, and in desperation, he pushed at it. The rough textured metal cut into his palms and made the bones of his paws ache. His arms shook and trembled, and then strained hard, thickening again. The bar budged.

He clenched his teeth, breath snorting through his nostrils, and pushed harder and harder. Inch by inch, eight hundred and seventy-five pounds of iron raised up off his chest, freeing it from its awful weight at last, his arms glad to finally stretch out. He lifted it to its full extension and hooked it in place.

"Holy shit," Ray said. "Holy fucking shit, did you just fucking see that?"

Trav moaned and pawed at his own erection. "Please let me teach him a lesson, too, Ray. Let him teach me a lesson."

"You can't," Ray sneered at him. "He's too big. It'd be too hard for you."

Matt sat up finally, feeling his new height and weight. He felt like a giant. He was pretty sure he was more built than Ray now. He gripped the wolf with both paws and lifted him up as if he weighed nothing, hefting him up as inch after inch of his cock slid out of the wolf, cum spilling out around his thighs, Ray groaning loudly at the sensation.

He put the wolf down on the bench and stood. Lust was still ratcheting through him; he had just climaxed, but he was ready to go again. He ached for it, like he had when chained up in Saul's basement. The Wholebutrin must not be entirely out of his system yet, or maybe this was just what he was like, now. Maybe it would take two or three times to satisfy him. He pulsed and strained with need, and so when the other wolf put his arms around him, panting into his chest, the point of his erection nudging up into his sac with urgent lust, and begged, "Please, please, *please* let me teach you a lesson," Matt obliged him.

He picked Trav up, carried him across the gym, and set him sprawling across the preacher curls pad, the grey-furred rump pushed up in the air toward him in an imitation of Devon's earlier. He expected the wolf to have more difficulty taking him, but he pushed his cock into him with much greater ease than he had with Ray, almost suspiciously so. The smaller bodybuilder whined in pleasure and wagged his tail against Matt's belly. It took him longer to finish this time. He fucked Trav across the preacher curl pad, and an incline bench, hammered him down into an exercise mat on the floor, and finally nailed him up against the mirrors, leaving streaks of Trav's precum across the surface, watching his massive, hulking body flex and rut powerfully, narcissistic fascination fueling him, until the mirror cracked, sending a long, broken rift across it, and then finally he came again, with less intensity this time, and stared in the mirror as his shoulders broadened to unnatural size, his chest pushed out beyond anything he'd seen before, arms stretching to incredible thickness, bulging so huge that his forearms pressed into his biceps if he curled up to ninety degrees. His heart began racing. If he were his old height, he'd be the size of some of the biggest pros out there, but he was far taller than that now.

He lifted the panting wolf up and up off his cock and more of his seed arced out and spattered across the floor. His shaft listed forward with its weight, but he could tell he rivaled most horses now. In every description, he was huge. Trav's ear tips barely reached the top of his chest. The wolf stared up at him in wonder. "What… what are you?" he panted.

Matt cast about for an answer to that question, the second time he'd been asked it today, and finally said, "Messy." He looked across the gym, where Ray was still sitting on the bench for the Smith machine, his head in his paws, obsessively running his fingers through his head fur and pushing his ears back.

"You guys think you can do anything to me now?" He shouted to Ray. The wolf looked up at that as if startled, and flinched backward. "You guys get the hell out of here. And don't ever mess with anyone again. You got me?"

Ray didn't answer. Matt marched across the gym. The machines shook with his footsteps. "I said you got me?" He stared into Ray's eyes.

The wolf nodded. "I—I got you, man." His ears were down, but Matt saw his gaze glance toward the paper Trav had dropped on the floor, the list of supplements, and then quickly look away again.

"Don't even think about it," Matt said. He crouched down, finding the new bulkiness of his body made this movement more difficult than it had been before, and picked up the piece of paper, wadded it up into a ball, chewed it, and swallowed it. Let them experiment with supplements all they wanted on their own. He grabbed his discarded clothes from the floor. "Go on," he said, "Get out of here. I'm gonna shower off, and when I come out, you better not be here."

Ray nodded again, and Matt headed back into the showers. Once inside, he started shaking with relief and exhaustion. The adrenaline was finally leaving him, and he felt trembly in its absence. In the space of an hour, he'd nearly lost his life, and then become a giant. It had been one hell of a day. All he'd ever wanted was to feel powerful and desirable. This hadn't been what he had in mind. For the first time since everything started, he wondered if it wouldn't be better just to be ordinary.

He stepped into the shower and closed his eyes, letting the water relax him, soak through his fur, soothe him. He had to crouch down to wet anything above his chest; the nozzle was just too low for him. Halfway through the shower, his stomach began growling with painful intensity, and he dashed for his supply of protein and began mixing it with the shower water, chugging it in gooey clumps directly out of the jugs, not even caring about the taste or texture. He didn't stop until it was gone, his belly feeling uncomfortably bloated and full. There was no noise from outside; he figured the wolves were probably gone, and then he thought about the mess he'd left in the gym. It wouldn't be fair to leave that for other people to clean up.

So he shook off, and headed back out into the gym. He was nude, but there was no one there anyway. Using paper towels and many trips to the fountain, he cleaned up as much of the mess as he could, and then got his clothes. He was surprised to find that they still fit him acceptably well; they were pretty well made after all, he supposed. Still. If he kept growing like had been, they wouldn't fit for very long.

He headed for the door with his bags, and then stopped in surprise. The cougar was behind the counter. One of the wolves had called him Tom.

"Dude!" the cat said. "You're still here? Ray and Trav said everyone was clearing out. Pro hour, you know. When the big boys wanna lift, you gotta say okay. They're what keeps everyone else coming here."

"You know, about that," Matt said. "I don't think guys like that make people want to come here. I think they make people want to leave. They're real assholes."

The cat's brows went up. "For real, brah? Shit. Man, I guess we should keep an eye on them, huh?"

"Yeah, you might wanna, Tom."

"ToMA," the cat corrected him.

"Right." He paused. Wait a minute. "Toma, do I look different to you at all?"

The cat scrunched up his forehead in thought. "Well, I mean you ARE way bigger than before. Must've been a great workout, huh?" He laughed.

"Um, are you serious?"

"Sure, you look like you really made some progress today, man. Good job. You're fuckin' huge now. Definitely top pro material." He looked back and forth, as if checking for people watching. "Man, speaking of that, I felt super lame about not just giving you that special rate. I mean, look at you. So what if you haven't won any contests. You might as well have. You're the biggest dude to come in here and no mistake. So… I was thinking maybe there's a way I could hook you up."

This sounded a bit dodgy, but the gear had been *awfully* expensive. "Yeah, how's that?"

"Well. I mean. If you hook me up."

Definitely dodgy. "Hook you up how?"

"Come on, man. You know. Show me what you got. I got a real good mouth."

Matt gaped at him. "You serious? You're gay?"

"Course I'm am, man, that's why I'm here. Get to look at all the thick bros walkin' through here, liftin', getting' all sweaty. It's a sweet gig. So watcha think? You show me your stuff, and then I let you walk out of here with your gear for free."

"I'm not gonna steal stuff!" Matt said in shock. "No way."

"Nonono, I mean, not the protein and drinks and stuff. But that gear? New line is coming out next month. All this stuff's getting trashed. We're supposed to just cut it up and toss it so that people will buy the new stuff, but we never do. It's a waste. Are you kidding, steal? I can't lose this job, man, I been fired way too much already."

Matt thought for a moment. The gear had cost an awful lot. And he was short on cash. What harm could a little posing do? "Okay," he said. "But I'm gonna quit if things get weird." Like they could get weirder.

"Sure bra, no prob."

Toma led him off into the aerobics room. It felt weird standing and flexing; Matt didn't exactly like it. It made him feel too self-conscious and showoffy, which was ridiculous, he knew, but still. It was kind of embarrassing. On the other hand, Toma may have been a dim bulb, but he knew his bodybuilding poses forward and backward, and he patiently guided Matt and showed him how to do it. By the time they were finished, Matt felt pretty confident he could handle himself at a bodybuilding competition if he had to.

And the cougar turned out to be right. He *did* have a really good mouth. He knew just how to use the rough parts of his tongue, and when to use the silky smooth bits, and his short fur made his muscled, compact body ripple nicely as he licked. Matt let him clean that mess up, though. He had to crouch and turn to the side to squeeze back through the aerobics room door, and when he headed out the front, he banged his head really hard on the top of the frame, and bent it.

Outside, he rummaged through his car for everything he wanted to keep from it, and shoved it in a sack. He again felt a twinge of sadness at leaving it, but there was no chance he would even begin to fit into it anymore.

He began jogging toward home. The movement felt odd. His thighs had difficulty moving past each other, and his weight came down heavily on each paw as he ran. His arms were properly musclebound now, sliding against his lats as he jogged, and his sheath and sac bounced with strange heaviness with each step, as did every muscle on his body, from his huge calves to the traps that rose up to either side of his neck. He could see people in their cars staring at him as he jogged past them, little erratic changes in their steering proving that they weren't entirely paying attention to the road. The people that he passed on the sidewalk looked strangely small. He wasn't sure how tall he was now, but he guessed it was over seven feet: a proper giant. And he had no idea what his weight was, now, but several times his paws landed on a concrete slabs and cracked them in half.

It had been a long and crazy day. He'd been fired from work, and had sex with his boss on the hood of his car, seriously denting in the thing in the process. He'd rutted with the nurse in the hospital after being told his condition could continue to increase in severity for a solid month. Then he'd gone to the gym and had his life threatened by a couple of freaky homophobes, and engaged in sexual conduct that had bordered dangerously along the lines of nonconsensual, albeit on their part, not his. He was nearly a foot taller, and probably twice as heavy, and the day wasn't even over. Maybe he could just hang out at home and try not to masturbate. But all this had happened in one day. And now he was a giant, a massive, powerful, sexual beast. What would happen tomorrow? And the day after? What would he be in a month's time?

If he stayed like this, he could make it work, somehow. He could enter in bodybuilding competitions. Toma had showed him how, and could probably coach him more. Hell, at this size, he could probably get some professional sponsors. There was a potential career in it. But if today was any indication, he wouldn't stay at this size.

He watched the traffic go by as he jogged, and realized he was running at a terrific rate. His powerful legs were able to propel him at a surprising speed, despite his weight. It was, he thought, kind of cool. Exciting, even. He didn't know what tomorrow would bring, but he'd made peace with it. He didn't know what he'd be in a month, but he couldn't worry about that.

No, his brain told him. You don't worry about it. But someone else is. What was it the nurse, Will, had told him? *This isn't all just about you.* No. It wasn't. He hadn't been the one worrying. It was Stetson that had been worrying for him. Stetson, who'd bent over backward to take care of him, to get him food, to take care of him. He'd been so selfish. He'd been running around town, having sex any time the urge—though it was admittedly almost uncontrollable—seized him. But Stetson was worried, afraid, even. Matt had made peace with the fact that their life was going to be different, but he hadn't shown Stetson that there was no need to be afraid. He needed to show him that everything was going to be all right, no matter what happened. No matter how big he got.

That was what he'd been forgetting all this time, and he cringed to think of it. Stetson was going to have a big—a *very* big—surprise when he got home, but they could work it out. He could let him know everything would be okay.

His home street came up. Had he really jogged however far it was, perhaps five or six miles, in so little time? It seemed like only thirty minutes or so. He didn't even feel tired. He slowed down as he walked down the street. It looked so different, so small. Fences barely reached over his knees. He could reach up to the roofs of some of these houses. He wondered, then, if he'd be able to squeeze into his own, still.

There was his and Stetson's house. He walked up the front path, looking at how his paws completely covered the flagstones. He couldn't wait to see Stetson; the rabbit would probably be home in a couple of hours.

Halfway to the door something stung at his neck. His paw darted to it instantly, feeling for a bee or wasp. Instead there was something solid and weighty there. He pulled at it and stared at what was in his paw. A dart? Where had that come from? He frowned, suddenly feeling very confused. There was another sting at his shoulder, and then at his arm. He looked down in hazy bewilderment to see two more darts sticking out of his fur.

The world turned sideways, and he felt his breath knocked out of him. He stared around at the sideways world. A little cat swayed into his vision, holding a small rifle. Saul. He tried to tell him to back the hell away, but his tongue was thick and stupid, and wouldn't make the words.

"Hello there, Matt," the cat said. His voice sounded like it was coming from deep underwater. "My, but you did make a monster of yourself, didn't you? Delightful. Let's find out just how much worse we can make things, shall we?"

Matt opened his mouth to tell him exactly what he thought of him, but instead a low, bestial groan came out.

"Stubborn one, aren't you?" Saul said. "Good thing I came prepared." He lifted his rifle. There was a hissing sound, and then the world spun away.

# Chapter 13

Matt's eyes opened. He felt like he hadn't really been asleep, but just too confused and lost to understand what was going on. He had vague memories of movement, of watching the sky go by above him. A dull headache throbbed behind his eyes, and he was growing increasingly aware of a sharp pain digging into his wrists.

The world before his eyes was a dizzying, foggy mess. "Where am I?" he tried to say, but it came out a deep, rumbling, "Whrrrrr."

"That's it," a thin voice purred. "Wake on up. You can do it."

Saul. Matt blinked his eyes, trying to clear and focus his vision. He was tilted forward, his weight pulling his chest and shoulders tight. Something was really digging into his wrists. His knees were scraping against the ground, his toes pressed up against a concrete wall. He struggled, trying to stand up, and managed to get to his paws. The pain in his wrists eased, accompanied by the clinking of metal. Before him, the blurry shape of a cat was seated in a chair. The room around him was brightly lit.

"Yeah," Saul said. "You're gonna be feeling much better in a minute or two. The tranquilizer I used has an antidote that lets you get back up and in the game. They use it on racehorses, but it works pretty good on big otter boys, too."

Matt shook his head, and the confusion seemed to slosh out of his ears. "You tranqed me? But... I don't... what's going on? Did I do something... bad?"

The cat tilted his head back and laughed at that. He was sitting in some kind of fold-up lawn chair and holding a martini glass with a couple of olives skewered in it. To his right stood a video camera mounted on a tall tripod, its red light glowing. On his left, a television on a stand. The camera was hooked up to it. "Oh, you've been pretty naughty, Matt. You've done a lot of bad things."

Looking around, Matt realized he was back in the basement, though apparently Saul had cleaned it up a lot. There were a lot of things piled around: snacks; lube; dildos; a stack of what appeared to be DVDs; and a laptop. To Matt's right, a large plastic bag hung from the ceiling, filled with a viscous, dark brown fluid. A clear plastic tube with a nozzle on the end dangled from it. Matt's fur stood on end, prickling up his tail, back, and neck. "What do you mean? What have I done?"

"We'll get to that." Saul got to his feet, still holding his glass. He took a sip and stepped forward, his tail moving behind him in a predatory sway—though from the exaggerated tilt of his movements, Matt guessed that he wasn't exactly working on his first martini. "But the important thing is that you and I are going to have a little fun." He came forward, and reached up to put his paw on Matt's chest. He looked so small, so frail. Matt blinked down at him, and realized suddenly that he was stripped of all his clothes. His head was clearing a bit. "Don't you want to have fun with me, Matt?"

"No," he answered. "What's going on? Why am I here? Where's Stetson?" He looked around, and then saw his arm, held out to the side, gripped by a manacle around his wrists. A thick chain extended up to a solid plate bolted into the wall. His other arm was similarly bound. He tugged at the chains. "Why am I chained up again? What happened?"

Saul took a step back, his expression darkening. "Like I told you, Matt, you were doing some bad things. You had to be stopped. I had to take precautions."

Matt furrowed his brow, remembering. "Wait. No, I wasn't doing bad things. I was going home. I was looking forward to seeing Stetson. And then… the dart. And then you—you *shot* me!"

The cat's tail twitched. He sighed. "All right, *technically* true. And it was quite the ordeal getting you down here, too. You're a monster, you know that? You must weigh a quarter of a ton at least. You should have seen how low my truck rode with you in the back."

"You shot me," Matt repeated, "and then drove me here? And… and chained me up?"

"Yes, yes, of course, my dear, sweet little muscle beast. But you know, I had to. You said yes to me, don't you remember? Two nights ago, when you were down here before, you said yes." His face twisted into a bitter scowl. "And then that *rabbit* interfered. He came between us." He softened his expression and looked up in a half smile. "It's not just the pheromones, you know. I've always wanted you. Even back when you were just a little strip of a thing. You were always beautiful to me."

This had to be some sort of weird nightmare, a disturbing sex dream. "This is crazy, Saul. I don't want to be down here with you. I want to go home. I don't want to do anything."

And for the first time in days, it was true. His cock was safely snugged away in his sheath. Well. Most of it. Not all of it seemed to fit inside his sheath anymore; a fat inch or two was poking out even though he felt completely soft. But the desire for sex was utterly absent.

The cat chuckled, his tail swaying as he walked away, looking up at the staircase as he drained his martini glass. One of the wooden railways up to the ground floor was broken. "You'll want me, stud. You'll want to feel everything I can do for you, all the amazing ways I can make you feel. It's just a matter of time."

Matt growled, and the rumbling, monstrous timbre of his own voice startled him a bit. It was going to take some getting used to. He tugged at his chains, feeling the manacles bite into his flesh again. They were pretty loose around his wrists, but his paws seemed thicker and meatier than before. There was no way he could slide the cuffs off. "No, Saul. I've learned a little self-control since then. I can resist sex when I want to. And believe me, I want to. Besides, when I said yes before, I was on drugs."

The cat turned toward him, his fangs bared in a predatory grin. "And that's how I know you'll say yes to me soon," he purred.

A heavy ball of nauseating fear formed in his belly. "What did you do?" His voice was shaking. "What did you give me?"

Saul drained his glass and licked the corners of his muzzle. "Not the stuff you were on before, sweetie. I thought about it, but it's hard to make an unconscious guy swallow pills. Besides, I wasn't really sure what filling you up with six or seven would do. No, this was just a little cocktail of my own devising," he said. "You learn a lot when you're hitting up seedy clubs for thirty years, you know. A little pinch of GHB, a dash of roofies, and my proprietary blend of other herbs and spices. Then I crank everything up to dose a guy four times as big as normal, and I'll have me an insatiably horny otter stud in… oh, about forty-five minutes now."

He couldn't believe what he was hearing. "This is sick, Saul. It's… it's just nuts. You know how strong I am now? How strong I'll be in… in an hour? I'm gonna break loose of this."

Saul laughed. He turned, slinking over to the wall, where he refilled his glass from a couple of clear bottles. "I don't think so, sweetie. Those manacles aren't the ones you were in before. The chains are rated to three thousand pounds. You're not breaking those, I'm afraid."

The chains did look thicker than the ones he'd been bound with before, now that he looked at them. He gave them a little tug, and they clinked heavily.

"That, by the way," Saul said, pointing to the large bag of liquid, "is a whole lot of very high-grade protein. Convenient for when you get hungry. As I suppose you will be doing a lot."

That was even more ominous. "So what are you going to do? Just keep me down here forever?"

"Forever?" Saul turned, flicking his gaze up and down Matt's body. It felt creepy now, unwholesome. "Don't be silly, boy. I'm not looking for commitment." He winked. "Just a little fun. Besides, you'll be too big for me soon enough."

"But you know I'll go to the police as soon as I get out of here!" He probably shouldn't be saying this, but he couldn't help himself. He was starting to panic now.

"Mmmm, no." Saul came back, tracing across the top of Matt's chest with one finger, the claw slightly extended. He gave a shuddering, hungry breath. "A little side effect of your medicine is the inability to form short-term memories. Amnesia. You won't remember most of what happens after the stuff kicks in. Go to the police, and what do you think I'll say?"

The cat stepped back then, his ears flattening back, his eyes widening in an expression of horror. He huddled in on himself, and began shaking violently. "Horrible. It was horrible. He… that—that monster. That *thing*. Attacked me. Attacked me in my home. He forced me to… forced me to do things. Please, I can't… don't make me talk about it." He looked up, his expression turning predatory once again. "Who are they gonna believe, the poor little cat? Or the terrifying brute without valid identification?"

Matt couldn't believe he was hearing this. "They can test my blood! They'll find the drugs!"

"Which you no doubt took as part of your supplementation routine. Look at you, with all that chemically-enhanced muscle. Who knows what other drugs you're on? My dear otter, even *you* don't know."

"But Stetson will vouch for me. He'll back me up."

Saul laughed at that. "Oh, you want to bring in witnesses, do you? Let's talk about witnesses." He walked back to the chair and bent down to pick up the remote, lifting his tail to flash Matt a glimpse of his ass. Matt looked away. The very idea of it was revolting now. Stepping back, Saul turned on the television and started a video. The picture that flickered into view was a black and white image of a small store. It took a moment for Matt to recognize it as the WNC he'd been to the other day. It took him a little longer to recognize the muscular, thrusting hips of the otter, pinning a raccoon up against shelves, ass flexing as he drove his cock into the smaller, writhing creature.

Saul let the footage run. "Look familiar? Turns out that having sex in a store like that is a firing offense." He clucked his tongue. "I know. This society with its barbaric laws and social niceties. All the same, your little playmate Terry there didn't want to lose his job. So guess what he'll tell the police if they ask if he was forced."

Matt stared, aghast.

"Or how about this little scene?" The cat clicked the remote again, and the image changed. This time, Matt could easily recognize his own car being recorded from a mounted dashboard camera: a horse in a police uniform tilting back his head, eyes squeezed shut, as an otter, even bigger and bulkier than the one before, rutted into him, half-crushing him against the car, the whole vehicle swaying as his hips pounded. Saul clucked again. "Assault of a police officer. Or so he'll say if this footage ever gets out." He grinned at Matt, wrinkling his muzzle as he feigned a friendly whisper. "Obviously he'll keep quiet if it doesn't."

"How did you even get this footage?" Matt stammered.

"Sweetie, you don't get to be where I am without making a few connections here and there. I followed you. And then I just talked to the right people. So let's see what other clips we have!" He changed the scene again. It was another top-down scene, obviously the parking garage. Right below the camera was a Porsche. Of course Gomez would park it right where it would be most easily viewed. A massive creature, barely recognizable as an otter, was gripping both sides of the hood, his whole body thrusting down and forward with terrific force, wide back rippling and bulging with impossible strength as his movements dented in the hood of the vehicle beneath him. The struggling lion pinned between the two could barely be seen.

"I understand he fired you just before that," Saul purred. "So there you even have motive." He shook his head in mock dismay. "Like I said before, Matt, you've been doing some very bad things. I bet I'll find even more to use against you if I find out what you did with the rest of your day today. And that's why you're not going to the police. You understand me? If you say one word to them about what's going on, I'll tell them you assaulted me. I'll have literal bucket loads of DNA evidence, recorded footage, and witness accounts all ready to say that you were an aggressor. A monster. Look at you. You'll be even bigger by then. More impossible. They will take one look and lock you up and throw. Away. The key."

He sighed through his nose. "I don't really understand why you're making this so difficult. You can ruin your life, or you can have a few good times with me. That's all I'm asking."

Matt slumped to the floor in despair—at least, as far as his chains would let him, his arms pulled out wide. "This… how could you do this to me, Saul? You're… you were our friend! This is rape. That's all it is."

Saul shrugged. "You guys were really shitty friends. Besides, it's not rape if you want it. And you're *really* going to want it. You're going to beg me for it."

"You're forcing me to want it!" Matt shouted.

"Oh really?" the cat sneered. "Does that make a difference? Isn't that what you did to those fun little toys of yours on the tapes? Didn't you, with your crazy, magic, sex-god scent, make *them* want it?" His face contorted in sudden regret. "Didn't you make *me* want it? If that's what makes the difference, then, my dear boy, you started it. You did it to me first."

"Don't even pretend that's the same! I never chained you up and shoved drugs down your throat while you were unconscious. I never shot you with a tranquilizer gun!"

Saul shrugged his narrow shoulders. "Semantics. I'm sure you'll feel better about things in, oh, about half an hour. But all this shouting and whining of yours is very unpleasant. I'll be back down when you're feeling a bit more agreeable." He looked around the room briefly. "I know what you're thinking, but there's nothing in reach. Your arms and legs are quite secure in those chains. I've left the key upstairs. So there's no point in struggling."

The cat's expression softened. "Look, I'm not... I'm not really a bad person. I'm just... I never get a turn, you know? You're... so gorgeous. I can't forget the way you looked from before, the way your scent drove me crazy. Your hungry face when you *begged* me for sex, before your little boyfriend stopped us. Besides, I need the money. I really need it."

Matt furrowed his brow. "Money? What money?"

Saul looked over toward the video camera set up next to his chair. "This whole thing you have going with you, it's got this... fetish... behind it. If I can get video of a guy like you growing like you do? Like, actually for real, and not some cheap computer-generated thing? If I go to the right people with that, I can name my price. It would help a lot." He gave an odd little laugh. "I mean, manacles and tranquilizer guns don't pay for themselves!"

Sighing, Matt said, "So that's it. You're gonna grow me huge and have sex with me. There's nothing I can do."

"Well, you could try to just accept it and enjoy it. But you know what? I'm a fair guy. If I come down once the drugs are *really* going, really roaring through your head, and you still say no to me, I promise I won't do anything. I won't touch you until you say yes, just like before. But Matt, you're going to say yes. So don't worry about it. It will be ecstasy."

Saul patted Matt's chest again, and he flinched away, his chains rattling. "Don't touch me."

The cat scowled. "I'm going upstairs now," he said. "And I'm not coming back until you're in a better mood." He turned, still holding his glass, and stalked up the stairs. At the top he paused. "Oh yes," he added. "Soundproofed room. So, you know, don't go wearing your voice out for nothing." He closed the door behind him.

Matt stared after him for a moment and then slumped again. His weight really tugged on his chest and arms, but it didn't hurt at all, except where the manacles chafed at his wrists. He stood up and pushed forcefully against the chains with both his arms, straining with all his might. His chest bulged out so thick that he couldn't put his arms all the way forward, his triceps mashing outward into the chain. It wobbled around as he pushed at it, but the metal itself showed no signs of stretching or breaking. Again and again he tried, but it was still no use. He sighed, leaning back against the wall and panting slowly; the exertion had heated him up. If each chain would really hold three thousand pounds, there was no way he could break them. He had been trapped with less than eight hundred pounds at the gym, unable to budge it until he grew, and even then it had taken a huge effort. There was no way, even if he grew many times.

He walked out to the ends of the chains, but that wasn't very far. Everything in the room was way, way out of reach, and besides, he couldn't see anything that would help him get free. The bottle of lube, maybe, but his paws looked far too big to slip out of the cuffs, and his feet definitely were. There was no way out.

He stared down at his feet—or at least in the direction of his feet, since he couldn't see them past his chest. There was nothing on the floor around him, nothing but white and gray dust, gritty under his webbed toes. Some kind of concrete dust, he guessed. Probably from when Saul had put in the new manacles, which only proved his claims from before. Rated to three thousand pounds each, then. The cuffs, the chains, and probably the bolts that clamped them to the wall, too. He froze.

But not the walls.

No, the walls were probably made of cinder block; that's what the dust under his toes felt like. And while he wasn't sure how much pulling a cinder block could take, it was probably a hell of a lot less than three thousand pounds. Still, it hadn't budged when he'd tugged at it. He wasn't strong enough to move it. But he had one surefire way to make himself stronger.

He hesitated at the thought of it. Did he really want to try to do this? As soon as he asked himself the question, the answer seemed obvious. It was grow now, of his own free will and escape, or grow later, at Saul's whim, and probably give in to him.

He closed his eyes and focused on drawing his lust. He waited. And waited. But it wasn't coming. Every moment of the past several days, his lust had been just a mere stray thought and a heartbeat away, but now he couldn't make himself get hard. It was his situation. It was Saul, and what he'd done. It just wasn't erotic at all; instead it was creepy and frightening. And still, lurking about his mind, was the faint haze of the tranquilizers.

He thought of the homophobic wolves in the gym, Ray and Trav, and how they'd threatened him because of the urges his scent had aroused in them. He thought of Devon, thrown into personal crisis over what he'd done. There was Gomez, his boss, who he'd practically ragefucked atop his car, and Will, who had reminded him that his life wasn't all just about him. There was Terry, the raccoon from the WNC, apparently ready to lie to the police because he'd risked his job, and Officer Cokie, who had threatened him with arrest if he didn't fuck him. Everything had occurred because Matt could create desire. He could make guys want him. And okay, maybe it wasn't bad like what Saul was doing to him now, but it was still just desire.

He'd always wanted to be desirable. He'd thought, back when he was a skinny little underwhelming otter, that having everyone look at you and crave you would be the best thing in the world. And true, it had been fun, most of the time. But now, because of it, he was trapped in a basement by some skeevy guy who couldn't say no. Desire wasn't enough. It was fun, but empty. It could even be monstrously selfish. It could make people just want to eat you whole. Cokie, Terry, Ray, Trav, Gomez, Devon, and Saul. And, of course, Stetson.

But then, Stetson had always desired him, even when he *was* that skinny little underwhelming otter. He sighed, suddenly remembering fondly the way he'd bent his boyfriend over the kitchen table, lathered up his buns with butter, and squeezed into him. He remembered his moans as he thrust, his whimpers as the tip of his cock hit the underside of the table.

His sheath pulsed. There was a sticky sound as his shaft rose an inch or two from it; he couldn't see it over his own chest to check. He wished the rabbit were here now. Even if he couldn't unlock the chains, just to have him here. The last time he'd been chained up here, Stetson had just climbed up him and rode him. Gods, that had felt good. His balls throbbed with the memory of it. He could feel the fur on his abs sliding against his cock as it rose. He closed his eyes, imagining Stetson's paws on his shoulders, his big ol' feet locked behind his waist, the tightness of the rabbit's rump as it squeezed down around him. Yes. His shaft ached with sudden hardness. A hot trail of precum oozed down his channel, and he sniffed the air, inhaling his intoxicating scent, still not opening his eyes, imagining a delicate pink rabbit tongue lightly tracing up his shaft, stroking him clean.

The soft touch of fur bumped against his tip and he opened his eyes in surprise, half-expecting to see the rabbit there, but no. There was no one. He tugged at his chains and felt the movement of fur against his tip again. It was his chest; the end of his cock nudging up against it. He gasped at the realization and braced his broad paws, pushing his hips upward a little. The top of his glans slid along the smooth cleft between his pecs. He drew his breath in sharply again, giving his hips a twitch. His cock flexed, almost by itself, bobbing downward—he could feel its weight tugging at his loins as it did— and then slapping up against his chest once more, wedging beneath its shelf and simultaneously painting the bottom of it with hot syrup. He could feel it seeping into his fur, crawling down his belly. His scent was getting to him now: his breaths were deeper, shuddering.

He pushed his hips up again, his tip stuck below the bottom of his chest, the shaft bowing outward as he did so. Again he pushed, and again, flexing his chest to squeeze at the sensitive flesh below. His sac bounced against his thighs, the weight of its contents drawing up. His cock flexed again; he felt his pre soaking down the fur of his belly, all the way to his legs, but also squeezing up between his pectorals until it glistened at the top of his chest. He breathed in deep, leaned forward, curled his tongue out, and licked the taste of himself off of his chest. It was utterly and overwhelmingly male. He wanted more of it. He mentally commanded his balls to make more of it, and felt, though surely it was only his imagination, a surge of heightened lust race through him. His cock pulsed several times, and with each, sent more pre soaking up over his chest, running down his shaft, each jet of it far more than he had once ever been able to cum. He felt drops of it on the floor, around his toes.

Almost deliriously he began to pump his hips again; he felt his tip slide free suddenly from below his chest, the fur too slippery now to keep it wedged there. It bobbed heavily in the air again, and then smacked against his chest and belly once more, and then the smell and the taste and the sensations overwhelmed him. His sac tightened his hips convulsed, and then he stared as a small fountain of white splashed up past his chest, soaking it, pleasure and satisfaction gripping his mind and making his back arch. His cock dipped as he thrust forward, sending thick ropes of his seed halfway across the room, splashing across Saul's chair. He craned his head forward eagerly, wanting to taste it, but his tip was out of reach. A few more splashes coated the floor in front of him, and then he felt it just bubbling out, streaming down his cock and dripping off of his balls onto his thighs.

The growth he had yearned for hit him then: he flexed his shaft hard, involuntarily, straining it, feeling the tip creep up higher against his chest, and then he saw the top of it beyond his pecs, broad as an orange, soaked in white with more oozing out. His body tensed, every muscle tightening, his wrists involuntarily pulling at the manacles about them, and he grew. His tail slid against the wall, and the rounding of his glutes pushed it up higher. His back pressed against the cinder blocks as it thickened, and he watched the floor drop further away. He could feel his traps bulking up higher behind his head, his neck widening. As he watched, his pecs jumped and twitched, his pelt stretching out as new fibers of muscle crawled beneath it, adding layer after layer of power, his still-dripping tip teased as the sinew shoved it out farther.

He panted for a second in the aftermath, and realized then that he wasn't satisfied in the slightest. He still yearned to cum. Had the drugs Saul had given him already begun to take effect? Or was this just what his libido was like, now? Maybe he had to cum more than once before he was finished, now. At any rate, his balls were still pulsing.

His stomach growled, and he sniffed the air, scenting the irresistible odor of his own cum. He hungered for his cock and he was determined to have it. There was no reason why he shouldn't; he was strong enough to get it. He shifted his grip in the manacles, turning his wrists to grasp the chains in his broad paws. He squeezed them tight and then hefted his own weight in them. Lifting himself was easy. It was as if he weighed nothing at all. He braced his thick tail against the wall and then pushed, using his abs to curl his hips upward. His knees rose up past his chest, and then the tip of his cock pushed forward, guided by the cleft between his pecs, trailing pre as it arched upward along his chest and into his waiting muzzle.

He had trouble squeezing it in at this point; it was pretty thick, but fortunately, an otter's muzzle was broad, and his was broader than most—perhaps more than any other's—thanks to his growth. His tongue lapped smoothly at the top of his glans and he groaned, sealing his lips around it. He could actually feel the load of pre traveling up his channel, pushing its way past his lips as it jetted into his throat, and he swallowed it hungrily. His mouth felt good, tight. He began to rock his hips upward, fucking into his own face, his body suspended by the chains gripped tightly in his paws. He realized, distantly, that he was both pulling up and crunching hundreds of pounds, but the effort was trivial. His back thumped against the wall as he pushed his hips upward, and pinched at it as the muscle flexed to support his weight. He could scarcely pay attention to that, though; he was lost in the sensation of suckling at his own tip.

Because it was his own cock in his muzzle, he quickly learned just how to slide his tongue, exactly how hard to suck, when to push into the back of his throat, when to avoid his teeth. He was learning more about oral sex than he ever could have on his own, and the sensations were quickly overwhelming him. His shaft jumped with sudden straining, filling his muzzle with mouthfuls of hot pre that he struggled to swallow in time, but his swallowing just made his throat and tongue tease him even more. Before he was ready, another climax was rapidly approaching. Some rational part of his mind told him he should pull his tip out of his muzzle in a hurry, but a more defiant (and pleasure-crazed) side of himself instead curled up his abdominals hard, pushing his tip into the back of his throat. His cock bulged slightly larger for a moment, and then his climax erupted into his own mouth. He choked on the first load, the wall of his throat spasming delightfully against his glans as he did so, and he barely managed to recover and swallow before the second load jetted out. His balls throbbed. Seed poured down his throat, making him feel bloated, the sensation of swallowing so much so quickly intensely uncomfortable, but he couldn't care. The pleasure was too great. Again and again he pulsed, humping up against his own face.

He felt his cock strain again, mid-eruption. In his mouth, he could feel it pulsing, feel the flesh moving against his tongue and palate as it stretched, forcing his jaws farther apart. It poured a little more seed down his throat, and then reeled out a bit, pushing deeper into his gullet and making him gag. He began lowering his hips to pull it out of his muzzle, and just then every muscle in his body flexed hard. His chest ballooned out in slow, stretching movements, pushing out against his shaft and prying it away from him, the tip popping free of his jaws. Cum drooled from the corners of his muzzle and spilled onto his chest. He could feel his back sliding against the wall again, the angle of his grip on the chains changing as his arms lengthened. The weight of his body seemed to decrease even further. He slowly uncurled his torso, lowering his toes to the floor and stood up. He was much broader than before, he could tell. Every muscle felt overstuffed, crowded. Looking down at himself he could tell that even were he back at his original height, he would still be enormously muscled, as much so as even the biggest guys he had ever seen. Every part of him was rounded bulges, stretching out his pelt with powerful sinew. He looked like a comic book hero, almost. He wondered if the rate of his growth could have increased even more than before.

His gut felt bloated and full, though, and it gurgled with the meal of seed he had just consumed. He tried to reach to touch it and the manacles gripped at his wrists, more tightly than they had before. He tugged at them in annoyance. Perhaps he was strong enough to pull them out. He ought to be, he thought, considering he was the size of

a forklift now. He lifted an arm and gave one chain an experimental tug, briefly distracted by the way his triceps pushed out, by the way his shoulders mounded. His cock had started to soften, but now it rose again. No. He couldn't give in to his appetites. He had to get free. He started to push again, but then his stomach growled once more. He was hungry. More than that, he was suddenly achingly, desperately hungry. He'd added so much mass so quickly. He needed food.

The protein bag was to his right, the feeding tube dangling below it. He couldn't reach it with his hands, but he could lean down and grab it in his jaws. His chest and shoulder bulged out, getting in his way as he tried to nip at the tube, but he finally got it. He worked it around with his tongue and teeth until he had the end in his muzzle, and then he sucked urgently at it. The thick fluid that filled his mouth was cold and sickly-sweet and foul-tasting, but he barely noticed, swallowing as rapidly as he could to stave off the intense hunger that clawed at him. He emptied a good quarter of the bag before the cravings left him.

Panting, he let go of the tube and looked around. He had been trying to get free. His panting breath made his chest slide up and down against his tip. The scents of musk and seed were heavy in the air. He felt his balls throbbing with need, his sac feeling like it was gripping them too tightly. A steady dripping came from the floor as pre trickled from his sac to puddle between his webbed feet. The urge to fuck… something… was overwhelming. But no.

No, he needed to escape. He wrested his attention away from his aching cock and lifted his right arm, eyeing the manacle around his wrist. With a quick movement, he twisted his body forward, pulling his right arm across his body to yank at the chain. The metal links held, jerking at his arm as he reached the end of it. The steel bit hard into his wrist, painfully, but it felt like the chain might have shifted a bit in the wall. He yanked again, just as hard. The bulge of his chest and biceps was making the movement more difficult, but he was learning how to move around them. Again the steel cut into his wrist, and again he felt the bolts shift in the wall. He put as much power as he could into the movement, tugging again, four times, five, and on the sixth, there was a crumbling sound and the chain pulled free, whipping forward across the room, the bolts still embedded in a chunk of cinder block that had torn out of the wall.

Matt stared at the chain for a moment, heart pounding in awe. He'd just ripped a steel chain out of a basement wall. He lifted his arm, ignoring the clinking sounds of the chain dragging on the ground, and stared at it, moving his hand from side to side, watching the overstuffed swells of muscle ripple like shifting iron beneath his short fur. No otter had ever been this big before; probably very few—if any—people ever had been this big. He was something new. He splayed his stubby fingers, pulling the webs tight, watching his forearm bulge with the casual movement. Trancelike, he lowered his paw to his cock and gripped it just under his glans, feeling heated precum bubble out and spill down across his knuckles. It felt so good. He could escape in a minute or two. Just now he needed to ease the pressure just a bit. He began stroking.

# Chapter 14

There was a loud thump. Saul opened his eyes. Something was hard under his cheek. The table. He'd fallen asleep on the table. His head swam with the dizziness of alcohol. He'd probably had too many martinis before the otter woke up. He frowned. Something. The otter. Matt. Matt was in his basement right now. How long had he been passed out on the table? He glanced over at the clock. It had been nearly an hour since he'd left the otter downstairs. Shit. He better not have started without Saul. But no, probably the tranqs would have slowed him down a bit. Saul got to his feet, picking up his martini glass. He'd come up here for something. What was it? Caramel sauce, that was it. If he was going to record this, might as well make it a good one. He grabbed it and swayed back to the basement. Shit. So much vodka. He opened the door down to the basement.

Hot air rushed out, heavy with the scent of sex. Damn it all, he *had* started without him. The scent moved through his lungs like electricity, made his nerves tingle, made his breath hover in aching anticipation at the edge of his lips. He stepped down the stairs.

And dropped the caramel sauce, barely having the wherewithal to hold onto his glass. Across the room stood a giant, his ears brushing the eight-foot-high ceiling, his body impossible, monstrous, filled with muscle, bulging with titanic strength. From one tightly-manacled wrist, a chain dangled, clinking as it was raised and lowered by a powerful paw that was stroking the biggest cock Saul had ever seen. The otter's other wrist was still bound to the wall, held there by strands that seemed a mere inconvenience to him, the massive shoulders and arms looking capable of snapping it free as casually as they might break a thread, each bulge of muscle twitching with barely contained strength, bigger than watermelons. The hulking beast was nearly as wide as Saul was tall. How could he have grown so much so quickly? The protein bag was empty; he'd apparently drained it.

Trembling, Saul descended to the bottom of the steps, and when he stepped forward, the huge beast turned, staring at him. "Saul?" it said. Its voice was rich and rumbling, with a lower, persistent growl, and the room seemed to shake when it spoke. Its brow furrowed. "I was… I was going to leave. Run home. But I just needed to ease the pressure." It stepped toward him, and the chain tugged at its still-bound arm. It looked toward its shoulder, frowning, and gave an almost casual pull. With a crack, the chain pulled free of the wall, ripping free a chunk of cinder block with it. Matt lifted a leg that looked powerful enough to crush a vehicle flat beneath it, and with a little kick tugged the chain binding it out of the wall. A second kick freed its other leg.

The beast came toward him; Saul was shaking more violently now, unable to control it. The beast loomed over him, igniting old flight instincts. Saul's ears pinned back. His fur bushed out. He hunched, fighting the urge to turn and scamper up the stairs, and instead reached up with one paw, tilting his head back to gaze up at the creature. Its huge torso expanded with its slow, deep breaths, chest shadowing his head.

He was only nose-level with the top of its abs, but those were obscured by its jutting erection. He leaned forward to give it a lick, but then the huge beast crouched toward him. He almost yelped and darted backward in sudden fright, but he held his ground. One huge arm moved toward him, a paw gripping around his chest more tightly than was comfortable, the digits as unyielding as steel clamps. He clutched at the fingers and arms, legs kicking and tail lashing as he was hefted into the air.

The floor was a good two feet below his paws, and he was staring into the eyes of an otter torn by desires. "Matt," he stammered. "Matt, put me down."

The otter's brow furrowed again. It tilted its head, thick neck rippling. "You did this to me," it accused him. "You wanted this."

Saul squirmed in the grip, which wasn't comfortable at all. He felt his tail curl against something, and watched the otter's expression flinch briefly into one of unexpected pleasure. "Yes," he said. "Yes, I did, but Matt, I didn't do anything that wouldn't have happened anyway."

The otter growled, his forearm bulging with a squeeze that made Saul's ribs creak. He yelped at the sudden pain, and saw surprise and regret flicker across the otter's face. Maybe there was something more than a monster in there still.

"I mean, how many times did you...?" He looked around meaningfully at the puddles of cum everywhere, the drops dripping from the ceiling.

The otter appeared to consider. "Four," it said. "Maybe five."

"You see?" Saul said. "You would have been like this by the end of tomorrow anyway, the way you've been going."

"No," the beast said, shaking its head. "No, I could have... stopped somehow. Done something." It narrowed its eyes. "I should punish you for what you did to me."

Saul's pulse quickened, though from fear or excitement, he couldn't tell. "You don't need to punish me," he said. "You're a good person, Matt. You wouldn't do that."

The beast narrowed its eyes. Saul frantically lashed his tail again, managing to curl it partway around the beast's cock. The huge creature shuddered in pleasure. It looked down at its shining tip, then back up at Saul. "I should punish you properly," it said, licking at its jaws.

Saul gaped, pushing more urgently at the fingers gripping him. "Matt, no." He looked back at the tip jutting up before him. That shaft had to be four inches in diameter. It would wreck him. "Matt, that thing will hurt me. You can't... you don't want this."

The otter lifted him higher, hunger burning in its eyes. The drugs were working on it quite plainly; he could see the urgent intensity in its expression, its inhibitions burned away. It was a creature of pure desire and power, consumed only with thoughts of its urgent need for the moment. "I do want it," it growled. "I want to fuck so much, so hard." It shuddered in lust, and more precum spilled out of it. It moved him toward its tip, its grip unyielding. It was just going to shove him down on top of it.

"Matt," he begged in panic. "Please, no, please. I don't want this. Don't do this to me." His body called him a liar: up from his sheath

jutted his slender, aching shaft. The pheromones were working on him now, he could feel it. A hunger was growing inside him. He tightened his tail around the cock below him. It was huge. It was too big. But it would feel amazing, wouldn't it? Stretching him as wide as he'd ever been stretched, stuffing inch after inch into him, filling him deeper and deeper, his own weight pulling him down around it as he was impaled by it. "I don't want this," he breathed again, but it was a lie.

He felt his hips rock toward the beast's slippery shaft of their own accord, trying to contort his body up and onto it. "I want this," he said suddenly. "I need it." He squirmed in the powerful grip. "Please, Matt. Fuck me. Fuck me hard. Punish me for what I did to you. Show me all that power. Show me what you can do with it."

Uncertainty fell across the face of the thing that used to be an otter. It frowned. It lifted him higher, nestling that broad trunk of a cock between his thighs. It held him there for a moment, tantalizingly close to pushing into him. A splash of preseed soaked the fur on his ass, its heat sinking into his skin. He tried to shove himself downward onto it, tail lashing. "Please," he begged it. "Punish me. Show me how mighty you are. You're not an otter anymore, Matt. You're not even mortal. Just look at you. You're a god now. Matt. Show me your divine retribution."

Emotion warred across the otter's face, conflicting desires twisting its expression. It lowered Saul down until he could feel that fist-sized tip beginning to spread his rump. "Yes," he groaned, excitement lancing through his mind. He should be concerned, he thought. Afraid. But he wasn't. He just wanted to be fucked. And he would lay it on just as thick as he had to in order to make sure that happened. "Yes, lord. Do what you desire tells you. You're a god, a divine being. You should use us mortals as you see fit. It's all that matters, your desire. All that matters is you."

The beast froze then. It stared at him, its eyes wide. It looked around the room, and then down at itself, and then, suddenly, put him down. He stumbled on the floor and then slipped in a slick puddle and fell backward onto his hands. What had just happened?

"What are you doing?" he demanded. "Come on, fuck me. Now!"

It snarled and took a step back away from him, chains dragging on the ground, erection bobbing and flicking drops to the floor. "No."

No? How could it say no with that much sex juice flooding its system? "Matt, you know you want to." He rolled to hands and knees, lifting his tail and arching his back in a practiced motion. "You know you want this." He looked back over his shoulder at the monster.

Its gaze flickered down to his rump, and he saw it twitch as if moving toward him. Then it shook its head. "No, I don't."

He couldn't believe what he was hearing. Nobody could say no after taking the stuff he'd given the otter, nobody. "Yes, you do!" he protested. "Look at your cock. Look at… look at all of you. You're made for sex. Every ounce of you is craving it. You'd do anything to fuck, anything."

The beast looked down at its hulking frame. "Maybe," it said. "But not with you."

Saul's face was hot with desire and fury. Not with him? How dare it say that? He deserved it. He'd earned it. "You're going to do it," he said, spluttering with frustration. "Or I'll say you attacked me. The place is covered with your cum. You tore chains out of the wall. You're a monster, and everyone will think so. You think they'll treat you like one of them? They'll throw you in prison. They'll cage you like the beast you are. I'll see to it. If you don't do what I want right now, I'll turn those recordings in to the police and get them to hunt you down. You'll be lucky if they don't just shoot you on sight."

The beast growled at him furiously, and then paused. "The recordings," it said. It turned away from him, looking at the camera on the tripod, the red light blinking atop it. Because, of course, Saul hadn't wanted to risk missing a minute of that otter fucking or growing. Damn it! How could he have forgotten that? It picked up the camera and tripod in one meaty paw, then stripped the tripod away and tossed it aside, its metal legs clattering against the far wall.

"Wait, no." Saul scrambled backward, getting to his feet. "Uh, it—it hadn't started recording yet, Matt. There's nothing on there. Don't… Just put it down, you're going to crush it."

The beast turned to him, showing its fangs in a terrible grin. "Oh, I'll be real careful with it," it rumbled. "Don't you worry about that." It stepped past him, then, heading toward the stairs up and out of the basement.

Panicking, Saul lunged after it, grabbing at one of its forearms and clinging. "Matt, gods damn it, give me that fucking camera. You can't do this. I'll hunt you down again. You fucking owe me, Matt. I can tranq you again. I can still send out that footage. Something could happen to you. Something could happen to Stetson—"

With a snarl, the beast whirled on him and leapt at him, knocking him to the floor as if he weighed nothing at all. He was underneath it then, one massive paw on his chest, pressing him to the floor, crushing the wind from his lungs with its impossible weight. He'd gone too far. Way too far. Its huge body expanded over him with its panting breaths, and it leaned down until the hot puffs of air dampened his muzzle fur. He tried to croak Matt's name, but he didn't have the air. Stars started to flash in front of his eyes. His paws beat feebly at a forearm bigger around than his own chest. He was going to die.

Then, abruptly, the beast let him go, standing up over him. Its bristling fur settled down, its ears went back, and it took a step backward. It turned and started back for the exit again, and this time, Saul had no intention of stopping it.

He took in huge gasps of breath, leaning up, dizzy. Matt ignored him, climbing the stairs, but the wooden planks snapped and caved under his weight. He gripped the railing, trying to climb up the sides, and with a splintering, crunching sound, the whole staircase broke down one side. The thing was too heavy for it. Undeterred, it reached up and pushed at the door, which was well within its long reach. Then it gripped both sides of the doorway and heaved itself up through, pushing off with its paws. Its shoulders slammed into either side of the frame, breaking it and punching through the drywall. The beast thrashed, trapped for a moment in the small doorframe, and then forced its way all the way through. It left a huge hole behind it where the doorway once was, and then the sides sagged in, caving, and the doorway collapsed.

Shaking, Saul got to his feet. He left sticky prints as he stumbled across the floor. In the room above, he could hear Matt stumping around, the basement ceiling shaking, dust drifting down. The stairway was utterly destroyed and unusable, and even if he could stack up bits of it to reach the doorway, he couldn't get through any time soon.

Cold realization of what he'd done crept through him. He'd kidnapped and drugged someone. He'd threatened extortion and blackmail. And now the otter was free, with a video camera full of incontrovertible, impossible proof. He slumped against a wall, feeling sick to his stomach. He could go to prison. Or maybe he'd pissed off the otter enough that one night it would just jump him in a dark alley and pound him into a smear. But no, the beast was sex-crazed, and growing more than any frame could hold. Give it a day or two, and it'd be so built up it wouldn't be able to move. Maybe its chest would even grow big enough to seal its damned muzzle closed so it couldn't speak a word.

Except it had that video camera. Stetson, at least, would see it. Saul was doomed. He sagged down against the wall in defeat. And to make matters worse, he was trapped in this room reeking with sex until he could figure a way out. He wasn't in the mood at all, but still, his erection ached.

"Would you just go down already?" he snapped at it. It just strained harder than ever.

\* \* \*

Free. Matt was free. He stood up in the hallway and hit his head on the ceiling, but it didn't hurt. He crouched, and looked up to see a dent there. The hallway wasn't wide enough to let him move down it normally, so he had to turn to the side and squeeze along it to get into the living room. He looked down at the front door to Saul's house, wondering how he was going to fit through it. He thought he remembered French doors in the kitchen, so he squeezed his way back down the hall, his shoulders and back knocking pictures off of the wall with crashes, one leg crushing a small table as if it were made of popsicle sticks. He looked down at the fragments, and saw, next to it, the tranquilizer gun and a little clear plastic case full of darts. No way was he going to leave those with Saul. He picked up the gun and snapped it between his paws like a matchstick. The dart case he took with him as he made his way to the end of the hall.

In the kitchen he could breathe easier, and was gratified to see there were, in fact, double doors there. He crouched and gave one knob a tug. It opened with a splintering sound, a deadbolt tearing through the wood. He blinked at it in astonishment. He hadn't even realized it was locked. His new strength was going to take some getting used to. The doors swung open (one listing to the side and scraping against the floor a bit), and he crouched to step out, and then paused.

Something wasn't right. That was it. He was naked. He wasn't hard anymore, for the moment at least, but naked still. He was going to draw attention no matter what his condition, but there was no point in getting obscenity charges. He cast about for something he could use to cover himself. He wasn't sure where Saul had put his clothes, if they would even fit him now. A towel would be too small. Maybe a bedsheet? He scanned the room, and his eyes settled on the floor-to-ceiling white curtains to either side of the doors. One of those would do nicely. He gave one a little tug, and the curtain rod popped off the wall. Oh well. He wasn't feeling too bad about Saul having to do repairs just now. He pulled the rod out of the curtains, having a little trouble gripping it with his thick fingers, and then tied the curtain around his waist. He checked himself over, hitting his head on the ceiling when he leaned up. He looked pretty silly, but at least he was decent.

He stooped down and crept out of the kitchen; even though his head cleared the doorframe, the mounds of muscle across his back struck and cracked it. Oh well. It hadn't been *his* idea to grow huge inside Saul's house… exactly. He stood fully upright, stretching out, feeling for the first time his body's breadth. The world looked so much smaller, now. He could see easily up onto the roof of Saul's house. It looked almost like a playhouse, made for a child. He went around the back and through the wooden gate, only to smash it as he tried to get through.

At the side of the house, Saul's pickup blocked his way. It seemed a trivial impediment; he crouched down, gripped the back bumper, and lifted the rear end of the truck easily into the air. Bracing his feet, he pushed forward, the truck skidding along the ground, step after step, until he had pushed it out of his way entirely. He had just *picked up a truck*. He felt a giddy sort of elation. He dropped the rear end and the little vehicle bounced in place.

The libido was beginning to rush back, and whatever drugs Saul had given him were fogging his mind more and more. He needed to get home. The sun was still high. Stetson probably wouldn't be back yet. Matt stepped past the truck and looked down the street. There were pedestrians staring at him. A car had stopped mid-traffic and people were gaping through the windshield at him. He needed to get out of here.

He turned in the direction of home and began to run. His first bound sent him sailing through the air, his arms waving as he leaped much farther than he was expecting to, and the sidewalk plates cracked under his toes when he landed. He felt so light when he walked. Only the terrific pressure on the pads of his feet betrayed his weight.

Something fluttered behind him; his sheet was coming undone and blowing in the wind like a dress. Embarrassed, he tied it around his middle like a loincloth so that all the objectionable bits were covered. His fingers brushed across his sheath as he tied, each of his huge balls cradled by the soft fabric, making his lust surge again, making his cock push farther out. He had to get home quickly.

He tried running again, and this time was more prepared for the leap forward. His thighs weren't well-suited for a steady run now; they crowded each other too much, and he found himself moving in a series of long bounds, sailing through the air, landing on both feet, crouching a bit, and bounding again. The sidewalk kept cracking beneath him, and on it, telephone poles and fire hydrants got in his way, so he ended up running on the street. He tried to ignore the people around him as he bounded by: pedestrians crying out in surprise, some dashing the other way, cars skidding to a stop when they caught sight of him. After a few minutes, though, it was obvious he was causing a disturbance. He really, really didn't want to see any police right now, so he detoured, taking back streets as much as possible, running down alleys.

He passed fences no higher than his knees, houses and cars that looked like toys, some of whose alarms went off as he thundered by them. He wasn't sure what size he was now, but he was definitely bigger than anyone he'd ever seen. He had to duck under low-hanging branches on the side streets, and even dip his head and not bound quite so much when passing under a bridge whose sign read "Clearance 8'0"—NO COMMERCIAL VEHICLES."

His libido was rising again. He could feel his cock sliding against his abdominals as he ran, poking up out of the top of the loincloth, and he tried to hide it with one paw, tried to focus on the road, on running, to take his mind away from thoughts of sex, of rut, of growing even larger and stronger. At this point, he thought, that would definitely be a bad thing. His range of motion was much lower than it used to be: when he tried to brush at his muzzle, his biceps, forearm, shoulder and chest all bulged out and made the motion more difficult.

When he reached his home street, he almost didn't recognize it. It looked so much smaller than he remembered it, so much smaller than this morning. His erection was rising higher. He couldn't cover the whole thing with one hand anymore. The street looked empty, so he dashed down it. His erection was aching now, rising higher.

He stepped over their house's fence and moved up to the door, then looked down at it in dismay. Of course. If Saul's house was too small, then his own would be, too. The top of his front door was below chin level. It looked like he would have trouble getting one arm through, much less his whole body. And then he'd be squeezed inside a tiny house.

His shoulders slumped. He couldn't fit inside his own house anymore.

He went into the back yard and sat there glumly, his eye level over the back fence even when sitting down. He'd never sleep in his own bed again. Never put his arm around Stetson on the couch while they watched old movies. Never rock out with games on his computer. Never sip coffee with his boyfriend in their breakfast nook. All those happy little moments of a normal life were gone to him forever.

The sadness broke in him like a wave, and then… dissipated pushed out of his mind by something else. Something artificial. Another mood was rising in him, unyieldingly strong, compelled by whatever drugs Saul had given him. His erection rose.

He put down everything that he was carrying and untied the curtains from around his middle, feeling better as his sac and sheath were freed. His erection pulsed higher, throbbing before his chest. It glistened with his natural lubricants. Maybe one more time would release him. Maybe that was all he needed before the drugs wore off. He leaned down and licked the head clean, and it throbbed and spat more precum toward his face. No. He would… he would lie on it, and crush the spirit out of himself with his own weight.

Turning, he lay belly down in the yard. The grass was deliciously soft against his shaft. He ground down into it. No, this wasn't working either. He rolled onto his back and stared up at the sky, deep blue, clouds drifting past, letting golden sunlight through. He watched them, let his mind drift with them. He let himself feel at peace. Despite how he felt, though, his cock was throbbing atop him. Of its own accord, it began to flex, bouncing against his belly and chest as if possessed. He tried to ignore it, but it made no difference. His balls churned and tightened. A deep, intense pleasure formed at the base of his shaft, and began rising higher and higher inside him. The drugs were going to force him to climax no matter what he did.

"No," he murmured in shock. "No, it's not fair, I'm not even doing anything, I'm not--—" he clenched his teeth, his massive back arching as his hips thrust upward, and the orgasm erupted unbidden from him, seed splashing across his chest and face, soaking into the grass behind him. He loosed the ropes of his climax again and again, hips pounding up and own, his upper body slippery with his seed, and growth overwhelmed him, sliding him through the grass, pushing his arms out so he could no longer rest them at his sides, his back elevating him up farther in the air as it thickened, his cock slithering farther up his chest.

He lay there, chest heaving with his breath, wondering how it could even have been possible for him to get any bigger. He smeared the cum out of his face with both paws, leaning up on his elbows. Could it be over now? Could he finally be done? He stared at his cock, waiting for it to feel spent, waiting for it to retreat back into his sheath once more. It pulsed. It started to go down. He sighed in relief, but then it began oozing clear fluid once more, straining back up to full erection. It ought to hurt, but it didn't. It just felt good. So intensely, overwhelmingly good. It began to throb again.

"Oh no," he breathed. "No, no, no. This can't keep happening, it can't." He pushed at it, trying to force it back down, but every touch only felt better than before. His balls, each looking the size of a cantaloupe by now, began pulsing again. There was nothing he could do. This was it. He was about to go too far. He felt the pleasure at the base of his cock once again, rising inexorably, and he looked aside.

His eyes lit on the case of tranquilizer darts. Reaching around his throbbing cock, he snatched it up. It was slippery with his pre, but he squeezed it open, and spilled out four darts into his paw. He wasn't sure how to use these things. Hopefully just getting stuck with them would be enough. His hips were starting to thrust with his overdriven mating instinct, pleasure burning at his brain. As the pleasure rose higher, as his cock flexed against his chest and strained with impending climax, he held all four needles point down in his fist and then jammed them into his thigh. He barely felt their stings. Pleasure wracked his frame; he fell back and rutted at the blue sky as he came again, white ropes sailing up past his vision. It seemed to him that they sailed higher and higher, mingling with the clouds, and that he was falling down, down, down into nothingness.

\* \* \*

Matt stirred. Wherever he was, it was soft and peaceful. He opened his eyes and saw fluorescent light. Something small touched his chest, and he turned his head to look at it. A paw. Connected to Stetson.

"Matt?" The rabbit's eyes were wide and concerned. He looked very tired. "Are you... are you feeling okay?"

There was no one in the world Matt wanted to see more. He reached over to him and froze at the sight of his arm looming up in his vision. It was massive. How could this have happened? He rested it on his belly instead. "Stetson—" He broke off, the sound of his voice startling him, a deep, bass, almost monstrous voice. "Stetson, I… I don't know how I got here. I don't know what happened." He turned back up to stare at the ceiling, frowning through hazy, barely recalled strands of memory. "I… I was coming back. And then Saul, I think he…"

Stetson's paw stroked at his shoulder. "Hush," he said. "I know. It's okay. You're probably not going to remember a lot that happened. He drugged you. And you got away."

Saul had drugged him? Could that be true? Why would he…? Matt frowned. "How do you know what happened?"

The rabbit crouched down and stood up with a video camera in his paw. "You had this with you. It had everything that happened on it. I don't want to bother you too much right now. But basically, Saul turned out to be… um, I guess a surprisingly bad person. I don't really understand why. But he wanted to get you to, you know, to do stuff with him. He chained you up, drugged you, and you escaped." His expression darkened. "If I ever get my paws on him, he'll be lucky if I don't wring his neck. The police were going to his house, last I heard."

A little of this sounded vaguely familiar to Matt, but nothing with any clarity. Concern tugged at him. "Did I… did I…"

"Did you have sex with him?" Stetson smiled warmly. "No. You were… astonishingly, sweetly faithful. Well. In that way, anyway." He chuckles. "I heard you had a lot of sex yesterday."

A series of images flickered before Matt's eyes. "Yeah," he said. "I guess I did." The sheet rose up below his chest an inch or two. He bit his lip. "Am I okay? Can we go now?"

His mate's ears went back. "Matt, I don't think that you're aware of what…" He sighed. "The drugs Saul gave you are out of your system. It was apparently a pretty nasty cocktail. If we hadn't found you when we did…" He shook his head. "But I don't think you realize that… you're pretty big now. I mean, you're really big. They don't… no one has ever seen or heard of anyone like you. You're over eight feet tall now. You weigh more than half a ton. They had to airlift you to the hospital under a helicopter. You're actually lying across several different beds right now. They want to keep you under observation. And find out what happened to you."

"Can they stop it?" Matt asked. Half a ton, seriously? It was impossible.

Stetson shook his head. "They don't even know what's causing it. I told them what happened to you, but without a list of ingredients..."

"I have a..." Matt began, and then faltered. No. No, he had eaten it.

He scooted up in the bed—*across the beds*—sitting up a bit. The room had curtains drawn around, but he must have been in an isolated area, as he didn't hear beeps from any heart monitoring equipment or anything. It was pretty quiet. The body sprawled out in front of him was unfathomably enormous. It didn't look real. He stared at the curtain, an ugly greenish blue. He took a deep breath, and watched his chest rise up until his chin nestled in the cleft between his pecs. "Stetson, am I... am I too big for you now? I mean, can you still like me like—"

The rabbit cut him off. "Yes," he said firmly. "Yes, absolutely."

"But I mean, can you still feel like you—"

Stetson gripped the sheets and pulled them aside, baring Matt's torso. With a little hop, he climbed up onto the bed and then crawled up onto Matt's chest. He straddled it, his arms reaching across as much of Matt's pecs as he could grab. He seemed to weigh nothing at all, so small that he couldn't even cover a fraction of Matt's torso. With both paws he took the sides of Matt's face and held him firmly. "It's you," he said. "You're amazing. On anyone else, I don't know that I'd be so excited, but this," he gestured backward with one paw, "is maybe what you've always been deep down. I love it. It drives me wild. You understand?"

Matt nodded.

"Are *you* too big for you?" Stetson asked, with a look of concern. "I mean, I know what you've always talked about. I know what kinds of things you look up on the Internet when you think I'm not paying attention. But now that you're this, is this... this is something you like, right?"

"I know I probably shouldn't, but I love it. I'm scared of getting bigger than this, but being like this makes me giddy. But Stets, I was going to ask... am I too big for you... down there?"

"Oh!" The rabbit's ears perked up. "Oh." He looked backward. "Um, sweetie, I don't know. I am pretty… good, but… you're… well, I just don't know if we can do that anymore. We could try."

Just the suggestion made Matt's cock crawl higher. It felt like it had been days since he'd had sex. It didn't have to crawl more than an inch or two before it nudged up against Stetson's pants. "Could we try now? I mean, at least just see if you can do it?" he asked hopefully.

Stetson stared at him. "Are you serious? Hon, I… you have had a hectic few days and you've just had a whole mess of drugs filtered out of your system. Ten hours ago you were passed out on our lawn. And now you want to… to…"

"I missed you," Matt smiled faintly at him. "A lot. And, well, if that's something that we can't do anymore, then I want to know now."

Stetson looked from side to side. "Someone could come in," he whispered.

"It's pretty quiet out there. And it's got to be late at night. I don't think anyone will. Um. We don't have to… you know. I just want to check. To see if we still *can* do it."

The rabbit snorted. "You know how you've been lately. If you get worked up, there will be no stopping either of us."

Matt grinned weakly. "I'll try to keep a lid on that." He didn't bother telling Stetson that the question of whether they could check now was about to be irrelevant. Just thinking about it was making his cock climb upward, and he felt it nudge up against the rabbit's shorts, making him start.

"Well, you don't waste any time anymore, do you, big guy?" Stetson gave him a bucktoothed grin.

Matt chuckled. "Remember like a week ago when I wasn't interested in sex that often?" He winced as his cock kept rising, pushing more firmly up against Stetson's pants.

"It's a huge improvement, I'll say that." The rabbit lifted his rump, his spade tail flicking as he watched the pulsing pillar throb up beneath him. "Holy fuck, Matt."

Matt felt his tip wedge up under his chest once more, the shaft bending upward as it continued to expand. With a gentle touch, Stetson slid his fingers beneath it and lifted it free, making Matt gasp and arch his back for a moment. Stetson let the thick member rest against Matt's belly, the tip against the bottom of his chest, where it pulsed and strained as if it had a will of its own. Then he looked down and back along the length of it. "Fuck, Matt, it's as big as my arm. You've definitely got a prize-winner there. I doubt the world has ever seen bigger. At the very least, you've got a career ahead you in porn."

He looked back at Matt, and Matt leaned forward, meeting him almost nose to nose above the tip, which was starting to glisten. "Can we… I mean, is it still possible for you to… fit it in?"

"Well not all of it!" Stetson exclaimed. "I mean, not the whole length." He took both paws and tried to encircle Matt's girth in them. His touch made Matt's cock strain again, and a stream leaked out of the tip. Quickly, he let it go. "Hon, I just don't know. It's really thick. I… maybe if I relaxed, and really tried. Maybe I could get about half of it into me. We could try." He sighed through his nose. "But if you grow again, even one more time, I think… I think you're just going to be too big for me, permanently."

One more time. Matt heard the words with a kind of shock. Maybe, *maybe* one more time he'd get to fuck his own mate, and then after that, no more. It wasn't so terrible as all that, he thought. There were plenty of other things they could do besides specifically that. But still. Only one more time.

"Then let's do it now," he said.

Stetson frowned at him, his ears going back. "Now? But if you grow again, I don't think we'll be able to again, ever."

Matt nodded. "I know. And that's why I want to do it now. Stets, I don't know what's going to happen over the next couple of days, but you've seen what I'm like now. You've seen what happens. I get irresistible urges. I suck myself in my sleep. Hell, sometimes I cum without doing anything just because I'm so horny I can't handle it. It's like my balls are just making too much for me, and they have to get rid of it."

"Well, I'm not surprised at that," Stetson said, looking back behind him. "I mean, they're like melons back there." He reached back and gave one a little squeeze. Pleasure surged through Matt— he arched his back and then pre spat from his tip and hit the wall behind him. He panted in sudden lust. "Sorry," the rabbit said, folding his ears again.

Matt clenched his teeth, trying to ignore the surge of desire running through him. "The point is," he said, "I'm gonna climax. Maybe not until tomorrow or the next day, but maybe even tonight, while I'm sleeping. And if there's only one more time that I can be inside you," he said, looking up to meet Stetson's eyes, "I don't want to miss it."

The rabbit's expression softened. "Oh, sweetie." He looked down at the thick cock pulsing beneath him, jutting up between his legs and arms, and back at Matt's face. He sighed. "You're right. We shouldn't miss the chance we have."

He gripped the bottom of his shirt with both paws and pulled it up over his shoulders, baring his white-furred chest, his lean, cut torso. Matt blinked at how slender and lean he looked; a week ago, he'd seemed pretty buff to him.

Stetson looked around for a moment, obviously nervous. "I hope no one comes in."

Matt shrugged. "If they do, so what? Fuck 'em."

"From the way things have gone the past few days," Stetson said in a wry tone, "that's the most likely scenario, yes. Speaking of which, you *know* this is going to make a mess."

Matt felt his cock straining with desire. He reached out to his mate, gripping at his sides with both paws. "I don't care," he breathed.

"Well, hold on, hold on, let me lose these pants." Stetson wriggled free and tugged down his shorts and boxers, baring a jutting pink erection that had once seemed huge to Matt. He shucked them to the floor and crouched, nude above the otter. Matt reached for him again, but he swatted his thick-fingered paws away. "You keep those paws to yourself until you learn your strength," he ordered. "Besides, if I'm going to get this in me, I'm going to have to work on it myself."

Matt nodded eagerly.

The rabbit climbed higher and braced his knees against Matt's shoulders, his sac brushing against Matt's chest, erection poking up past Matt's whiskers. Matt gave it an impish lick and was rewarded with a squirm from the rabbit and a drip from his tip. "Not now!" Stetson groaned. "Let me concentrate." He reached behind himself, and then Matt felt fingers groping awkwardly at his length, finally getting a grip on it and lifting it up. Rabbit fur was softer than any other, and it teased his tip delightfully as Stetson nudged it up under his tail. He felt himself pushing the curves of Stetson's rump apart, furrowing through the fur until his tip was pressed up against the twitch of the rabbit's ring, and at that point he was unable to stop himself from flexing his cock again, a hot splash soaking his tip and dripping down from his mate's backside onto Matt's chest.

Stetson started at that, and then nodded, patting his shoulders. "Yeah… we're gonna need plenty of that, big guy. Almost like your body knows you need it, huh?"

"Uh huh." Matt found he got a real thrill from Stetson calling him that.

Stetson breathed in and out a few times, with a focused expression. "Okay. Okay. Here we go." Slowly he leaned back, putting more and more pressure against Matt's tip. Stetson's warm ring parted steadily but it felt almost like a pinch on Matt's tip. He held still, trying to keep his hips from twitching or nudging upward. The last thing he wanted to do was hurt Stetson.

Paws clenched on his shoulders. Stetson bared his gritted teeth, ears forward and twitching as he concentrated. He breathed in and out a few more times and then leaned back again. Matt's tip pushed farther, starting to squeeze into a place that was warm, and very, very tight.

Stetson's fingers tightened on his shoulders, clutching. "Oh gods. Oh gods," he groaned. He made a fist, beat against Matt's left shoulder for a moment, and then pushed back again. Matt's cock flexed, making Stetson emit a low, wordless groan, and then he felt pre squeeze into the rabbit's rump; Stetson twitched in surprise, giving a little push back and a yelp, and then with a kind of pop, the whole of Matt's cock head was inside him. He leaned forward on Matt's shoulders, chest pressed against the otter's face as he panted, and then he pushed up again. His ring was twitching spasmodically around Matt's shaft, and Matt was having to try very hard not to push up and in.

"We did it," Stetson said through a half grin. "You're inside me, sweetie. Ugh, but I'm… I'm gonna be feeling this for a while. I'm not even sure I can get it out."

He wiggled his hips from side to side and then began pushing back, gritting his teeth. It went more quickly than before, and he crawled backward as he squeezed inch after inch into him, pausing every moment or so to pant. On about his third push back he suddenly froze, groaning loudly, his ring gripping around tightly around Matt's girth, then sliding down another inch, his cock twitching as a mixture of cum and pre was squeezed out of it, spattering across Matt's face and dribbling in thick gobs down the rabbit's cock. "Gods," he groaned. "That was everything in there… you just… squeezed it out." He panted heavily and then pushed down, inch after inch, until he was lying across Matt's chest again, his slippery cock nestled between the pecs. "That's it," he panted. "That's as far as I can go."

"It feels amazing," Matt said truthfully. He gave his cock a flex and was surprised to see Stetson cry out, his rump lifting upward.

"Aaah! I, uh, it'd take some getting used to for me," the rabbit panted. "It's… it's mostly good." His paws gripped at the sides of Matt's pecs, his ears folded back, he closed his eyes, and began to grind, driving his erection up between the massive plates of Matt's chest, down along the ridges between his abs, his small body twitching and clenching against him, breath coming in half-whimpered, shuddering gasps into Matt's neck. The tight grip of his rump slid up and down Matt's cock, his passage hot, slick, squeezing, and below that, the luxuriantly soft brush of his thighs against the exposed part of his shaft, fuzzy toes tickling at his sac.

Matt kept still, letting Stetson move in the way that felt the best for him, and for once, his libido did not accelerate him to a quick climax. He wanted to roll Stetson over on the bed and ease in and out of him, but instead he just put an arm across the rabbit's back, holding him firmly to his chest, feeling him shiver and keen, nuzzling into his ears. It seemed an hour or more that they were like that, Stetson slowly rocking atop him, and after a while his movements seemed to grow easier.

"Matt," Stetson breathed finally into his chest, and then he nudged the rabbit's chin up with one paw, leaning down to press his muzzle to the rabbit's, kissing firmly. It was like kissing him for the first time, perhaps because they were now so different in size. The rabbit's fur tingled with electric sensitivity against his lips, the taste of his mouth hot and soft and firm and sweet. Their tongues lapped against each other, his own barely able to squeeze between Stetson's teeth. He broke the kiss and immediately hungered for it again, pressing muzzle to muzzle once more. Stetson clenched around him a few times, shuddering, and then Matt felt his climax rising.

"Quick," he groaned. "Pull off. If I grow inside you, I'll hurt you!"

Stetson shook his head and gripped more tightly at his chest. "I don't care," he breathed. "I don't want to lose the feeling of you here. I don't want it to end."

"I don't want to hurt you!" Matt clenched his teeth. He could feel his balls tightening, his hips beginning to jump despite his attempt to control them.

"You won't," Stetson sighed, his voice sounding peaceful.

Matt could do nothing else. His heavy arm gripped tightly across his mate's back, his hips twitching as the pleasure reached its peak. And then he erupted, his cock flexing with powerful blasts that made Stetson yelp, his fingers digging into the sides of Matt's pecs, claws piercing the skin. Matt tugged him forward just a bit, trying to make more room, and then fired again and again into the rabbit, who was softly groaning.

The growth was about to come; he could feel it. Every muscle in his body was tightening. "This… this is it," he managed. "The last time." He leaned back to gaze at Stetson's face. "I love you."

"I love you too," the rabbit whispered.

He stared into the rabbit's eyes, savoring the feeling of his fur against his chest, the tight squeeze around his shaft, the rabbit's heat enfolding him, the join of the two of them together, one inside the other, the perfect intimacy. He held onto it for as long as he could. His body flexed, strained… and then relaxed. He waited for a moment. He could still feel his cock pulsing inside the rabbit, still oozing cum. He panted, a warm glow of supreme satisfaction settling over him. Nothing else happened.

Stetson looked back. "Um," he said. "Was that it? Did it, you know… did you grow?"

212

Matt knitted his brows. "No," he said. "I didn't. Nothing… nothing happened."

"You didn't grow?" Stetson leaned up a little bit, hope stirring his voice. "You didn't grow!"

"I didn't." Matt could hardly believe it. "Maybe it just wore off. Or maybe something in all that crap Saul gave me, maybe even the tranquilizers, had some sort of… contraindications… or something."

"So this is it? This is as big as you get?" Stetson's ears twitched. "I mean, not that you're not plenty big, but… you think you're done?"

"It should have happened by now." Matt gave his cock an experimental flex, and Stetson yelped.

"Don't do that!"

"Sorry." A giddy rush of elation flooded through him. It was over. He laughed, and kissed his rabbit's cheeks and whiskers and muzzle, and Stetson sighed happily, kissing back, reaching up with both paws to tug at Matt's broad neck.

Finally Matt leaned up, looking down at the small rabbit sprawled across his mountainous chest, about half a foot of thick pink cock sticking out behind him. "Do you, uh, do you want me to help you off?"

Stetson looked over his shoulder, twisting around Matt in a way that teased his sensitive flesh once again, and then grimaced. "I, uh, I think maybe that's not such a good idea, until you get less excited."

His libido pulsed through him. "Well, I don't think that's going to happen with you on top of me like this. I don't… I don't think I really ever lose interest anymore."

The rabbit's ears went back, his eyes widening. "You can't be serious."

"I mean, I don't *need* it all the time. But I'm pretty much always ready." He tried pulling his hips back a little, and Stetson gasped through clenched teeth. "Is it… I mean, was it really that bad?"

Sharp claws gripped at his neck as Stetson's fingers tightened. "No. I mean, it was… it was rough. It felt good, mostly." Ear tips brushed against Matt's face as the rabbit looked down at the soaked fur across his chest and abs, and he nipped at one playfully. "Obviously." Stetson twitched and flicked his ears away again. "But I think with a little practice, I can get used to it, and it will be all good."

Someone pulled the curtain open behind them. He saw a bored-looking badger step halfway in, and then stare in shock. "Oh! Oh my g--! Oh, sorry!" She darted backward in a hurry, pulling the curtain closed. They could hear footsteps running quickly away.

Matt laughed, his deep voice booming, chest bouncing Stetson atop it.

Stetson poked him in the chin. "Are you positive that's you, Matt? You used to be so shy, embarrassed! I mean, she's probably going to go report that. And I don't think I'm ready to get off of this yet. Maybe a few minutes more."

Shrugging, the otter answered, "I guess it's just hard to be too embarrassed anymore, after everything that's happened." He sighed. "I lost my job. I got attacked at the gym. A policeman forced me to fuck him. It's been crazy. I just want to go home now. Do we really have to stay here for observation?"

Stetson looked down. "Well, I don't think they can force you to stay. And we know chaining you up doesn't work. They had to cut those off of you when you got here. So if you want to leave, I guess we can. But… we can't really go home, hon. You're just… There's no way you're going to even fit through the door. I don't think you can live there anymore. We're going to have to figure out something else."

The memories of all the good times they'd had in that house flooded back to him. He remembered when they'd first bought it, remembered breaking in the bedroom, remembered trying, and failing, to learn to cook. He remembered curling up on their bed on lazy Sunday mornings, and rocking into Stetson across the kitchen table. So many memories. "Where will we live?" he asked.

Murmuring the words into his chest and neck between kisses, Stetson said, "I don't know. We'll find something. We'll be happy, wherever we live."

# Epilogue

Matt sat up at a clattering sound echoing through the cave. It was dark, constantly dripping, and it smelled musty and unpleasant. The rocks he had been lying on were uncomfortable and jagged even against his solid bulk.

Silhouetted in the light of the entrance, a cat lashed his tail. "So this is where you've been hiding out, monster," it hissed. It sauntered into the darkness of the cave with a swaying gait. "Took me quite a while to find you." It had something long and sharp in its paw. A sword.

"Get out of here," Matt shouted. "Get out of here or I'll destroy you. You know you are no match for me."

"Oh, I'm not." The cat stepped forward into a ray of light, revealing an eye that was scarred milky white. "Not on my own. But I brought help." He grinned a mouthful of needle sharp teeth. Behind him, silhouette after silhouette appeared in the mouth of the cave, more than a score of growling, hissing cats, some with knives, others with torches that flickered and illuminated their twisted faces, and two that moved in eerie precision with each other, twirling their fine-bladed swords in a syncopated martial dance. "Now," said the cat, "you're going to die."

This was what Matt had been training for four weeks now. He reached down and hefted up a huge axe in one hand. It was nearly as long as he was tall, and they told him it weighed over three hundred pounds, but the weight was inconsequential. He lifted it and twirled it over his head once. With a clang, the blade hit a chunk of rock in the ceiling and was yanked out of Matt's paw, clattering to the cave floor.

The cat rolled his eyes. "Oh, for crying out—"

"Cut!" a voice shouted. A clunking sound came as bright, artificial light flooded the cave.

Fuck. Matt slumped his shoulders.

The cat scowled and turned to a pudgy, weary-faced Doberman who was walking up behind Matt. "It's the fortieth take, Stephen. The *fortieth*."

The Doberman pressed his fingers to his forehead. "I know."

"I've got three Oscar nominations now. Three. I don't need to be doing this. I don't need the paycheck this badly."

The Doberman put his arm across the cat's shoulders, and turned him away, walking with him. "We're all grateful for your work here, Russ. You're a consummate professional." He turned and looked back over his shoulder at Matt, earnestly mouthing the words, "I'm sorry!"

Matt nodded back.

"I mean," the cat continued in quieter tones, but not so quiet Matt couldn't hear him, which was probably the point, "he can't do the choreography. He doesn't know his blocking. I've seen four-year-olds with better acting. And three times a day *minimum* he's off to his trailer so some PA can give him a blowjob. It's just… it's intolerable. The only thing he is *is* big. Can't we just get some computer whiz to *make* one for us?"

The director said something back, but Matt couldn't hear it. He sighed, picked up the axe and put it back into place, and walked to the back of the cave, where there were folding tables set up with beer, soda, juice, and just for him, several huge slabs of seared ahi. He cut off a wedge with a knife and munched on it. Acting was proving to be a lot harder than he thought. Russ was right: he wasn't very good at it. But it was fun anyway, even when he screwed it up.

"Mister Stafford?" said a voice. He looked down to see a little squirrel, his tail twitching, a clipboard tucked under one arm.

"Oh, hi, er…" he tried to remember the squirrel's name. There were dozens of people on set, and he had trouble with them all. He hazarded a guess. "Benny."

The squirrel lit up like a sparkler. "Yes sir!" He beamed.

Matt waited a minute. "Did you want something?"

"Oh! Stephen says we're done for the day. He said he's sorry for the fuss and that we'll just start again tomorrow." He looked down at his clipboard. "And uh, that we're going to see if we can move the shot so that you have room. To swing. He said we'll be hitting the trailers for tonight."

"Okay, well, thanks, Benny. I appreciate it." He took another bite of the fish. Whoever their caterers were here, they knew just how to sear an ahi.

The squirrel nodded, backed off a step, and then paused. Matt knew what this was. He'd seen this routine from different people dozens of times. "Uh, sir?"

"Matt," Matt said around a mouthful of tuna.

"Matt," the squirrel said. His gaze drifted up and down Matt's frame, and then his ears went back. He stared fixedly to one side. "Uh, I'd heard, from some of the crew that sometimes you like... company... in your trailer. I mean while you're away from home and all."

Matt nodded, looking the squirrel over. He was pretty cute, actually. If he didn't know better, he would have suspected that Stephen was hiring hot PAs just to keep him happy. Not like hiring people based on their looks was frowned on in the film industry. "Sometimes," he said.

The squirrel looked up at him hopefully. "Only we're a long way from the states, and my boyfriend says it's okay when I'm on the tour. And if he knew it was you... he'd flip his shit."

"Let's grab some food first," Matt said. "Maybe eight?"

Benny's expression waffled between disbelief and elation. "For real? Thank you sir! Matt! I can't wait! I'll... I'll see you at eight! On the dot!" He backed away in short, ecstatic little steps, and turned to go, then froze. "Oh! Your mail!" He turned back, shoved a wad of letters into Matt's paw, and then dashed off.

Chuckling, Matt finished off his fish and set down the plate. He took the letters and made his way toward the entrance of the cave, having to duck down pretty low to clear the overhang. Outside, the wind was still hot, whipping through the palm trees, churning up the water on the beach. He stretched out his arms and shoulders, now that he had room, and gave a wave to the small group of people who had clustered around the security barriers. They cheered and waved back, jumping. He ought to do autographs, but he hadn't got a pen with him, so it would have to wait.

On his way back to his trailer, which they'd had to construct custom to fit him, he opened his mail, using a thumb claw to slit open the letters. A hefty stack of fan mail, forwarded from Sam, his agent, he set aside for later. There were a few personal requests from supplement and workout gear companies requesting he sponsor them. Most of these were supposed to go through Sam as well, but the persistent ones always seemed to find his personal address and contact him directly. In packets, a few scripts that Sam had selected. A remake of Bonan the Barbarian. A tv pilot for the Incredible Bulk, which was weird, since everyone knew the Bulk was supposed to be a wolf, not an otter, but whatever. And a number of different blockbuster types in which he was supposed to be the bad guy. He usually turned those down; his agent said those were career death. Some weird Japanese ad for whiskey. He'd have to discuss it all with Sam later. And, of course, with Stetson.

There was a weird little pocket on the island where cell phones had reception, and nowhere else. He pulled out his phone. The interface was so tiny for his fingers that he had trouble using it. He'd heard there were mods that could upsize the icons and everything. He'd have to look into it. Or switch to a tablet.

The phone rang, and Stetson picked up. "Hey there, big guy!"

"Stets! How's the book tour?"

"Going good, going good. I'm on my break between Chicago and New York now. How's filming going? You having fun?"

"Yeah, I mean, it's beautiful here. The island's gorgeous. Nice to be away from most of the crowds for a change too, you know?"

"Yeah. Is the movie good?"

"I dunno. I'm not good in it, but they didn't hire me 'cause I could act. And you know, they treat me great. There are diversions."

He could hear the grin in Stetson's voice. "I bet there are, you beast."

They laughed.

Stetson's voice sobered. "I dunno if you heard, but Saul got convicted. Six years. Assault and kidnapping, first degree."

"Took them damned long enough."

"Yeah, well. At least we can forget about him now. When he gets out he'll be closer to sixty than fifty."

"Yeah." Matt paused. "How's the house coming?"

"It's great. I mean, it's huge, but it's great. I walk through it and I feel like a little kid. It's enormous. Thank god you're making fat bank or we'd never afford it. It'll be done when you get back"

Matt sighed, walking up to his trailer. He was looking forward to the air conditioning and a cool bath about now. Maybe if there weren't people around later he'd try the ocean. "I can't wait to see it. I can't wait to see *you*." He opened the door to the trailer.

Stetson stood just inside, phone to his ear. He was buck naked. "Then don't."

"Stets!" Matt scooped him up in both arms and crushed him fondly to his chest.

The rabbit's feet kicked against his thighs. "Don't break me!"

Matt eased up, held him at arms' length. "How did you get here?"

"I told you, the publishing company gave me a break from the tour. Thank god we're making mad bank, or I'd never have been able to afford a plane to… what's this place called again?"

"Balu." Matt grinned. "I'm glad you're here. Russ has been bitching everyone out over my horrible acting. Can you beat him up for me?"

Stetson growled, puffing out his chest. "Let me at him. I'll show him he can't mess with poor, defenseless otters!"

Matt closed the door behind him. "If you kick his ass, I promise to fuck you senseless."

"Hmm." The rabbit frowned. "No dice. Fuck me senseless, and then I'll kick his ass."

"Senseless ass-kicking? That's basically the plot of this whole movie I'm in! Maybe you should be the star!"

Stetson nodded toward the bed. "I'm already a star. I've got a best-selling book and a pet monster. You can keep your terrible movie. Let's go, groupie. I've got needs."

"Groupie." Matt paused. "Shit. I've got some squirrel coming over tonight. Benny. He's so excited I think he might pop halfway through the door."

"Well, too bad for Benny." Stetson slapped at his chest. "You can do what you want on the road, but when I'm in town, you're mine." He grinned. "Maybe if you're real good, I'll let him play too."

"Oh, I'll be good." Matt carried him across the trailer and set him down on the bed. He stripped away the huge loincloth costuming had made for him. It had a prosthetic to cover the portion of his sheath and cock that would normally show above the waistline.

Stetson grinned back at him, rolling onto his elbows and knees, wiggling his tail at him.

Matt gave a fake growl that shook the room, waggling his own massive rudder, and pounced atop him. The trailer bounced on its springs, and a glass fell off the sink in the kitchenette, but he ignored it. His lust mingled with his adoration, and together they rose and swelled, expanding larger and larger within him. It felt like it might never stop.

# About the Author

<u>Pen Darke</u>

Pen Darke is an enigmatic but cuddly giant snow leopard who is completely unrelated to anyone you might have met on the Internet. He enjoys dinner, dancing, long walks by frozen lakes, and being too buff for clothes.

# About the Artist

<u>Ash Finley</u>

Ash Finley was born in a Showbiz Pizza Place. He is an illustrator who uses his knowledge of the craft mostly to draw big animal-men. He likes open shirts and boxer briefs. He may look familiar to you, but he is his own olinguito.

# About the Publisher

<u>FurPlanet Productions</u>

FurPlanet is a small press publisher serving the niche market that is furry fiction. We sell furry-themed books and comics published by us and most major publishers in the community. If you can't get to a furry convention where we are selling in the dealers room, visit *www. FurPlanet.com* to shop online.

9 781614 504573